STRIPPED BARE

STRIPPED BARE

SHANNON BAKER

A TOM DOHERTY ASSOCIATES BOOK
NEW YORK

This is a work of fiction. All of the characters, organizations, and events portrayed in this novel are either products of the author's imagination or are used fictitiously.

STRIPPED BARE

A Forge Book
Published by Tom Doherty Associates, LLC
175 Fifth Avenue
New York, NY 10010

www.tor-forge.com

Forge® is a registered trademark of Tom Doherty Associates, LLC.

The Library of Congress Cataloging-in-Publication Data is available upon request.

ISBN 978-0-7653-8544-4 (hardcover)
ISBN 978-0-7653-8545-1 (e-book)

Our books may be purchased in bulk for promotional, educational, or business use. Please contact your local bookseller or the Macmillan Corporate and Premium Sales Department at 1-800-221-7945, extension 5442, or by e-mail at MacmillanSpecial Markets@macmillan.com.

First Edition: September 2016

Printed in the United States of America

0 9 8 7 6 5 4 3 2 1

To Terri Bischoff, who makes dreams come true,
and
Catriona McPherson, who wouldn't let this one die

ACKNOWLEDGMENTS

Sometimes life takes us on unexpected journeys. I couldn't have predicted I'd find my way to the Nebraska Sandhills and that I'd be so happy for my time there. First, a thank-you to the warm, loving, fun, and friendly people of Grant County, who welcomed me and gave me a home for nearly twenty years. (Also, thank you to those others because they gave me lots of great conflict to write about.) There is no place quite like the Sandhills, full of beauty and challenge. The gifts of the Sandhills aren't always obvious and might take some effort, but the rewards of loving this landscape are worth it. I will always be grateful for getting to know the people and the land.

An enormous thank-you goes to Sheriff Shawn Hebbert. Always willing to answer my craziest questions, never once laughing at my ideas, and the first person besides me who talked about Kate like she's a real person. Where I've gotten it wrong, it's because I didn't ask the right questions, not because Shawn gave the wrong answer. Kate wouldn't exist without you.

Thank you to Alan Larson for egging me on and for reading early drafts. A most heartfelt thanks to Janet Fogg for not only all the great writing advice but also for being who you are. Jess Lourey gave me a nudge and the confidence to keep going. And to the electric minds of Karen Linn and Julie Kaewart, your brainstorming is nothing less than magic.

To my amazing agent, Marlene Stringer, who found the perfect editor, Kristin Sevick. I'm the luckiest writer in the world to have you both in my corner. And to Bess Cozby, who rides herd on me; Todd Manza, who keeps me and Kate from being too crude; Jessica Katz, who is paying attention to all the dead people; and everyone at Forge who labors behind the scenes, thank you, thank you. You make me look better than I deserve. A special hug to Alexis Saarela, the Big Gun. And to art director Seth Lerner, who captured the heart of the Sandhills; no wonder they call you an artist.

A special thank-you to Bob Gentry, a true Sandhiller, and to Chris Gentry, who is taking up the reins. Thanks to my Uncle Mike, who grumbled to me about L1 and L2 vertebrae and the effects of bullet holes and why don't I look it up on WebMD.

The book world is a whole lot better for Ron and Nina Else from the Broadway Book Mall in Denver. They love and are loved in return. Jessica Morrell gives a good edit and if I did everything she told me to do, I'd be a writing wonder. Rocky Mountain Fiction Writers gets the bulk of the credit and none of the blame for any skill I've gained as a writer. Thank you to Sisters in Crime and Mystery Writers of America for all the knowledge and support you dish up daily.

To my daughters, Joslyn and Erin, who inspire me every day. And mostly, thank you to Dave, the saint who listens (or at least pretends to listen) to plots and plans, anxieties, and excitements. And listens. And listens.

STRIPPED BARE

1

I've never trusted happiness. Just when you think you've corralled that mustang, she busts through the fence and leaves you with splinters. I should have seen it coming.

Still, when I tromped across the back porch, feeling grateful to be out of the frosty night air, I wasn't worrying about my world turning into a sloppy, wet pile of manure. My calving ratio sat at a hundred percent so far this year. Maybe I could convince Ted to take a week off after the election and head down to a beach someplace, anyplace away from cattle and family and sheriffing.

The house lights weren't on when I'd trudged from the barn. Carly was supposed to be home working on the term paper she'd blown off last semester. Using her charm, Carly had convinced the English teacher to give her another chance. If she didn't finish the paper this time, though, she wouldn't graduate, and my dear niece would be living with me forever.

I pried off one cowboy boot and dropped it to the porch floor, wondering how to motivate Carly without pushing too hard. The jangle of the phone penetrated the door to the house. I could have ignored it, but if Ted didn't answer his cell, the county sheriff's number rolled over to the landline installed in our house. I burst through the door and thudded across the kitchen. With one boot on, one boot off, I flew into the closet-turned-office and grabbed the old-fashioned receiver. "Sheriff's phone."

"Listen, Kate, Uncle Bud and Aunt Twyla are planning Easter at their place and I told them you'd bring that seven-layer salad."

As far as the Fox family was concerned, you can run but you can't hide. "Hi, Louise." My older sister. One of them, anyway. "We've talked about you using the sheriff's phone only for emergencies. Right?"

The reminder was as effective as ever. "You won't answer your cell. Let me talk to Carly."

"Carly's not here." Where was she, anyway? And where was Ted?

I stretched the phone cord. Grand County didn't believe in fancy equipment like cordless phones. They sprang for Ted's cell phone, but he wasn't supposed to use it for personal calls. I slapped on the light, squinting into the tiny living room. Several books were scattered on the floor. A potted plant spilled dirt onto the worn carpet and the throw from the threadbare couch puddled in the middle of the living room. The chaos seemed unusual, even for Hurricane Carly.

"Where is she?" Louise asked.

"Not sure." Maybe I wasn't fit to be a guardian, but I thought a girl destined to graduate from high school in a month ought to have a fair bit of autonomy. Course, with Carly's history, I was balancing on barbed wire there.

Louise paused to build up steam. "You should supervise her better. She needs—"

A syllable blanked from her lecture. "Gotta cut you off," I said. "The sheriff's second line."

I punched line two, expecting another one of my siblings, who'd also been warned against using the official sheriff's line. "Sheriff's office."

"Oh God, oh God, oh God!" Sobbing, hysterical. A woman blubbered into the phone. "Oh God!"

It took a moment to recognize the voice. It wasn't one of my favorites. "Roxy?"

More sobbing. "He's dead. He's dead. I think. Oh God."

"It's Kate. Who's dead? Where are you?"

"Kate. Oh my God. Blood!"

My skin chilled and my scalp prickled, despite knowing Roxy's penchant for drama. As Ted's old high-school girlfriend, and by some unfortunate quirk of fate, Carly's stepmother, she'd been plaguing me for years. "Roxy!" I yelled, trying to shock her hysterics away.

It didn't work. "I don't know who to call. I came home and the door was open. There's blood everywhere."

"Whose blood? Where are you?"

She finally sounded as if someone caught her with a grappling hook and dragged her slowly down to the ground. "I'm at Eldon's."

Eldon Edwards was her father-in-law. Their houses were only one hundred yards apart and a good half hour from the nearest town. "Is he hurt?"

She started to sob again. "He's dead. He's been shot."

Dead? Eldon? No. My brain tried to push the words away. This was definitely a job for the sheriff. "Okay, hang on. I don't know where Ted is, but I'll find him and get him out there right away."

"He's shot." Roxy sounded like she jumped on the panic wagon again.

"I'll get an ambulance and find Ted."

She wailed out his name. "Ted."

"Stay calm and he'll be there soon."

"He's bleeding. Oh God, he's dying!"

I'd often wanted to slap Roxy, but this time I could probably get away with it. "I thought you said he's dead."

"No, Eldon is dead." Sob, sob.

"Then who is dying?" Maybe Ted was buying drinks at the Long Branch, since it was campaign season. Or visiting his mother in Broken Butte, more than an hour's drive away. I ran through a list of places he might be.

"Ted!" Roxy shrieked into the phone.

That's when her stampeding words started to make sense. "Ted what?"

"He's shot. And there's blood everywhere!"

I dropped the phone and didn't hear whatever else she said.

2

It took me about ten seconds to push my foot into my muddy cowboy boot, grab my barn coat, jump down the back steps, and hurl myself into the nearest vehicle, my '73 Ford Ranchero.

Night had set in, and with low clouds masking the moon, the headlights of the Ranchero didn't light up much. I wrestled with the phone while maneuvering around the hay meadow in front of our house on Frog Creek Ranch. The Hodgekiss village emergency number picked up after two rings. Rocks pinged from the dirt road and the back wheels slid as I careened around the sharp curves of our one-track ranch road and relayed the scant details.

By the time I hung up, I'd made it the five miles to the highway, burying the speedometer on the straightaway. Speed might be Elvis's finest quality—Elvis being the Ranchero I'd owned since before I could drive.

It took me a couple of tries to get Milo Ferguson, Choker County sheriff. Even though the Bar J was in Grand County, where Ted was sheriff, Milo was closer to the scene than me or the ambulance.

Before I made it to Hodgekiss, twelve miles from home, I punched in Carly's speed dial. No answer.

I didn't let off the gas as I barreled through Hodgekiss. Light spilled from the open doors of the firehouse and the bay sat vacant. The ambulance should be far ahead of me.

A few pickups and four-wheel-drive SUVs lined the highway in front of the Long Branch Bar and Grill, but the rest of the town, population one thousand, had hunkered in for the chilly night. Fortunately I didn't need to dodge any traffic.

Snow sparked in the headlights. The dried-out, sharp kind that couldn't really be called flakes. More like minuscule butcher knives. I'd left the heavies—cows about ready to calve—out in the calving lot for the night. If the snow got after it, as it often did in April, the cows could be in trouble. I could tolerate ears and tails frozen off, a common casualty of spring snowstorms, but on a night like this the calves might freeze to death. I'd planned on going back out after supper to bring in any critters that might be at risk. Nothing I could do about it now. I had to go to Ted.

I sped to the edge of town and jerked the wheel a hard right, catching the highway running north. Elvis's back tires slid on the pavement before I floored it, flattening my spine in the seat and racing down the deserted stretch of road.

In the midst of Roxy's hysterics I'd learned that Eldon was dead. The thought bounced in my brain, not settling into reality. Someone must have called Ted out to the Bar J when trouble broke out. Sheriffing was supposed to be an easy job in Grand County, not one where you got shot.

The more worried and wrapped up I got, the slower the drive to the Bar J felt. It was like Elvis's wheels spun in molasses.

Dizzying ground blizzards swirled along the black highway. The twenty miles north only took seven years before I swung a quick right onto the dirt Bar J ranch road. The wheels rattled across the

AutoGate, the steel bars embedded in the road at the fence line, designed to keep cows on one side or the other. The back tires slid and the momentum smacked the Ranchero's bed into an anchor fence post. The post didn't break, but it tilted out, drawing barbed wire with it and snapping the line post six feet away. "Sorry, Elvis."

The Ranchero rode low, like an El Camino. Too bad I hadn't jumped into a four-wheel-drive pickup, instead.

I fought to stay on the slightly raised dirt road but bounced into frozen pasture. Elvis didn't hesitate, especially since I kept pressing on the gas. I raced alongside the road, swerving to avoid the biggest soap weeds. The rough ground and clump grass ricocheted me from the seat to bump my head on the ceiling and back down. Each time, it forced my foot lighter on the gas and then pressed it back down. The engine roared and faded. I finally found a shallow entry spot and climbed back to the relative smoothness of the road.

Three miles from the highway I reached another AutoGate and a sharp turn to the left that led around a shallow lake the size of the Broncos' stadium in Denver. The ranch headquarters snugged under a hill on the other side. Red and blue flashed against the barn and houses with frantic urgency. Eldon's boxy two-story, built in the early twenties, looked like a shack compared to Roxy's McMansion, which dominated everything at the other end of the compound. I gunned across the frozen yard to Milo Ferguson's police cruiser. He hadn't wasted any time getting to the crime scene.

Crime scene. In Grand County? Here, "crime" meant an angry kid egging Principal Barkley's car. Or Leonard Bingham getting another DUI. A *bad* crime was a fistfight at the annual street dance.

Not murder. Not a cop shot.

I sailed over the final AutoGate, into the ranch yard, and skirted the barn with the calving lot behind. Two dozen cows bedded down in fresh hay. Tire tracks showed in the damp sand. Someone had been out checking the heavies recently. Why would I even notice that, when every thought should be on Ted?

Harold Graham and Eunice Fleenor, two of the best EMTs on the squad, wheeled a gurney out the front door and hauled it down the steps. The floor of the Ranchero probably buckled, I stomped the brakes so hard.

Roxy followed them out of the open door She sobbed with abandon and clutched a wool blanket to her chest. One of the EMTs had probably handed it to her, and for once her pride-and-joy of a cleavage disappeared.

I rammed the gearshift into Park and pulled the door latch. It didn't catch. I pulled harder and slammed my whole one hundred and twenty pounds into the door. Still, it didn't budge. The temperamental SOB sometimes balked for no good reason. "Not now, Elvis!"

I struggled out of the driver's bucket seat, across the console, and into the passenger seat. I threw myself against the door and it creaked open.

By the time I ran around the Ranchero, Eunice Fleenor slammed the back doors and sprinted for the cab.

Ted was inside. I wasn't. "Wait!"

Eunice jumped in the ambulance and turned the key. "Meet us at the hospital."

I gripped the ambulance door with both hands. "Let me go with you."

Eunice wrenched the door from my hands like she was swiping a cigarette from the mouth of one of her teenagers. "Can't. Got Roxy riding along already."

She gunned the motor and jerked away, closing the door on the run.

I darted back to Elvis. Before I could pry the door open to follow the ambulance the ninety miles to Broken Butte, Milo Ferguson stopped me.

"Kate," he hollered above the frosty wind, from the front porch of the old house.

Like a worn guitar string, I vibrated, ready to snap. I needed to get to Ted, but I had no information. All Roxy's *Oh my Gods* didn't tell me much. How badly was he hurt? Who shot him? Why was he out here? Was Eldon really dead?

I took off for the house. A slash of light from the open front door silhouetted Milo as he stood at the top of the wide wooden porch steps. His stomach billowed over the top of his pants, belted so far down on his hips it was a wonder they stayed on. Like other old cowboys I knew, when Milo's belly got bigger and his butt disappeared, he simply hitched his Levi's lower and kept the same pants size.

Squinting into the driving snow pellets, I stopped at the base of the stairs to hear the story and dash. "Roxy said someone shot Ted. Is that true?"

He descended the steps. "Come on inside."

No. I had to get on the road. I inched backward.

"Let's get out of the storm." He clamped a beefy hand on my arm and pulled me up the stairs.

I resisted, but short of throwing a punch, I couldn't escape. To the right of the front door, yellow crime scene tape blocked the steps leading to the second story. I didn't see any blood or bodies or signs of struggle.

Rope Hayward and his wife, Nat, sat on two vinyl kitchen chairs across the room. Nat was Dad's mother's sister's cousin by marriage, twice removed. She'd gone to grade school with Dad and married Rope when he got her pregnant, around the time Buddy Holly fell from the sky. They moved out to the Bar J, where Rope took up the job of ranch hand for Eldon. Nat cooked for the hay crew in the summer, for the extra calving help in the spring, and for Eldon, after his wife died.

Looking like a faded scarecrow, Rope rested his hand on the back of Nat's bent head. Her weeping sounded like a hungry kitten. I dipped my head in their direction. Rope nodded back in a disjointed way. Nat blew her nose.

The ranch house appeared even older and less modernized than ours. Cracked, dry leather covered the couch and recliner. They might be pieces purchased by Eldon Edwards's parents, the original homesteaders. Dark, glossy, varnished wood outlined the window sashes and served as floorboards. Whatever color the wall-to-wall carpet started out, it was now a dirty gray, worn nearly to the backing in some places. The living room opened into a kitchen, with a two-burner gas stove visible, sitting on cracked linoleum.

Mom would say the house had good bones. It certainly had plenty of space. Bedrooms and Eldon's office filled a second story, with only Eldon to occupy them.

This was the house Eldon grew up in, and from what everyone around town said, he hadn't changed a thing since. They said—and I didn't hold much with what "they" said—he hadn't let his bride spend a dime on upgrades. But that saintly woman—again, a "they said" sentiment—had passed away so many years ago I had only a vague recollection of her. The house had the musty basement smell old houses are prone to. Tonight, a faint odor of burned meat and gunpowder lingered in the air.

I shivered and stayed close to the front door. I wrenched my arm free from Milo's grasp and decided I'd give him three seconds. "What about Ted?"

Milo clicked the front door against the rising wind. "Not sure."

My heart bounced to my stomach floor. Two seconds down. "How bad is it?"

Milo sucked on his teeth. "He was shot from the front. Bullet went into his midsection but there wasn't an exit wound. He was unconscious."

Two seconds more than I was willing to give. "I've got to go!" I lunged for the door.

Milo leaned against the front door so I couldn't leave. "He was breathing, and the EMTs'll git him stable. Nothing you can do, for right now."

I fidgeted like a horse in the starting gate. Even if I shoved him, I'd probably not be able to do more than jiggle his belly.

"Just listen to me a sec. You're gonna have to tell Carly that her granddad is gone. Sooner the better, before somebody spills the news first."

His words smacked me upside the head. Of course. Carly. She'd already lost her mother, my oldest sister, Glenda. When her father died, Eldon's son, a couple of years after that, it had nearly broken her. Would she hold up after she learned her granddad was murdered? With her mother and father dead and a stepmother like Roxy, I was the closest thing to a parent she had. Poor girl.

"I don't know where Carly is." I blurted it out before thinking.

He narrowed his eyes. "Aren't you her guardian?"

My fingers closed on the doorknob.

He frowned. "Seems a girl like that might bear a little closer watching."

I'd been accused of negligence in the matter of my niece twice in the course of an hour. I focused on the door, thoughtless words dribbling from my mouth. "She's much better these days."

Milo let out a *harrumph*. "She's gotta know about her granddad."

Some of Milo's concern seeped deeper into me. "He's really dead? Who shot him? Why?"

Milo's frown deepened. "Don't know. Gonna find out." Milo wheezed as if he couldn't get enough air past his big belly. "I couldn't make heads nor tails out of all Roxy's wailing."

"When Ted wakes up . . ." He would wake up. He'd be okay. I gulped down the doubts. No sense getting worked up until I knew his condition. "When he comes to, he can tell you what happened. Whoever shot Eldon must have shot Ted."

Milo's graying eyebrows drew together. "Maybe."

"I've got to go." I put a hand on his tree trunk of an arm to urge him away from the door.

He hesitated, and the look in his hazel eyes softened. "I've known you since you was no bigger'n a bug. You're a good and honest one, that's for sure."

What was that about? Did he think Ted was going to die?

"I'd haul you to Broken Butte, but I got to secure the scene. You gonna be all right?"

I swallowed hard. An hour-plus drive to Broken Butte to worry that I might be greeted with the grim news that I was a widow? I nodded and he stepped out of the way.

I jumped down the rickety porch steps and raced for the Ranchero.

Milo pushed outside and raised his voice against the wind. "Get hold of Carly."

3

I managed to stay on the dirt road out from the Bar J, but the highway felt like a belt of frozen black snot. I needed to tell Carly about Eldon. I needed to be with Ted. No way to split me in two.

With one hand gripping the wheel, and praying I didn't end up ass over teacup in the barrow ditch, I felt for my phone in the console, then the passenger seat. Despite the freezing temperatures and the iffy quality of Elvis's heat, sweat trickled down from my armpits and dampened my flannel shirt. A smell of wet manure from my boots mingled with the musty fragrance of Elvis's heater.

Clouds blocked out the scant moon, and the dash lights didn't do much to help me locate the phone. I leaned way to the right to snatch it off the passenger side floor, which made me steer across the centerline. After all that, I held it up and pushed speed dial with my thumb.

Robert answered on the second ring. Only fifteen months older than me, we'd grown up as close as twins. We might be the only sane ones in the Fox clan, but that was giving me a lot of credit.

"Kate." Robert's voice hung heavy with sleep.

"Sorry to wake you up, but I need your help." The back wheels slid to the left and I tossed the phone aside to use both hands to steady Elvis. He was never any good on snow and ice. When I fished the phone from the seat, Robert sounded fully awake.

"What's going on? Where are you?"

Trying to ignore my overactive heartbeat, I explained the situation as I knew it.

"Do you want us to come down to the hospital?" The squeak of a closet door told me he was already reaching for a shirt. Sarah, his wife and my best friend, mumbled something in the background.

Yes. "No. I don't know how Ted is or what's going on. I've got about fifty head in the calving lot. If I don't get home by morning, can you check on them and throw them some hay?"

"I'll go out there first thing. Who's with Carly?"

My wipers swiped at flakes, smearing moisture along the windshield. "Well. Um."

He paused. "You don't know where she is?"

I didn't need more judgment on that score. "I tried calling but she's not answering her phone."

"Does she know about Eldon?"

"I don't know. If she's home when you get there, tell her Ted was shot, but don't tell her anything else. And don't let her answer her phone or the house phone. I'll tell her about Eldon."

"Okay. You sure you don't want us to come to the hospital? Dahlia is bound to be a handful."

Ah, Dahlia. Ted's mother. Much as I'd like a posse with me, I'd wait to rally reinforcements until I needed them. "I'll call Ted's folks when I know more."

We signed off and I put all my energy into arriving in Broken Butte without killing myself in the storm. I blinked away tears at the thought of Ted in all his tall, broad-shouldered good looks, bending down to give me a teasing kiss.

From the moment Ted had noticed me, I'd never believed my good fortune. He was a Hodgekiss legend, my older sister's age, and the hero of every little girl's fantasy. Okay, maybe not every girl, but certainly mine.

He was my first crush, as true and impossible as my younger sister's love for Justin Bieber. Of course, I'd grown out of it, but when I'd returned home with my shiny BA and no clue what to do with my life, he'd appeared as if by magic and literally became my dream come true.

He'd better be all right. That's all.

An hour later, Elvis's brakes squealed as I stopped under the covered driveway in front of the emergency room entrance. Bright lights glared through the glass automatic doors. Elvis obliged me by not sticking the driver's door this time. I jumped out and flew for the hospital. The darn doors took their time sliding open, and I was tempted to crash through them. My boots clacking on the linoleum sounded like a parade in the empty corridor.

"Hello!"

I took the first turn to the right. Somebody had to be moving or making noise somewhere in this damned hospital.

I loped down a corridor. The Broken Butte Community Hospital was a two-hundred-bed facility. How hard could it be to find the single emergency case?

I returned the way I'd come, hit the emergency entrance, and sprinted the opposite way from my first try, skidding around another corner. If I'd stepped on a rattler, I wouldn't have gasped any louder.

Ted's loving mother, Dahlia, stood cradled in her husband, Sid's, arms. They guarded a set of closed metal double doors. Midsob,

Dahlia buried her face in Sid's broad chest. "Oh God, oh God, oh God."

Déjà Roxy.

Sid's face held the resigned expression he usually wore when dealing with Dahlia. He noticed me and raised his eyebrows in greeting.

A small window centered in each of the swinging doors revealed an empty hallway. On a normal day I'd retreat. The less time I spend around Dahlia, the better for everyone. But this wasn't a church fund-raiser or a baby shower.

Sid's eyes opened in alarm as I strode toward the doors. "Is Ted in there?" I asked.

Dahlia jerked away from Sid as if stuck with a hot poker. She glared at me.

I placed my palm on the cool metal panel of one door.

Dahlia's voice sounded hard as ice on a water trough in January. "You can't go in there. They're operating." She crumpled into Sid's chest. "On my baby."

"Where's a nurse or doctor or anyone?" I pressed my nose to the window to view the deserted hallway.

Dahlia managed to speak through her tears. "If they won't allow his own mother beyond those doors, then you can't go."

It was times like these I hated my diminutive, five-foot-five stature. With a good four inches on me, Dahlia always seemed to have the regal advantage.

Drawing up my shoulders made me feel courageous, like a Komodo dragons. "He's my husband and I need to know what's happening."

Sid, a giant in his own right at six foot three, put his arm around Dahlia's shoulders. "Let's all calm down."

Dahlia shrugged it off. "My baby is in there fighting for his life. I'm as calm as I can be."

"How did you get here so fast?" I always suspected Dahlia of chipping Ted, so she'd be in constant contact.

Dahlia stepped away from Sid. "Roxy called us."

Thank you, Roxy. "Where is she?" Maybe she could tell me something about Ted's condition.

Dahlia shifted her eyes to the window in the door and her voice grew husky. "They took her someplace so she could wash off the blood." She gulped a sob. "Ted's blood."

A quick punch to Dahlia's nose would go a long way to relieving my frustration. I didn't use that approach often, not since eighth grade, when I'd sliced my knuckles on Diane's—another older sister—braces.

I might be edging that close to my limit now. I made for the door again.

Dahlia threw herself in front of me. "You will not interfere!" She stood in front of the double doors, arms wide, chest stuck out.

I fought to keep calm. "I'm his wife. I'm going in."

Sid took a step in retreat.

Dahlia thrust her chin out and flared her nostrils. She all but said "Over my dead body."

That was it. I'd be polite and respectful up to a point, but I was beyond that now. I reached up, slammed my hand onto her shoulder, and shoved. If I could manhandle thousand-pound cows and wrangle razor-hooved horses, Dahlia Conner wouldn't stop me.

Though Dahlia stumbled to the side, she recovered before I pushed through the doors. She latched onto my barn coat and jerked me back, just far enough that, when the door swung open, it caught me in the chin.

A middle-aged woman in lavender scrubs, her graying hair cut short and highlighting her triple chins, stood with arms akimbo. She sniffed. "Kate Fox. What would your father say if I told him you were causing a stink in public like this?"

"Aunt Tutti. Thank God." I wanted to hug her, right after I corrected her that my last name had been Conner since I'd married Ted, eight years ago. "I need to see Ted."

Aunt Tutti heaved her sizable bosom in a show of authority. "Ted's out of surgery. They went ahead and took him to ICU. Doc Kennedy'll meet you there."

"He's already out? Is he okay? I want to talk to the surgeon." I'm pretty sure that's what I asked, but my mouth was moving much slower than my racing brain.

Aunt Tutti patted my arm. "The EMTs did a good job and the bullet was easy to get to. The surgeon said he's heading back to North Platte tonight, since he won't be able to go back to sleep. Believe me, you're better off talking to Doc Kennedy. This guy thinks he's gooder than God."

I planted a quick kiss on Aunt Tutti's cheek and whirled around to face a choice of directions. There was no sign of Dahlia and Sid.

Aunt Tutti pointed to the corridor on the right and I galloped down the hallway.

I took a few turns, remembering the hospital layout. Unfortunately, I'd been to the ICU waiting room before. I finally approached another set of double doors. I burst through them, not waiting for Dahlia or anyone else to stand in my way.

A circular nurses' station took up the center of the open area, with three curtained rooms off to the right. Sid stood midway between the nurses' station and one of the rooms.

Dahlia and Roxy huddled together, their arms around each other. As far as I knew, there was no shared genetics between them, but they looked and acted so similar it made me wonder.

Ted and Roxy had made a perfect couple in high school, all shiny and beautiful. Ted told me they broke up because he couldn't handle Roxy's drama, but Dahlia obviously preferred Roxy over me. They both inhabited the high-drama zone.

Like Dahlia, Roxy was tall and slender. I'd never seen either one without impeccable makeup and hair fluffed, curled, and sprayed. And sprayed. Even now, they both wore crisp jeans, heeled boots, and fancy blouses. No bloodstains marred Roxy's appearance. I hurried toward them in my old barn coat over faded flannel, work-weary jeans, and boots I'd worn tromping through the calving lot. With the combination of a long day of physical labor and manure-caked boots, I might overpower their perfume. But I doubted it.

I squinted through the window into the darkened hospital room full of blinking machines. My breath caught in my chest as my sight narrowed to Ted's pale face lying motionless on the pillow. I wanted to yank out the tube taped to his cheek and shoved down his throat. A scruff of dark whiskers dotted his chin, as it always did by the end of the day. An IV attached to his arm dripped clear liquid, and a bank of monitors flashed numbers and graphs behind the bed.

Without conscious thought, my boots carried me toward the door to his room.

"Don't," Roxy said, somehow finding the ability to speak despite her trauma. "They said we can't go in."

That must be true or Dahlia would have taken her place next to his bed.

I planted my open palm on the window. The cold glass was no substitute for my husband's warm skin.

The squeak of rubber soles made me turn as Doc Kennedy approached. He moved as if a lightning rod ran straight down his back, and his white hair stuck out as if it had been struck. He'd delivered both me and Ted, all of my eight brothers and sisters, and a collection of nieces and nephews. When we had a baby, I figured he'd deliver that, too.

Doc Kennedy nodded to me and shifted his gaze to glare briefly at Roxy and Dahlia. "We don't know much right now."

With each beat my heart grew heavier. It would pop through my chest any moment.

"The bullet entered close to the L2 vertebra. We were able to extract it. Because the shock wave from the bullet caused swelling, we won't know if there is nerve damage until later. I can't give you a definite prognosis."

"Oh God, oh God, oh God." The chorus to my side ratcheted up.

I clamped my back teeth for a second to get control. "You mean he might not make it?"

Doc Kennedy shook his head. "Oh, no. He's not in danger of dying. The uncertainty is whether he'll walk again."

There was more, of course. But my ears dammed up and kept the words from entering my brain. Ted might not walk again. How would I break that to him?

After telling me that Ted probably wouldn't wake up for another twenty-four hours, Doc Kennedy ushered us from the ICU to a nearby waiting room. He suggested we go home and get some rest. Instead, I prowled the waiting room for the next three hours, anxious for Aunt Tutti to pop in every hour and allow me five minutes to stand outside Ted's window and look at him, sending healing and love with every breath.

Aunt Tutti even allowed Dahlia and Roxy one visit each. They telegraphed their resentment of my special treatment with heated glares whenever I returned to the waiting room. I ignored them, for the most part.

Eventually, weeping and gnashing of feminine teeth drove me from the room. Sid leaned against the wall just to the right side of the door. He buried his chin in his chest and stared at the waxed linoleum floor.

I picked a spot next to him, nearly touching his arm. "He's strong. It'll be okay."

"Yep." He sniffed. "If he doesn't walk, he's going to need you by his side."

I was sure Sid didn't think I'd leave Ted at any sign of trouble. He knew me better than that. "Ted's going to be fine. Even if he's not, we'll face it together."

From far down the hall the heavy clump of boots on industrial hospital tile made slow progress toward us. It reminded me of the campfire story where the monster trudges up the stairs, saying, "Give me back my bloody arm."

Sid and I both stared down the hall, waiting for doom. We weren't disappointed when Milo Ferguson came into view. His pace didn't alter as he made his way to us.

He nodded at Sid. "Any word on Ted's condition?"

Sid's head hung low as a hound's on a hot August afternoon. "He's in ICU."

Milo expressed deep sympathy by clapping Sid's shoulder. He eyed me. "Can I have a word with you, Kate?"

I glanced down the hallway to the double doors guarding Ted. I hated moving any farther away from him, but I followed Milo.

He led me to a dark hallway lined with closed office doors. My numb brain only halfway questioned his need for privacy.

He rummaged in his shirt pocket, pulled out a tiny plastic cylinder, and pried off the cap. He shook a toothpick into his hand, popped it into the side of his mouth, and sucked on it.

That's when his actions struck me as odd. "What's going on?"

Even isolated as we were, he spoke in a low voice. He worried the toothpick. "I don't know how to tell you this."

Fear jabbed me. "Carly? What's happened?"

He hesitated as if he'd had a new thought. "Far's I know, little Carly's fine."

He looked at the ground and rocked back on his heels, chewing on the toothpick. I wanted to throttle him to get him to speak. I clenched my teeth and pinned him with my gaze. "Then what?"

The toothpick snapped from the left corner of his mouth to the right. "The crime scene is confusing."

"But you have some idea who killed Eldon and shot Ted?" Of course he did. Grand County wasn't a metropolis with a million suspects. This kind of crime would be easy to solve here.

He nodded slowly, with his whole body. "Can't say as I figured the whole thing out, but the logical thing would be . . . Well, it kinda looks like it could . . . I'm not saying it's definite yet, but all the clues point . . ." He stopped again and looked at the wall above my head.

"What?" My voice echoed in the empty hall, startling the both of us.

He held my eyes and inhaled. "I'm gonna have to arrest Ted for Eldon's murder."

4

My laughter barked in the silence. “Are you crazy?”

He frowned at me, and the toothpick bounced. “I’m not any happier about this than you are. But I’m gonna have to go with what I’ve got.”

I folded my arms across my chest. “And what is it you think you’ve got?”

Milo lowered his eyebrows. “I’m going to keep the details to myself for now.”

I scrubbed hair from my face with both hands. “Ted had no reason to shoot Eldon.”

Milo studied me. “Might be he did.”

This was beyond absurd. “You’re going to accuse my husband—the sheriff of Grand County—of murder, but you’re not going to tell me why he would do such a thing?”

He shrugged. “It’ll all come out sooner or later, but for now it’s police business.”

On a normal day I’d keep my thoughts to myself. But tonight

was as far from normal as snow in July. "Maybe you ought to do some true sheriffing and find out who really shot Eldon?"

Milo backed away from me, his face cloudy. "I understand you're upset. Rightly so. But until I see something else convincing, it looks pretty clear to me."

"You're not even going to investigate?"

"I'm gonna head home and get some sleep. My advice is that you do the same."

I trailed Milo down the hall and we stopped at the intersection where he'd head to the outside door and I'd go back to ICU. "He didn't do it. You know that."

Milo dropped his hands to his sides and they bent at the elbows to outline his belly. "Might be you don't know Ted as well as you think you do."

That put me on the fight. "I know he didn't kill Eldon. And if you won't find out who did, I'm going to have to."

Milo rocked back on his heels. "Now you just stay out of this."

If Milo thought I'd stand back and do nothing while he arrested my husband for murder, well, he didn't know a damn thing about the Foxes. "You don't honestly think Ted did it."

Milo sucked his toothpick. "I don't know, Kate. Hard to dispute the signs."

I focused long and hard on Milo. "How many times has Ted covered for you when you were on vacation or needed some time off?"

Milo scowled at me. "I can't do favors just because we're friends."

"This isn't a favor. Ted didn't kill Eldon. All I'm asking is to hold off anything official until Ted wakes up and can tell you what happened."

Milo took the toothpick out and jammed it into his pocket. He hemmed and hawed for a few seconds. "Fair enough. I'll have the hospital call me when Ted comes around."

Satisfied that I'd kicked that can down the road, I inhaled. "Thank you."

Milo gave me another of his caring looks. "Yep."

I watched Milo's elephant-trundle to the front door before I headed back to ICU.

I had several more turns to stand beside Ted's bed and watch the machines flash and see him not move. Aunt Tutti urged me more than a half dozen times to go home. "You need to take care of yourself or you'll be no good to him when he wakes up."

A couple of hours later, with no change in Ted's condition and little indication he'd wake soon, I took Aunt Tutti's advice. I left Dahlia and Roxy at the hospital to guard over Ted. I needed to be back here when Milo showed up. If Ted didn't know who shot them, I'd best have a suspect or two to toss to Milo.

A ribbon of pink outlined the eastern horizon. I had a lot to do before I made it back to Ted's side, and I couldn't do it without a little sleep.

After countersteering across a patch of black ice, I tried Carly's phone again. Robert answered. "I found her phone under a blanket on the living room floor. No Carly, just the phone. Looks like you had a wrestling match in here."

"She's not much of a housekeeper." Carly was all bursts of passion, mixed with moments of wisdom and insight, swirling in motion. No telling what prompted her flight this time, or how far she'd gone.

Robert gave me the update. "I threw a few bales of hay to the cows in the lot and fed the barn cats. You had three new calves and everyone looks happy."

Everyone but Ted and Carly and a whole herd of other people, including me. "You're the best brother in the world."

I heard the smile in his voice. "Why, yes. Yes, I am."

"But if you tell Michael, Douglas, or Jeremy"—my other brothers—"I said so, I'll call you a liar."

Cupboard doors squeaked open and banged closed. "Jeez, you have nothing to eat here. Aren't you supposed to be raising a kid? How do you manage that without feeding her?"

"Carly's capable of grocery shopping and cooking. I'm preparing her for the real world."

He laughed. "In true Fox fashion." He crunched something, probably a handful of cereal. "When are you going to get another dog? The place feels lonely without Boomer."

Our old boxer hadn't made it through the winter, and my broken heart had barely scarred over. "Maybe later this spring, after brandings."

He smacked his lips. "A place needs a dog. Keeps the bad element at bay."

Right now, the worst element in my life was a suspicious county sheriff. A ranch dog wouldn't chase him away.

"How's Ted?" Robert asked. "Wait. Before you answer, let me hang up Carly's phone and call you on mine. I need to get back to my own cows."

When Robert called back I gave him the medical assessment and left out the bit about Milo fixing to arrest Ted. I hoped I'd get that straightened out soon enough and wouldn't have to bother anyone with it. All I needed was another suspect or two, to get Milo off Ted's back.

His pickup door slammed and the engine started. "You don't know who shot them?"

"Nope."

The farm report blasted on the radio before he turned it down. "People are going to want to know why Eldon got shot and who did it. If you can't come up with something to calm them down, they're going to think a Charlie Starkweather is on the loose."

We didn't need people getting all panicky and recalling Starkweather, Nebraska's most infamous criminal, who went on a statewide random-killing spree in the late fifties. "I'm not the sheriff. Why would they ask me?"

Robert guffawed. "Because they can't ask Ted, for one. And because everyone knows you're the brains of the Frog Creek outfit."

I needed to deflect Milo's suspicions. With elections coming up, that kind of gossip wouldn't do Ted any good.

"Sarah's calling. Talk to you later." Robert hung up.

I liked Milo, had known him all my life, but he never struck me as a go-getter. I pictured him having coffee and sweet rolls with his cronies, more than chasing clues and hunting a murderer. Robert was right. If someone was going to sleuth out the real criminal, it was going to have to be me.

Exhausted but wired, I slowed to idle through Hodgekiss and noticed Dad's old Dodge pickup parked in front of the house, with no frost on the windows. I ought to get some sleep before I tackled the job of tracking Eldon's killer, but Dad knew the history of Grand County—who had grudges and might wish Eldon harm. If I could get him to talk, it might expedite my search.

Really, I just wanted the comfort of my parents' warm kitchen. I pulled Elvis in front of the paint-challenged house by the side of the railroad tracks as the brittle April sun struggled to rise.

Because the railroad depot was the first building in Hodgekiss, in 1889, and the main reason for the settlement, the town had grown up along the tracks. In Hodgekiss, there was no "wrong" side of the tracks.

I dodged a tricycle, a faded plastic wagon, and other toys strewn by Fox grandkids. Even before I opened the door I nearly gagged on the smell of bacon. Guess maybe I wasn't as immune to trauma as I thought. Instead of turning into a blubbering heap like Roxy,

I fell apart intestinally. As I'd learned in Psych 101, stuffing feelings could lead to all kinds of gastric difficulties.

I entered from the side door. Mom's joke on herself was to decorate the kitchen like a sixties sitcom. As is typical in houses nearing their century mark, the kitchen was huge. Handmade cabinets, soft from countless layers of paint and currently a bright white, rose to the ceiling above red composite countertops that lined two of the walls. A recently installed island with a butcher-block top added more work space—something that was needed when all nine Fox kids, their spouses, and a gaggle of grandkids gathered.

White curtains with red polka dots hung at the windows in the door and above the sink, but the picture window along the front of the house remained bare, letting in maximum light. Even though she didn't use them often, all the small appliances were red and retro or covered with vintage cozies.

Dad stood at the stove in his canvas Dickies, stocking feet, and faded hoodie. He glanced up with tired eyes. "Hi, Katie. How about some eggs?"

Even the word brought bile to my throat. "No, thanks." I dropped onto a step stool next to the butcher block. "Did you just get in?" For almost forty years Dad had been a conductor on the BNSF. We grew up with his intermittent presence. Out on the road for twenty-four to forty-eight hours, home the same, sometimes more, sometimes less. Taking calls to go to work at all hours. Unpredictable and variable. Still, he was the most stable parent of the two.

He cracked two eggs into the pan and poked at the sizzling bacon with a fork. "Worked all night from Lincoln." Ropey, with thinning gray hair, Dad spoke low and slow, never raising his voice. "They" said he was one tough cowboy, riding barebacks on the rodeo circuit before he went into the army, but he only showed us kids a gentle side.

"I heard about Eldon. And Ted." Yeah, I'd figured. Even though he was on the rails half the time, Dad's sources kept him informed through a system that would make the CIA envious.

A desert of sand drifted in my eyes, and my shoulders knotted tighter than a pony's backside in a dust storm. I slumped over my knees. Between Eldon's death, Carly's disappearance, Ted's prognosis, and the stomach-churning thought of Milo's suspicions, I didn't know which problem to focus on first.

Dad lifted a slice of bacon with a fork and laid it on a paper towel. He tilted the pan and slid his eggs onto a plate. "What do you suppose happened out there?"

Not whatever fantasy Milo dreamed up, that's for sure. I closed my eyes. I figured Eldon was the main target and Ted got in the way. Eldon owned one of the oldest and biggest spreads in the Nebraska Sandhills, probably close to one hundred thousand acres. Land didn't necessarily translate into big cash flow, though. Even if it did, Eldon was so tight he'd squeeze an ant for the tallow.

I looked up at Dad, hoping he'd cough up some gossip. "I thought everyone liked Eldon."

Dad carried his plate to the rustic picnic table. The table didn't match Mom's decor, but she bowed to practicality. With a bench along the wall and mismatched chairs on the outside edges, the picnic table accommodated a whole passel of Foxes. Dad built it after Michael and Douglas, the twins, numbers six and seven, were born. As Fox number five, I'd been squeezing onto that bench most of my life.

Dad sounded more sad than tired. "I can't think of anything worth shooting someone over." He'd spent a year in Vietnam and had returned a pacifist.

I stared at the black kitty-cat clock with its rhinestone-encrusted tail that ticked the seconds. I intended to ask Dad about Eldon's enemies, but my mind shifted.

Carly hadn't been home last night. My concern registered about a five on the Carly scale. Unfortunately, Carly had the tendencies of a beagle: at any moment, she'd slip out the open door and make a run for it. Mostly, she made her way home on her own. Sometimes I had to grab the leash and go after her.

Dad worked on his breakfast while bright sunshine streaked across the floor from the picture window.

When I found Carly, what could I tell her? She'd been close to Eldon, and his death would flatten her. I had no clue who shot Eldon, and she'd want answers.

The basement door creaked open and a phantom drifted into the kitchen. In her silky blue kimono and bare feet, Mom floated toward Dad and bent to kiss his rough cheek. "I thought I heard you." She flicked her wild snaggle of wavy hair from her face. She'd thrown me the chromosome for the same hair, only mine was still dark; hers shimmered in a silver halo. She smiled at me with even, white teeth. "Good morning, love." She glanced at Dad's plate. "It's morning, right?"

Without waiting for an answer, she wafted to the refrigerator and opened the door. "Is there any tofu left?"

Dad soaked up egg yolk with his toast, knowing Mom didn't expect an answer. "How's the new piece coming?" he asked.

Mom turned red-rimmed eyes to him. "It's taking my very soul." This meant that the sculpture she was crafting in her basement studio was probably pretty good. Mom pulled out a Mason jar half full of green liquid and walked to the sink to gaze out the window. She unscrewed the lid and drank the thick concoction. Bright bits—maybe spinach, maybe kale, maybe chunks of vegetable-coated granular protein—stuck to the sides of the jar.

Dad took his plate to the sink, and they stood so close together their hips touched. No words, no deep, soul-searching glances, but total trust, respect, and understanding flowed between them, almost palpable enough to smell.

I picked up my phone from where I'd dropped it on the butcher block. The number I wanted fell to the bottom of my Favorites list, not because I didn't love her as much, but because Susan was Fox number nine. I punched, knowing it was way too early for a college kid to be up.

A groggy voice answered after several rings. "Christ, Kate, you couldn't wait until daytime to call?"

"Better not let Dad hear you talk like that."

"Go to hell."

Enough of this small talk. "Have you seen Carly?"

Slight pause. "Carly?" Obviously, Susan was stalling, trying to think how to answer.

"Is she there?"

"Is she supposed to be?"

Lincoln, where half the Foxes had attended the University of Nebraska, was a three-hour drive from Hodgekiss. Maybe Carly drove there last night, or was on the way. "If she shows up have her call me."

Susan sounded alert now. "You don't know where she is?"

That was becoming an irritating question. "I haven't talked to her since yesterday morning, and she left her phone at home."

At nineteen, Susan knew it all. "Way to be a responsible guardian."

"Just let me know if she shows up."

Susan yawned. "Okay."

I wanted her to understand the importance of my request. "Eldon died last night."

It sounded like Susan's lungs collapsed. "Oh, shit."

"Yeah."

With only two years separating them, Carly and Susan were as close as sisters. "That'll kill her."

I filled Susan in on the sketchy details and hung up to the sound of Mom and Dad's kiss.

Fortified with her vegan protein shake, Mom started back downstairs, where she'd shed the kimono and resume work.

Dad poured himself another cup of coffee and took the lid off the cobalt-blue ceramic cookie jar. Mom's artwork popped up all over the house. He swung the jar in my direction and offered me a sample. I shook my head.

He set it down, reached in, pulled out two plate-sized chocolate chip cookies, and hauled them to the table with his coffee. He lowered himself down.

I had more than sugar on my mind. Once I gave Milo a better suspect for Eldon's murder, I could concentrate on finding Carly and breaking the news about his death, and then move on to Ted's recovery. "Do you know anyone who had a grudge against Eldon?"

Dad slurped hot coffee and set the cup in front of him. "A man doesn't live to be as old as Eldon and not have someone mad at him from time to time."

That was too diplomatic for my purposes. "Who, specifically?"

Dad collected gossip, but prying it loose from him was harder than getting black off coal. "I wouldn't be able to say." He bit into a cookie.

I pushed myself from the stool. "Guess I'd better head home."

Dad met me at the back door and kissed my forehead. "It'll all be okay in the end. If it's not okay . . ."

"It's not the end," I finished with him. It was a saying he repeated often.

Someone knocked on the front door. Dad shot me a puzzled glance. No one from Hodgekiss used the front door. *Carly.*

I sped from the kitchen into the dark living room. Dad followed. I crossed the closed-in porch, with its two barber chairs, old-time hair dryer that fit over the entire head, and hair-washing station. This was a holdover from the previous generation, when Dad's mother, my Grandma Ardith, owned this house and ran her beauty parlor here.

I flung open the door to Milo Ferguson, who was standing on the cracked concrete steps, in his brown sheriff pants and shirt. He nodded at Dad and addressed me. "I saw your rig out front."

I stepped back to let him in.

"Come in the kitchen. I've got a pot on." Dad led the way.

What was Milo doing here? Hadn't he done enough with accusing Ted? I felt like Dad was giving aid to the enemy—except I hadn't told him that Milo suspected Ted. One of Dad's favorite sayings was "You catch more flies with honey than with vinegar." Maybe if I didn't rub Milo wrong, it'd go better for Ted.

While Dad poured coffee and set the cookie jar on the table, I fidgeted in the doorway.

Milo let out an *umph* as he slid onto the picnic bench and sucked in his belly. Peppery whiskers covered his face, and bags drooped under his bloodshot eyes. It looked like he hadn't been to bed either.

"Have you figured out who killed Eldon? Who shot Ted?" Guess I didn't have much honey in me.

Dad set Milo's coffee on the table and floated a paper napkin to him. He pulled the lid off the jar, and Milo reached in and brought out a golden-brown chocolate chip cookie. My guess is that Louise, Fox number two and the self-proclaimed mother of the clan, filled the jar for Mom and Dad.

Milo bit, chewed, and followed it with a swallow of coffee, while my nerves jangled. He motioned me to sit.

I stayed by the doorway.

He swallowed another bite and set the cookie down. "I need to ask you some questions."

"Questions?" I barked.

Dad pulled out his stern face. The one he used right before sending us to the corner.

Milo waved his hand. "I'm just getting some background. State patrol is sending someone out from Omaha. But I imagine they'll mostly handle the newspeople."

My stomach flipped. "News?"

Milo looked miserable, but not so much he couldn't munch Louise's cookie. "The state patrol guys advised me to refer those bloodhounds to them. That suits me."

I shifted to my other foot. What if the news media caught wind of Ted being under suspicion? That would jeopardize the election, and that would devastate Ted.

Milo folded his hands on the table in front of him. "What do you know about Glenn Baxter?"

Huh? Dad and I didn't offer a reply.

Mom surprised all of us by stepping into the kitchen. "He's obscenely wealthy from his cable news station. And even if he's a typical East Coast dick smoker pandering to overconsumption, I do approve of his plan to buy up ranches in the Sandhills and convert the whole area to a buffalo common."

Mom might often be distracted, but she wasn't stupid or uninformed. Apparently she'd been hiding on the stairs and felt compelled to join us.

I cringed at her term for rich, entitled businesspeople who made outrageous wealth buying and selling paper, and had no compunction against screwing someone else. It wasn't a slam against sexual orientation, any more than others use the term brown-noser, but I wasn't sure anyone would know that. Mom believed in Karma and goodness, so her using this term, which she did often enough, seemed out of character. We didn't know Mom's parents and we speculated this prejudice of hers came from her upbringing.

Milo looked startled. Maybe it was Mom's decidedly un-Sandhills kimono, her gray Medusa tresses, or her crude terminology. Maybe all of it. He took a moment to get his breath and address me, as if he were afraid of Mom. "They say he's one of the ten wealthiest people in the country."

"What does Glenn Baxter have to do with who shot Ted and Eldon?" I ignored Dad's frown at my impatience.

Milo's eyes shifted to Mom hovering by the stairs, then back at me. "Talk is that Baxter wants a half dozen spreads, and figures Eldon's as the cornerstone."

I eased into a chair, too tired to stay upright. "Carly told me Baxter had approached Eldon to sell."

Milo sat upright. "Did she say what Eldon thought about it?"

Mom took a few steps toward Milo and he stared at the table.

Dad leaned on the butcher block. "Eldon wouldn't sell the Bar J. It'd be like selling his legs."

Milo nodded. "I 'spect you're right. But what if Eldon had decided to sell? S'pose that might upset some people? People who might inherit a piece of the Bar J?"

There was only one heir to the Bar J. That was Carly, unless, as Brian's wife, Roxy snagged a few acres. No "supposing" about Carly being upset if Eldon sold the ranch. But completely irrelevant. I shrugged.

Milo picked up the cookie and set it down. "I'd like to talk to Carly if I could."

I leaned forward. "Why do you want to talk to Carly?"

"For one thing, she might know some things about her granddad that would be useful. And after that, it's worrisome if she's run off again. Teenagers have all these . . ." He screwed up his eyes and moved his hands as if twisting an imaginary Rubik's Cube. "Hormones. It can make them do some crazy things, especially if they're troubled."

Mom stepped toward Milo, thunderclouds gathering in her face.

Warning frosted my words. "Carly's not troubled."

One eyebrow cocked. "But she was upset that Eldon thought about selling the ranch? Anything else that might disturb her?"

I stood, my chair scraping the floor. Milo pushed himself from the bench.

Dad and Milo passed some kind of communicating look between them, but it was a language I didn't understand.

Mom advanced on Milo. "You couldn't be insinuating Carly has anything to do with this." She picked up a wooden spoon from a utensil canister next to the stove and waved it like a sword.

Milo backed toward the outside door, keeping ahead of Mom's lethal spoon. He eyed me. "Have Carly call me by the end of the day."

5

Mom might have chased Milo off, but he was shaping up to be a definite burr under my saddle. First accusing Ted and now creeping up on Carly. That last would be an easy fix. I'd find Carly—okay, maybe not as easy as it should be—and drag her to Milo. He'd ask her a few questions and that would be that.

On a better day, witnessing Milo's reaction to Mom would have tickled me. Not many people saw Mom in her full-on working stage, when she didn't sleep, barely ate, didn't bathe for days, and her eyes had a glow like plum-crazy glaucoma. My college psych books told me she was probably manic. Folks in Grand County shook their heads and dismissed her as an artist. For us, Mom was just Mom.

Mom and Dad showed mild concern about Carly's disappearance. They probably accepted, as I did, that Carly had a knack for survival.

"Try not to worry too much about Carly," Mom said. "When I was her age I hitchhiked from Chicago to San Francisco. She's a smart girl with an open heart. She needs to find her own way."

A light tapping came from the window on the kitchen door. We all turned to see the outline of Aunt Twyla's head through the curtains. Mom slipped from her chair like a cat slinking from a roomful of dogs. She caught Dad's eye before disappearing downstairs.

He nodded and pushed himself to his feet. A genuine smile lit his face before he opened the door to his older sister.

Aunt Twyla zipped into the kitchen. Unlike Dad's thinning, gray hair, Twyla's curls stayed thick and long, like a teenager's, but one look at her face showed the ravages of a life of booze and cigarettes. She shoved a casserole dish into Dad's hands. "I don't know where to take the condolence food. I'll be damned if I take anything to that floozy Roxy, and I'm not craving a drive out to Frog Creek."

Did Aunt Twyla dislike Roxy because she'd been Ted's old girlfriend, or was the animosity merited? Aunt Twyla and Uncle Bud owned the Long Branch, the most popular restaurant and watering hole in Hodgekiss, so Twyla knew most of the goings-on—if not from firsthand witnessing, then through gossip.

Dad nodded and took the casserole dish. "Here's as good a place as any."

"Where's Marguerite?" Twyla's cigarette-smoke-husky voice demanded.

Dad didn't hesitate. "Sick headache."

Twyla huffed her disbelief. She focused on me. "What happened at the Bar J?"

Robert was right. It didn't take people long to start asking. "Milo Ferguson is in charge of the investigation, and the state patrol will be involved. They have some theories."

Twyla eyed me. "I see the state patrol sent a woman. She got a room at the Long Branch. Channel 10 from Omaha grabbed up the other two."

That was fast. I hoped Milo would keep his mouth as tightly clamped about Ted, with the media, as he was with me. I planted my hands on the table and pushed myself up. "Guess the best we can do is go about our business and let them work."

Twyla considered me a while longer. "If you hear anything, let me know."

"Sure will," I said to her back, as she hustled out the door, nearly knocking into Mom's geriatric next-door neighbor, Beverly.

Beverly held a rectangular cake pan in her shaking hand. "I was afraid it might be too early, but since I saw Twyla over here, I thought I'd best bring the cake."

I took the cold pan Beverly had obviously just pulled from her freezer. The early bird gets the gossip. "Thanks, Beverly."

I had a half foot of height on Beverly and she leaned toward me, pointing her face up. "I heard you were out at the Bar J. Did you see who did it?"

I repeated my line about staying out of the investigators' way. Before I got free from the kitchen, though, neighbors had dropped off a ham, a five-pound can of coffee, two loaves of home-baked bread, and a batch of warm cookies. All excuses to find out who killed Eldon Edwards. Sure, they were motivated by morbid curiosity, but a thin shellac of fear coated their faces, and more than that, sorrow floated in their eyes.

The ice had already melted from the highway, so it didn't take long to hit our turnoff. I pointed Elvis down our narrow dirt road, watching, as always, the sky, the grasses, and the hills. Last night's storm and this morning's sunshine seemed to encourage green tints in the meadows, while the hills remained winter gold. No loose cattle or coyotes dotted the hills. Nothing appeared out of the ordinary. Water ran in the windmills I passed, so I wouldn't have to pitch ice. The blue sky held no warning of bad weather. My mind bounced between Eldon and Ted. Carly. Milo. Ted. Carly.

I drove through a narrow spot between two hills, across an Auto-Gate, and eased on Elvis's brakes. Out of habit, I stopped here, where our home valley opened up in front of me. The house, the barn, several outbuildings, and the plowed garden spot stretched below a hill on the west. A cultivated alfalfa field spread from the headquarters across the meadow to hills on the east, with a center pivot irrigation sprinkler at rest, waiting for summer.

A red-tailed hawk hunting for mice soared in lazy circles over the hay meadow in front of our house. I breathed in some of his freedom. The skiff of snow from last night was a memory, and only a bit of frost lingered in shadowed hoofprints in the frozen mud of the road. The sun hovered just east of center.

The first time I saw this view was on my third date with Ted, nine years ago. I'd come home from the University of Nebraska with a bachelor's in psychology, a truly useless degree, unless you planned on grad school and beyond. I liked school, but I couldn't get enthused about where it would lead me: a city, an office, someone else's schedule, wearing heels and dresses every day. Prison.

I knew Ted, of course. In a town of a thousand, you know everyone. But he was six years older than me, in Louise's class. Louise disliked him, which was good enough reason for me to be interested.

After my grade-school fantasy had faded I hadn't given Ted much thought, until he burst into my life on New Year's Eve. He and Roxy had broken up for the final time—they broke up every year or so, just to stay in practice. But this time it seemed to take. Roxy had moved to Colorado to work on a dude ranch.

Ted was smart and funny. He loved to take me riding in the hills around Frog Creek. I can't say why I fell so hard for Ted. I did. When I was with him I felt special. I was his one and only. After a lifetime of being the invisible middle child who always shared a bed and clothes, food and toys, it felt wonderful to be the focus of someone else's life.

I continued around the curve, toward the headquarters, and followed the drive to park behind the house. If Robert had been here at sunrise to check the cows, that meant they'd been on their own for over four hours. I might be ready to collapse from exhaustion, but I wouldn't sleep until I saw to the state of my ladies.

I stepped out of Elvis and reached inside for my old Carhartt barn coat. The calving lot took up three acres halfway up the hill behind our house. A worn dirt path led from our back walk, across the drive, and up a steep climb to a gate in the barbed wire fence. The most I kept in the lot was fifty head, the cows I predicted would calve the soonest. I could check on them every two hours. I adhered to common knowledge: if a cow started to calve and hadn't finished within two hours, she likely needed an intervention.

I trekked up the hill and into the lot. Crisp air brought scents of freshly fed hay, the musky dust of cowhide, and the hint of manure, only starting to ripen with the day's thaw. The cows paid scant attention to me as I meandered along the softening ground, checking to make sure none needed my help. Robins celebrated spring in the soft morning air. The cows munched hay Robert had fed them earlier, their grinding teeth and their huffing breaths adding a beat to the birds' song. At least here, peace reigned.

Assuring myself the ladies would be okay without me for a spell, I plodded to the house. The whistle from a BNSF coal train floated from the tracks that ran along the highway twelve miles north. Some mornings, the air at Frog Creek was so still and magical that the sound made the long, impossible journey to be here in this special place. I understood how it felt.

I stumped up the back steps, closed my fingers around the wooden door handle, and pulled, slipping into the covered porch. Worn pegs crowded with coats and jackets lined two walls. A simple bench with peeling paint flanked one wall, with boots, old tennis shoes, and even a collection of mismatched flip-flops tossed underneath. I peeled off my coat and manure-crusted boots, kicked them out of the way, and padded to the back door.

I entered the sunny kitchen and slid along the old linoleum. I only got as far as the fridge before I stalled out. Most of my brothers and sisters have real, grown-up refrigerators. The kind that stand taller than a barefoot preteen. A modern appliance with two doors and shelves and drawers and even a separate freezer compartment. I was sure my fridge was the same as the model in *I Love Lucy*'s kitchen. I couldn't use the freezer nestled in the top because it frosted over so quickly.

I slipped from the kitchen. The house, not counting the unfinished basement, was probably spacious by homesteaders' standards. I loved all one thousand square feet of it, even if most folks would find it dowdy and cramped.

The silence nearly crushed me. Was it only yesterday that Carly's annoying rap music competed with Ted's complaints that we were out of eggs? What had Carly said about her plans? She wasn't much of a morning person. But she'd seemed even more growly than usual. She'd refused breakfast, finished off the milk by drinking from the carton and shoving it back in the fridge. With a "See ya," she tromped out the back door. Ted hadn't been far behind her. Then, I'd been happy for the peace.

How would I tell Carly she'd lost another loved one?

A creak from above sent a zing shooting through me. I tore through the dining room to the short hallway leading to the bedroom and bathroom. I wrenched open the door to the attic. "Carly?"

"Yeah," she hollered back.

Cool relief showered me. "I didn't know you were home." I started up the steep stairs where I piled her folded laundry, books, shoes, and any other things I cleared from the rest of the house. "Where's your pickup?"

Her head appeared around the top of the stairs, long blonde hair draping across her face. Puffy eyes and a red nose paired with her hoarse voice. "By the fuel tanks. Just a sec. I'll be down."

She knew. I'd dreaded telling her, but I didn't trust the job to anyone else. What had they said? What would I say now? I backed down and waited for her by the front door, where I strained to see to the far side of the barn, to the fuel tanks.

The attic door clicked shut and Carly trudged from the hall, shoulders slumped under her backpack, hands thrust deep into her jeans pockets. "Hey."

I stood in the living room between the office we'd converted from a closet, and the couch. I held my arms out and she walked into them. But she seemed done crying and impatient with my touch. She straightened quickly.

"I'm so sorry, Bird," I said.

Her eyes swam, but the tears stayed put. "Yeah. It sucks." She looked above my head, out the window.

I gave a quick glance outside, then back at her. "Is someone filling up your pickup?"

Her gaze dropped to the floor, over to the wall, and with a sigh of resignation she answered, "Yeah. Danny."

Danny Hayward. Her sometimes boyfriend. Though not since last spring. I didn't put much effort into hiding my surprise or disappointment. "He's the one who told you?"

She frowned. "He called me from town last night and I went to get him."

"And you stayed out all night?" That wasn't what I wanted to say, but I couldn't find the words to show how sorry I was for not being here to tell her. Sorry it happened at all.

Carly's sweet face hardened in defense. Most folks said Carly took after the Edwardses, with her Swedish blonde, blue-eyed beauty. But one look in her intelligent, fiery eyes branded her as a

Fox, and more specifically, as my oldest sister, Glenda's, daughter. "We sort of needed each other."

As Rope and Nat's grandson and ward, Danny lived at the Bar J. He'd care about Eldon, too. But Danny wasn't a solid friend. "Okay. I'm home now. Maybe Danny can take your pickup home and we'll get it later."

She shifted her backpack and her eyes darted to the office, then back to me. "Danny's pretty upset about Granddad and he doesn't want to go home."

"I'm sure he's sad, but what about you? Eldon was your granddad. Besides, being with Rope and Nat might be the best thing for him." What lame reasoning. But Carly should be with me or the rest of the Foxes. Not with a kid who had dragged her into trouble before.

Her face closed like a window in a storm. "He needs a friend, okay?"

"And you're the only friend he has?" Damn. I wasn't helping her one bit.

She thrust out a hip in annoyance. "No. But I'm the best one."

Danny drove Carly's ten-year-old Ford in front of the house and tapped on the horn. She'd inherited the black F-150 when Brian died four years ago. She rarely let mud cake its sides or dust settle inside. For her, it was a gas-powered shrine.

Carly struggled too hard to be tough. I sighed. "You don't have to be strong for everyone."

She frowned at me, then out the window at the pickup. Danny rested his forehead against the steering wheel, looking limp as a pile of dirty laundry. "Danny." She paused. "He's not so strong."

I backed up a little to give her space, both physically and in conversation. "What are you planning to do?"

Gallant young man that he was, Danny held the horn down a little longer this time.

She stepped around me and put a hand on the front doorknob. "We're going to school. Be around our friends."

Apparently tired of waiting, Danny climbed from the pickup. Instead of looking frail like Nat or lanky like Rope, Danny resembled a rhinoceros. He had about as much charm and wit as one, too. His dirt-colored hair always looked like it needed to be washed, and stains pocked his T-shirts. He clomped up the porch steps and flung the front door open, yelling, before he saw me, "Come on."

When he recognized me standing in front of the window, he paled and his mouth went slack. His red-rimmed and veiny eyes testified to his tears.

I ought to show some sympathy for the kid, but my main concern was Carly. "Go on to school. I'll bring Carly."

His eyes lumbered from me to Carly. A whine crept into his voice. "I thought she'd come with me."

Carly's expression put up the generational fence, planting her on one side, sword raised in defense of Danny, and me on the other, no weapons handy. "I want to be with my friends. Don't you get that?"

Sure I did. "Okay. Milo Ferguson needs to talk to you first, then I'll take you to school."

Danny drew in a quick breath. Of course, he naturally feared the law.

Carly stuck out her chin. "What does he want?"

A cat shrieked and I jumped out of my socks. My heart slammed into my ribs before I realized it was my phone. Carly loved to change the ringtone. Last week it had been a baby crying. Before that, some awful rap song. I scowled at her and her mouth ticked into a hint of a smile before grief quashed it. I pulled my phone from my shirt pocket.

"Kate Conner?" a male voice more stated than asked. "This is Glenn Baxter."

Not what I expected. I held up my hand to Carly in a wait-a-second gesture.

"I understand you're Carly Edwards's guardian," the voice continued.

"That's right." Was I really talking to one of the world's wealthiest men? I pictured Glenn Baxter from the few images I'd seen on TV. He had a lanky build and the pasty complexion of someone who spends his days behind a desk. Dark hair with dashes of salt at the thin temples. He was probably somewhere in his midforties.

"First of all, my condolences for Eldon Edwards's death."

Murder. Eldon's murder. Ted's injury. Reality threatened to surge past my feeble wall. "Thank you." Now I held up one finger to Carly and padded into the kitchen so they wouldn't have to listen.

He cleared his throat as if in a funeral parlor. "You may know Eldon and I had an agreement in place for the sale of the Bar J."

His respect for the dead only created an avenue to talk business. Mom might be right about him being an East Coast . . . well, what she said. "Nope. Didn't know that."

Oil dripped from his voice. "The problem is that he passed away before he signed the agreement."

"Passed away" sounded so much better than "murdered."

I was only slightly more hospitable than Mom would have been. "My niece lost someone she loves. We've all lost a respected member of our community. What is it I can do for you, Mr. Baxter?"

Again, that sorrowful voice felt like biting on aluminum foil. "I'd like to conclude the sale of the Bar J with Carly Edwards. I understand she's Eldon's only surviving heir. Five million dollars would go a long way to ensuring your niece a fine future."

That was the price Eldon settled on? If he had the hundred thousand acres "they" said he did, five million was about one-tenth of the market value. Sounded like the upstanding Mr. Baxter was fixing to swindle Carly. "I'm not convinced Eldon wanted to sell. Not at that price, anyway."

"Oh, believe me, Eldon agreed. He had good reason to get out while he could." It sounded like those threats used car salesmen toss out: *I've got three people interested in this beauty. They're getting their credit checked right now.*

"I'll let Carly know you called."

His voice crawled from my phone on eight spindly legs. "Her grandfather told me working a ranch was no life for a young girl."

This had the coppery taste of a lie. Carly spent a good portion of her weekends at the Bar J. She loved working cattle with Eldon. Carly would probably be living full-time at the Bar J if she didn't have to be at school five days a week.

"Thank you for passing that along."

An undercurrent of frustration soured Baxter's sweet words. "Of course. I only hope you'll let me talk to Carly so she can consider carrying on Eldon's final wishes in good faith."

I said something nice that Dad would have approved of, and severed our connection. I stood for a moment. Would Eldon really have sold the Bar J?

I returned to the living room. The front door stood open, letting in the crisp morning air. Danny and Carly headed for the idling pickup. She was probably telling him she'd see him later. Except she climbed into the driver's side and Danny ran to the passenger door.

I took off for the porch. "Carly! Wait!"

She didn't. Gravel spewed from her tires before Danny even closed his door.

Dust rose as Carly gunned it around the bend and rattled over the AutoGate, disappearing between the gap. My fingers tingled with cold before I turned and walked back inside.

I woke up to the smell of chocolate chip cookies, something that ought to draw me to the kitchen with anticipation. Instead, I wanted to run to the toilet and puke. The clock told me I'd been asleep for four hours. I rolled over and grabbed my phone from the bedside table. Because Ted is sheriff and I sometimes acted as dispatch, the number for Broken Butte Community Hospital was programmed into my phone. They told me Ted's condition was stable and that he hadn't regained consciousness yet.

I flopped onto my back again and stared at the ceiling for a second.

Damn it, Carly.

I'd stood in the living room after she and Danny drove away. Maybe it would be better for her to be with friends. Teenagers often leaned on each other more than on parents or someone like me, a sad excuse for a surrogate mother.

No one could love her more than I did, though. Trust that she could deal with this new tragedy in her own way warred with my desire to help her. She'd call if she wanted me. That wasn't enough, but what else could I do?

I climbed from my cocoon and padded to the dresser for clean underwear.

"Oh, good, you're awake," Louise said from the doorway.

I jumped and yelped before turning to see my older sister advancing on me. All boobs and belly and outstretched arms, dressed in her mom jeans and decorated sweatshirt. "Louise, what are—"

"I dropped the kids at school this morning and heard about Ted. I came right out, but you were sleeping. Oh, honey, I'm sorry. How is he?"

I backed away, but not quickly enough.

Louise yanked me into a smothering hug. "Oh, you poor thing. Do Mom and Dad know?"

I disengaged myself. "Yep."

"I don't suppose they were sympathetic." She folded her arms in disapproval. "That's why I'm here. At a time like this, family needs to pull together."

Or not.

"You slept so long that now I've got to pick up the kids. But we can come back out if you want."

Sending the kids out here and leaving herself at home had more appeal. "No. Thanks anyway." I started pulling on my clothes. If you grow up with four sisters wedged into one bedroom and a bathroom with no door, you've got nothing to hide.

Louise wore her disaster face. "For Pete's sake. You don't have any groceries. Carly needs nutrition to grow right."

How nice of all my siblings to worry over Carly's nutritional well-being. Opting for a fresh pair of jeans and clean flannel shirt, I continued dressing.

"Thank the good Lord I stopped at Dutch's before I came out. I managed something yummy from what I brought."

Of course. For Louise, Dutch's Grocery was like a pharmacy.

"How did Carly take the news?" Louise asked.

I looked for a hair elastic on the dresser top. I mumbled syllables into the mirror, in a useless attempt to avoid the inevitable.

Louise wasn't fooled. "You didn't tell her, did you?"

"She knows." I opened a dresser drawer, then closed it.

"Where is she?" Louise's voice rose.

I pretended great concentration on my hair, smoothing it back despite having no ponytail holder.

She gasped. "You don't know where she is."

I left the mirror and eased out the doorway into the hall. I shouldn't have let Carly go. I'd need to hog-tie her soon and drag her to see Milo. "She's with friends."

Louise slapped the dresser. In a falsetto voice, she said, "Let Kate be her guardian. She understands her best."

I did, actually. Understand Carly best. But that didn't mean much.

Louise chased me from the bedroom. "You don't know the first thing about raising kids. You go after it like Mom and Dad. Letting kids do what they want, never giving them boundaries and discipline."

Campaign posters for Ted's reelection had been knocked helter-skelter from the dining room table. I picked them up and stacked them.

VOTE FOR TED CONNER

GRAND COUNTY SHERIFF

TRUSTED AND EXPERIENCED

I'd meant to plant those posters in Hodgekiss and the four other little towns in sprawling across Grand County. The primary election was only two weeks away. As incumbent, Ted ought to win, especially with the weight of the Fox clan behind him. Of course, that was before Milo planned to charge Ted with murder. Dahlia had spent a fortune on the signs, and she insisted I place them, since I was related to a high percentage of people with yards and storefronts.

Louise hounded me to the kitchen. Her lecture gained steam. "It's like in kindergarten, when the other kids were making fun of her about that stupid stuffed toucan."

I'd given it to Carly when she was born and she'd loved it immediately. She'd carried it with her everywhere, talked to it, fed and cleaned it. Carly called it Birdy Bird.

As far as I knew, Birdy Bird lived on Carly's bed, upstairs in the attic.

Louise's lecture was like little hammers in my brain. But, as a gossip hound, she might be useful. Fortunately for me, Louise didn't hoard her information. "Who do you suppose might want Eldon dead?" I asked.

She switched gears without a hitch. "I heard Milo Ferguson is investigating what happened." Louise picked up a plate of cookies from the counter and set it on the table. She'd left cookies at Mom and

Dad's, which Milo had munched, and now she supplied them here. They were like turds of love that she dropped wherever she went.

The cookies had all the appeal of day-old roadkill. Emotional upheaval as a diet aid might be effective, but it couldn't be healthy.

Louise helped herself to a cookie. Melted chocolate dabbed her upper lip like an edible beauty mark. She lowered her voice, almost to a whisper. "Who do you think did it?"

Not Ted. Not Carly, either. I brushed my hair from my face and searched my pocket for a ponytail holder. "A thief, maybe."

She waved one hand and reached for another cookie with the other. "Eldon didn't have anything to steal."

Glenda told me Eldon kept a boatload of cash on the ranch someplace. He's not the only old-timer who didn't fully trust banks. "What else could it be?"

Louise predictably warmed to the gossip. "They say murder is always committed for love or money. So if it wasn't money, what about love? I've always thought May Keller had a thing for Eldon."

"May Keller?" The woman was six days older than dirt and a widow for most of that time.

Wrinkles lined Louise's forehead. "Or maybe Eldon was carrying on with Aileen Carson and Jack found out. That's one creepy guy. He could have shot Eldon without a thought."

"Jack's not creepy. He's just quiet." I rummaged in the kitchen junk drawer and found a ponytail holder. "Besides, why do you think Aileen and Eldon had an affair?"

Louise leaned in. "It's the way they look at each other."

Oh, brother. I smoothed my wild waves and flipped them through the elastic. "I've got to check the cows." And go find Carly, drive to the hospital and see Ted, find out who killed Eldon so Milo would stand down, and in the meantime, keep Frog Creek running during the busiest time of year.

No hill for a climber, as Dad would say.

6

One of my best cows stood alone in the northwest corner of the lot, her tail kinked. That was a sure sign she'd started labor. I stared at her for a long while and finally decided she'd be okay on her own. This would be her sixth calf and I'd never had problems with her before. It rankled, leaving her now, when so much could go wrong.

While I debated abandoning her, Louise had climbed into her Suburban and headed out. My innards tied and twisted and roped together. Just yesterday I'd mentally complained about calving season dragging on and had wished that this busy time of year would come to an end. If I'd known what was in store, I'd have clung to the fatigue of regular overwork.

First things first. I climbed into Elvis and pointed him after Louise. I had to check on Carly and somehow get her to talk to Milo.

Twenty minutes later, Elvis buzzed through Hodgekiss, now bustling with morning activity. Okay, maybe "bustling" was generous, but there were several outfits in front of the Long Branch, and most parking spots on Main Street were full.

I was surprised to see Rope Hayward's pickup heading into town as I coasted out the west side. Rope didn't venture off the Bar J often, and coming to town today would expose him to packs of gossip hounds. Maybe he had business relating to Eldon's death.

Grand County Consolidated High School squatted on several acres to the west of town. Since the school couldn't afford to bus students who lived an hour or more from town, most kids drove themselves. Old beaters filled the lot, and Elvis fit right in.

I parked and bounded to the school and into the carpeted lobby. Louise's class was the first to graduate from this building, so compared to the courthouse or most businesses downtown, it felt new. They didn't serve cooked spinach every day, so why did the school always smell like it? Even though the wonderful aroma of the bread the cafeteria ladies prepared almost daily hovered over the top of everything, my stomach rolled over.

Mary Ellen Butterbaugh rose from her desk when she saw me approach the office window. Easily the smartest and most cultured person in town, she'd been school secretary since the dawn of time. "You didn't need to come all the way in. I know why Carly isn't here."

Drat. I hadn't really expected her to be in class, but it would have been nice not to have to track her.

"Thanks," I said. Then, without hope, I asked, "Danny Hayward's not here today, is he?"

Mary Ellen twitched an eyebrow in interest. "Oh, dear." Mary Ellen was a good egg. She knew all and kept her own counsel. Insightful enough to know Carly shouldn't be with Danny, she wisely never tried to change a teen's mind.

"Is anyone else out today?"

She shook her head. "Sorry. Just the two of them."

I didn't like that.

I zipped my coat as I crossed the parking lot toward Elvis. The sun shone bright but acted stingy with the heat. Typical April, full of tricks and contradictions.

I drove back into town, thinking about Rope Hayward. As Eldon's ranch foreman, he'd know who came and went and who might have it out for Eldon. And as Danny's guardian, he might know where the kids went. I turned onto Main Street and found a parking spot next to the Bar J pickup, in front of the post office. Rope strode out with a fistful of mail, face lined with shadowed crevices, all scowls and squints. Faded Wranglers draped from his bony hips and he wore no coat over his plaid Western shirt.

It looked like he walked slowly, but those long legs ate up the ground, so I had to scurry from Elvis to intercept him. He'd already climbed inside the pickup and had the engine rumbling when I tapped on his window.

His deepening frown created a series of Grand Canyons along his chin and cheeks. He rolled down the window but didn't say anything.

"How's it going?" I hadn't meant to start with meaningless small talk, but the darkness of his eyes unnerved me.

He wasn't going to play the inane game with me. "What do you need?"

Social skills weren't Rope's strong suit, so I took the direct route. "Do you know where Danny is?"

He growled in the back of his throat, not a full-on rabid dog sound, but maybe that of an annoyed cat. "I guessed he's at school. If he's not, I can't say."

And people accused me of detached parenting. "How about Nat? Would she know?"

He stared straight ahead, and his fingers squeezed the steering wheel so hard that his knuckles whitened. "Can't say."

I tried again. "I didn't get a chance to talk to Carly about Eldon, and I think she's with Danny. I really need to see her."

His lips barely moved. "I don't see as that's my business."

Eldon's murder would naturally be hard on Rope, but my sympathy only ran so deep. "Danny was out at Frog Creek this morning, and he looked pretty broken up. I thought maybe they'd need some help processing Eldon's passing."

His head pivoted slowly toward me. "I gotta get back to the ranch."

"I understand. I'll give Nat a call."

His jaw flinched and the growl came out as rough words. "Just give 'em a bit and they'll be fine." He shoved the gearshift into Drive.

I reached in through the window and laid a hand on his arm. "I really need to get in touch with Carly. Milo Ferguson wants to ask her about Eldon."

He closed his eyes. "He thinks she shot Eldon?"

"No! Of course not. He just wants to talk to her." I nosed into the topic. "Can you think of anyone with a grudge against Eldon?"

He reopened his eyes and locked them with mine. "I can." He planted his boot on the accelerator and jerked backward.

"Wait!" My protest was lost in the squeal of tires. I could call Milo and try to get him to talk to Rope, but my guess was that it'd do little good. Maybe I couldn't get more out of Rope, but I might get Nat to talk to me.

Rope gunned the engine and turned onto the highway. I followed, walking down the sidewalk to the Long Branch. I pulled out my phone and checked the time. I needed to get to Broken Butte and see Ted. Priorities warred inside me. I could help Ted more by finding Eldon's killer than by staring at his sleeping face.

Rope's comment about others wanting Eldon dead piqued my curiosity. Aunt Twyla might have something interesting to add.

I pushed through the glass door, into the vestibule of the Long Branch. About the size of two old-time phone booths, the vestibule separated the restaurant from the bar area, though that didn't make much difference. Anyone, including minors, could eat and drink on either side. I barreled into the restaurant.

The place smelled like deep-fry grease and stale beer, enough to make me pause and swallow down nausea. Not much put me off my feed but, apparently, having a husband shot and accused of murder introduced me to new territory. Maybe the nausea would subside when I found Eldon's real killer. Thank you, Psych 101.

The building was divided roughly in half. The bar side of the Long Branch occupied twice the space of the restaurant because the kitchen and restaurant shared the other side. A dozen red molded-plastic booths flanked the long, narrow dining room, along the windows that looked out onto the highway. The opening into the kitchen, the silverware station, the drinks dispenser, and the rest of the serving equipment took up the opposite wall, allowing for a walkway, about six feet wide, from the door to the end of the room.

Most of the booths were empty, because it was nearing two o'clock and dinner in the Sandhills arrived at noon. Always. Supper could run anywhere from five to seven in the evening. Breakfast ended by the super-late hour of seven. That left afternoons and mornings reserved for the coffee klatch. Today, two groups of gray hairs occupied separate booths.

Aunt Twyla stood in the kitchen. She looked up through the servers' window and waved. She yelled, her voice gravelly, "How're you doing, honey?"

I leaned toward the window so I wouldn't be shouting in the restaurant. "Do you have a minute?"

She came around a shelf to talk in a normal level. "I wish I did. The danged dishwasher busted and I've got Bud repairing it. If I don't stand by for him to cuss at, he might start growling at the new waitress and she'll quit and I'll be stuck waiting tables until we hire some other fool."

Some things never changed.

"Kate," a voice surpassing Twyla's on the cigarette-scratch scale called out. May Keller, a hardened little woman who looked like wet rope left to dry in the sun sat at one of the booths facing me. “What have you heard about Eldon?”

I wandered to her table. May Keller’s ranch neighbored the Bar J. She was old enough to have swapped nursery school stories with Methuselah. “How’re you doing, May?”

May cackled, following it up with a gurgling kind of cigarette cough. “I been better, hon. At my age, you’d think I’d get used to friends dying. But I gotta tell you, Eldon’s passing has hit me hard. Couldn’t stand to be out on the ranch by myself, so I come to town for groceries and one of Twyla’s finest.” She pushed a plate with sticky frosting and cinnamon stuck to it.

Her bony hand closed around my wrist and she yanked me down to sit next to her. “I heard about Ted and that tramp.”

If NASA could replicate the speed of gossip in Grand County, they’d be able to reach the moon in three hours. Problem was, the message could get distorted. Like now. I didn’t understand the tramp reference but assumed it had something to do with Roxy. Since Ted was at the Bar J and that’s where Roxy lives and Ted and Roxy had been high school sweethearts, the tongue-waggers would conclude they were having an affair. Or that’s how May’s oxygen-deprived brain summed it up.

May pounded a fist on the table. “Men can be such asses. My husband tried that with me once and I fixed his wagon. Ain’t bothered to hook up permanent since.” She winked at me. “Don’t mean I don’t have me some fun now and again.”

“They” said May’s husband disappeared mysteriously and never showed his face around Grand County again. Maybe May did him in, as rumor had it, and she’d done Eldon the same when he didn’t return her affection. I didn’t buy it.

May harrumphed in disgust. “There seems to be a lot of it going around. You heard about Aileen Carson?”

This was my chance to slow the speed of gossip. "Aunt Twyla makes the best rolls."

May patted my hand. "Don't let that fool get you down. I always thought you were too good for him, anyway."

Was I supposed to say thank you?

She seemed to have covered that topic and jumped to another. "At least with Eldon being gone it might get Glenn Baxter out of my hair." May was a lifelong smoker with diminished lung capacity. I thought all that tobacco had not only shriveled her up but also sucked out some of her smarts.

"He's been bothering you?"

She coughed again. That deep gurgle didn't bode well for her own mortality. "He's been jawing at all of us out north. At first he was all sugar and sweetness, offering us gobs of cash for his crazy buffalo scheme. Then he threatened us."

"What do you mean?"

She played with her fork, probably craving a cigarette. "First he said Eldon agreed to sell and, if I didn't join them, I'd be surrounded by buffalo who'd tear down my fences." She stabbed at the table. "But I know good and well Eldon wouldn't sell. So then Baxter said—in that barely-a-whisper kind of criminal voice—about my health not being so good and he hoped my affairs were in order."

I wanted to take the fork away before she accidently stabbed me. "Why would he say that?"

She cackled/coughed/gurgled again. "Oh, hon, he was trying to scare me. Make me think he'd kill me to get my land."

How many *CSI* episodes had May watched out there alone on her ranch?

She tapped the tines of the fork on the table. "Listen, I want to know how's Carly doing?"

One of the best things about Grand County is the way people care for each other. "She's upset, of course."

May nodded. "Anyone could see that filly loved her granddad. But here's the thing: young 'uns, they don't always understand the whole picture. They get an idea into their heads and can't see anything else."

Milo had an interest in Carly. Rope had commented about her involvement. And now May. It made me want to offer her a smoke. "Right."

She jiggled her foot now, making the bench vibrate. Her eyebrows wagged up and down, as if telling me more than her words. "You know? Carly. And Eldon."

She was starting to ruffle my feathers. "I'm sorry?"

She leaned close, and her breath smelled like coffee, cigarettes, and cinnamon roll. "I won't say anything. I know how passion can lead you to do things you wouldn't otherwise do. Bad things."

I couldn't help moving back a little. "You lost me, May."

She glanced around to make sure no one was listening. "At that meeting. You know, the one where Baxter sent his fancy lawyer. Carly went to speechifying—mighty good at that—about how no one should sell their ranches. I think she got it into her head Eldon was fixing to sell. Which he wasn't."

May stopped to cough, and I waited.

When she got her breath, she continued. "I won't tell Milo or anyone else about that."

Knowing she suspected Carly capable of murder made me rethink my position on May offing her philandering husband.

From the way she inched toward me, I assumed May needed to get outside to light up. I unfolded from the booth. "It's been good talking to you. I'm sorry about Eldon."

She scooted out after me. "We all have to go sometime." She nearly ran me down, getting out of the Long Branch.

I didn't know who killed Eldon, but May Keller, Glenn Baxter, or even Rope Hayward seemed more plausible suspects than Carly or Ted. But would anyone else, especially Milo, think that?

Ted would know who had shot him and Eldon. Maybe he was awake now and I could stop all this useless searching.

I started off on another trek to Broken Butte. I had to drive over most of Grand County and into Butte County, sliding just a mile or two through Choker County, which ran along Grand's eastern edge and north to Nebraska's border with South Dakota. We're a bunch of square states, and Grand County copies that pattern. Sprawling over six thousand square miles, it's bigger than Connecticut, Delaware, or Rhode Island, with about as many people living inside its borders as there are square miles. Foxes are related to most of them. In a county where cattle outnumber humans by more than sixty to one, Ted had captured one of the steadiest and best-paying gigs around. Not a bad job.

Unless you got yourself shot.

One of the largest towns in Grand County, Hodgekiss mainly existed to support the BNSF railroad and to give the far-flung ranches a central gathering spot. It sported a few businesses, but those carried only essentials. It was a town version of a highway convenience store; a little of this and that.

Normally, therefore, a trip to Broken Butte was an occasion. Broken Butte had a Kmart, a Maurice's dress shop, Hardee's, and Pizza Hut. A few other mom-and-pop businesses specialized in everything from new cars to farm equipment to carpeting, and most necessities. At a whopping population of fifteen thousand, Broken Butte was, for us, the City. Mom always made us clean up and wear good clothes when we made the trip.

Today, the sixty miles from Hodgekiss dragged. I shouldn't have stayed so long in town. Ted might be awake right now, and I wanted to be there before Milo showed up. Ted would need me. I drove too fast. If I arrived by Ted's bedside just five minutes sooner I could spare him that much more misery. The hills stayed the same dull yellow and brown, with only a promise of the spring green. Here and there, cows and their young calves stood in pastures next to the highway. I normally loved to watch the babies. Their white faces looked pristine, their black bodies all shiny. But my eyes stayed on the road and my mind looped and spun twelve ways to sundown.

I finally hit the last ten miles of flat road, and soon Broken Butte's water tower loomed in my windshield. I had to cruise through ten blocks and tap my palms on the steering wheel while waiting for a geriatric woman with a scarf tied on her head to cross the street. I punched the gas and turned north onto Main Street, then drove to the edge of town, to the "new" hospital—meaning it was built just after World War II. I spun Elvis into a parking spot and was halfway across the parking lot while he still ticked and sighed and settled in.

Aunt Tutti plodded across the lobby, deep bags hanging under her eyes. This afternoon she wore gray-blue scrubs that nearly matched her permed head. I probably looked as frantic as I felt. She paused when she spotted me, and waited until I caught up to her. "They just got Ted moved to his room. Two thirteen. Down that way."

Thank the stars they hadn't put Ted in the same wing where Glenda had died. I reached out a hand and squeezed Aunt Tutti's plump shoulder, trying to be polite, even if I'd rather sprint to Ted's room. "Don't you ever go home?"

She graced me with an exhausted smile. "I pulled a double. Lots of staff out with the flu. Happens at calving season every year. Don't ask why."

I didn't. I barely held myself back from running, and when I closed in on Ted's room, I actually did trot. I swung into the room, surprised not to see Dahlia and Sid.

Ted lay on his back, head turned toward the window. I probably made some kind of squeaky noise, or maybe the sound of my running in boots made him turn his head. I didn't register anything except that my husband was alive and awake and moving. I flew across the room and made a tent over his face with my arms. Maybe I shouldn't touch him, but I had to kiss him.

He mumbled something against my lips. Maybe I'd surprised him, or he was trying to greet me. There would be time for words after I did this one thing.

His lips felt cold against mine. Poor Ted. Shot, alone in the hospital. Probably frightened and upset. I drew away and gently placed my hand on his hair, smoothing it with the slightest touch. "How are you?" It wasn't the greatest thing to say. What about *I love you, I'm sorry you're shot, I want to make it better*? But words were too shallow for the sea of feelings.

Ted's voice sounded like it had been run over with a tractor. "I'm full of painkillers, but I'm not feeling anything yet. That's not a good thing."

Beneath the dusting of dark whiskers, Ted's skin took on the color of chicken fat. Fatigue and worry rimmed his eyes. He smelled sort of like a forgotten load of laundry left to dry in the washer, with a spritz of bleach and old oatmeal.

"Have you talked to Doc Kennedy?"

"He stopped in this morning while I was sleeping. He told Dahlia . . ."

He broke off and I waited. An unwanted image of his over-involved, fluffed, and pressed mother flashed in front of me. It bothered me that he always called her Dahlia, like she was his friend, not his mother.

He swallowed and his Adam's apple bounced. "They won't know anything until the swelling goes down."

Okay. We needed to stay calm and upbeat. "That makes sense. So we'll wait and see."

I acted nonchalant by gazing around. Ted's private room contained his bed and two hard chairs with orange vinyl cushions.

Nothing in the room dragged it from sterile, typical hospital, not even the cheap seascape print on the wall. Why would anyone slap an ocean on the wall in landlocked Nebraska?

His lips shook. "What if I never walk again? What will we do?"

I flicked my attention from the tube of a catheter peeking from his blanket. "No sense in getting all upset if we don't have to."

If I'd been Dahlia, or even that flibbertigibbet Roxy, I'd succumb to panic and start bawling. Instead, I whispered, "It'll be okay." In the silence that followed, I looked out the large window at a wheat field stretching north of the hospital, the emerald grain standing about a foot high and waving in the breeze.

He reached for my hand—a good sign, since it meant he wasn't totally paralyzed, even if he missed it on the first try. "Thank you for always being so strong."

I let that sit for half a beat, then said, "Has Milo Ferguson been in to see you?"

He looked confused. "I just woke up. I haven't seen anyone but Dahlia and . . ." He paused. "And the nurses."

"Did Dahlia and Sid go home?" I asked.

He gave his head a slight shake and swallowed. "I think Dad left last night sometime. The nurse came in and she chased them to the cafeteria for coffee. Dahlia threw a fit, but she finally left."

Them? Anyway, it was good we were alone. I could get this all taken care of without having to deal with Dahlia. "Who shot you?"

He looked startled. "I. Uh."

Maybe I'd been too abrupt. "Do you remember who called you and why you went to the Bar J?"

His hand dropped to the bed and he blinked several times. "No. I don't remember anything."

"Nothing?" This wasn't going to help his cause. "You need to concentrate, because it's really important."

Without hesitating to give himself time to consider, he answered quickly. "No. I don't remember anything."

He wasn't taking this seriously. I'd have to tell him more. "You have to remember, because here's the crazy thing: Milo Ferguson thinks you shot Eldon."

His eyes flicked from side to side as if they were trying to read his brain. A thin stream of panic seeped in. "What?" He squinted at me and said again, "What?"

Maybe I could back him into it. "Okay. Think. Did you or Eldon get shot first?"

"Eldon was shot? Where were we?" His voice creaked. "We were together? I swear, I don't remember."

"You were in Eldon's office."

"At the Bar J?"

I counted to three. "Yes. Why don't you talk it through with me. Step by step."

He wrinkled his forehead in concentration. "I can't remember being in Eldon's house."

I spoke as calmly as possible. "Going to the Bar J. You got there quickly. Who called?"

He blinked again. "Why don't you ask Eldon who shot us?"

I took hold of his hand and lowered my voice even more. "Because Eldon is dead."

His mouth dropped open. "No. That can't be."

Several moments of silence followed, and Ted sniffed and wiped at his eyes. The wind slammed against the window and sent a tumbleweed scurrying from the wheat field. Clouds scuttled across the sky, making the light grow and fade.

A clack of heels and the rapid staccato of a female voice warned us of Dahlia's approach. I took the opportunity for one more kiss before she invaded. Ted's eyes remained open, and they took on a wild gleam, so I pulled back before we connected. "What's wrong?"

Then I recognized another set of clacks on the floor and another female voice answering Dahlia. Roxy was still here?

"Honey, I'm home." Roxy sailed around the corner, and her wide, glossy-lipped smile dropped from her face.

Dahlia bumped into her. They both froze.

I turned to Ted, who stared at me, his mouth and eyes wide.

My blood felt like fresh cement hardening, as certain thoughts I didn't want to think crowded into my brain. "Milo said Roxy found you and Eldon."

He didn't move.

"Did Eldon call you to the Bar J or were you already there?" I asked, even though I figured Ted wouldn't answer.

He didn't.

My brain was a runaway, and no matter how hard I yanked at the reins, it galloped onward. "I didn't see your squad car at the Bar J."

Ted's mouth opened and closed in perfect imitation of a bass.

I might not have put it all together if Ted hadn't been on pain meds and therefore not up to his peak cover-up performance.

No one moved for several seconds, as if waiting to see whether something or someone would explode. Finally, I shook my head. "My guess is that your squad car is hidden out back of Roxy's house, and if there was any delay in you responding to an emergency at Eldon's, it was only as long as it took you to put your pants on."

Ted's gravelly voice pulled up the least original phrase in the world: "I'm sorry."

With all the dignity I could muster, I skirted the two women and marched out the door.

I wasn't more than a few feet from his room when the cold hatchet of Dahlia's voice landed between my shoulder blades. "Where are you going?"

7

"I need to talk to you," Dahlia said. General Patton couldn't issue a firmer command.

I kept walking. Ted and Roxy. I knew it. I goddamned knew it. Or I should have figured out May Keller wasn't as addled as I'd thought. The world around me seemed squishy, sounds warped. My skin felt split open, leaving my insides free to spill onto the floor.

I slumped against the corridor wall and squeezed my eyes closed. I collected my guts, zipped them back into my skin, and took several deep breaths. When I opened my eyes, Dahlia advanced on me.

Her long legs unfolded and contracted like a tarantula. Why did I always go to the dark side where Dahlia was concerned? She had a fierce love for her only child. What was so evil about that? Her lying, cheating, no-good bastard of an only child.

One manicured hand, nails painted cherry red, brushed through her hair. "You need to pull yourself together. I have something to say." She took me by the arm and marched us into the minuscule chapel. Her sweet perfume swirled up my nose and into my gut, threating to make me upchuck.

Two six-foot pews faced a raised platform. Muted lighting, immaculate furniture, and subdued colors didn't come close to soothing my devastated soul.

Dahlia released my arm. "Did Ted talk to you about the sheriff's debate?"

"The? What? No. What?" I couldn't unhitch my mind from the whole Roxy/Ted revelation. My husband, who was just shot and might not walk again, the one accused of murder, the one I'd been determined to prove innocent, had been sleeping with his old girlfriend. My husb—

She looked down her nose at me. I don't mean in the clichéd kind of way. She stood close to me, with her chin raised, and sighted down her pointy nose until her eyes nailed mine. "You need to take his place at the debate and then schmooze."

Hysterical? Probably. But her suggestion was so ludicrous I cracked up. "Schmooze?"

That broke her stare, and she stepped back. She looked as if she considered using me for target practice. Close-range target practice. "You *have* to. Ted needs you to step up for him. Support him."

"Seriously? Not two minutes ago I found out he was having an affair." That's not the vernacular I wanted to use, but I spared Dahlia the four-letter description. "I thought not shooting him would be pretty awesome of me."

She looked like she had slapped the cylinder and cocked the hammer. "Awesome. Sure. As if there's nothing in this for you."

Wait. Milo had said I didn't know Ted. May had talked about "that tramp." Even Dad had acted weird when Milo mentioned Ted. They knew. Everyone knew . . . except me. "How does total humiliation translate into anything good for me?"

She sighted down the barrel. "It's your obligation."

I nearly choked. "For the amazingly wonderful way Ted treated me?"

She seemed truly perplexed. "You don't think you owe Ted anything? After eight years of living off of him and never having a job?"

Was she delusional? Who did she think ran Frog Creek? Who brought in a more than 98 percent calf crop every year? Who managed the hay crew and put up record yields? "I've worked Frog Creek every day of those eight years." And for this, Ted rips the rug out from under my life. Crumbling foundation, broken heart, crushed—every cliché I'd ever heard, revealed its truth.

She waved that off. "You told me more than once that you've always wanted to be a rancher. Ted gave you the opportunity you could never afford without him."

I needed to get the hell away from this woman. "Good-bye."

She glared. "After all this family has done for you, you're going to walk away?"

I stepped around her, heading for the door.

Her aim narrowed. "That's fine. But know that if this is the way you're going to be, we're going to quit doing for you, too."

Fine. I kept walking.

She fired a shot. "If you don't help Ted, your marriage is over."

I stopped to count to ten. I only got to five. I turned back to her, wanting to slap her smug grin. "What makes you think I want it to survive?"

She raised one eyebrow. "Do you think you're the first wife to have a wandering husband? Tell me: Until yesterday, were you satisfied with your life?"

I held my hand up as if it could stop her.

She got off a second round. "You had a good relationship with Ted, and you loved being at the ranch."

Until Roxy's phone call, yesterday had been pretty nice. But I couldn't unring any Roxy bells.

She sported her superior smile. Her third shot nicked my flesh. "You can stay on the ranch if you help Ted get reelected."

"Maybe I don't want to stay." And maybe I didn't want to keep breathing.

Dahlia sighed. "No games here. The only thing Ted ever wanted was to be sheriff. Even as a kid. He looked cute with his cowboy boots and little six-shooter."

Somehow, I couldn't give a sparrow's fart what Ted wanted.

"We were so proud of him when he won the election. Daddy nearly burst his buttons." "Daddy" being the exacting father of the three Flower girls—Dahlia and her sisters, Rose and Violet.

I desperately wanted to stay on Frog Creek, but I couldn't live there without Ted. And I didn't know how I felt about Ted. I hated him. I loved him. He'd betrayed me. He'd been my best friend. Was it over? Was this a terrible time we'd look back on while we sat on our front porch and watched our great-grandkids search for Easter eggs? Or was this when I cut my losses?

I'd had enough of Dahlia's insanity. The door opened and closed while she still spouted nonsense.

I escaped from the hospital. I beelined to Elvis, fighting tears and hoping my shredded heart would keep beating. Dusk dropped a thick curtain, and wind tugged my hair. I held back the flying strands with one hand while my other hand fished in my pocket for keys.

"Well, howdy, Kate." Milo's heavy footsteps and wheezing sounded behind me.

Not now. I needed to dive into Elvis and slam the world out before the dam burst and I flooded everything with my pain. I braced myself, hoping I had enough steel to talk to Milo without falling apart. I opened Elvis's door, though, ready for a quick retreat. "Milo."

"Been in to see Ted?" He held a Mountain Dew can, which he

brought to his lips and spit tobacco into. A nauseating wintergreen smell floated to me.

The wind bit at my hands as I clutched the Ranchero's door. "I just came from there."

"How's he doing?" Milo spit into the can.

Whatever jumble of noxious emotions churned inside me, it was anger that rose to the top. "Why not see for yourself? The day's nearly over and you're finally getting around to hearing Ted's story before you throw cuffs on him and drag him from his hospital bed."

Milo cocked his head back as if I'd slapped him. "I'm not fixing to haul him to jail. And I'm sorry if it offends you I hit the rack for a few hours. And it happens I had cause to do a little investigating."

I didn't want to have this discussion. I didn't want to talk to anyone about anything. "Don't bother. Go ahead and throw his carcass behind bars and let him rot. I'll testify that the lying SOB wasn't with me."

"Oh." Milo only had the one word.

Darn bless it. I tried to pull everything in close, tighten down the cinch, and keep the reins steady. But a piece deep inside me loosened and caused everything to fall apart. Without warning, tears gushed, and I let out a sound as if I'd been punched in the belly.

Milo stepped back and gulped.

I spewed like a geyser. "You knew. You knew all about Ted and Roxy and you didn't say anything." I gasped in a sob and the tears rained down.

He must have thought that if he moved I'd start in again. I don't think he even breathed. I felt bad about putting Milo in this awkward place, but I felt a lot worse for what Ted had done to me.

I leaned my forehead on my arm, letting Elvis take my weight, and I sucked in two giant gulps of icy air. I sniffed, wiped my eyes on my coat sleeve, and looked up at Milo. "I don't think Ted shot Eldon, but I'm not going to do anything about finding out who did."

He spit into the Mountain Dew can. "I'm on my way in to talk to him about that." Before I could throw myself into Elvis, Milo stopped me. "Have you got hold of Carly?"

I shook my head.

He spit. "Think she knew about Ted and Roxy?"

I glared at him.

"Think that might chap her, Ted messing around behind your back?"

The wind yanked at my hair. "Carly isn't involved in this."

He rocked back on the heels of his cowboy boots. "Maybe."

My head throbbed with everything pent up inside. "If you've got something on Carly, just tell me."

Deep shadows of sunset hid his face. "Seems Eldon kept a mountain of cash in his office."

I rubbed my forehead with frozen fingers. "What's that got to do with Carly?"

"The money's gone missing."

He seemed full of information. "How would you know about this?"

He lifted the pop can and spit. "I got a glimpse at Eldon's will. He intended Carly to have that cash, and specified the sum. It's a goodly amount. He allowed as how only him and her had the combination to the safe."

Of course Milo had seen the will. Eldon's lawyer was probably Niles Ferguson, Milo's brother. "So how do you know the money is missing?"

"Eldon's attorney turned over the combination to me and I checked. Safe is dry as the Sahara."

My skin heated from the inside out. "So now Ted's off the suspect list and you think Carly killed Eldon, shot Ted, and stole the money?"

"I've seen murders committed for less."

8

By the time I got back to the ranch, night had swallowed the day. A blanket of clouds coated the sky, making it feel as dense and heavy as my heart. The radio weatherman predicted no precipitation, so the cloud cover would provide insulation, keeping the killing cold from my baby calves. In the same way, a sort of numbness padded my thoughts of Ted and Roxy. Contrary to how I had felt an hour ago, I decided news of their affair probably wouldn't kill me.

It was too early to think spring had arrived for good, but she was inching toward us. Likewise, I knew I'd eventually come out the other end of this sorrow, but it was too soon to really believe it.

After a check on the cows—no new calves—I made my way to the house and into the kitchen. The tub of cookies and the clean dishes neatly stacked in the strainer were the only indication that Louise had been there again.

No sign of Carly. Even though I wanted to be alone to process the shock of Ted and Roxy, Carly needed me. We'd have to get in touch with Milo soon. But more than that, I wanted to touch her, to see that she would get through this latest grief.

When I was a junior in high school, Steve Misner had run his car into an oncoming semi after a party. When we heard the news, all of his classmates gathered at the shallow lake north of town. We stayed out there for two days, drawing comfort from one another that we'd never be able to get from our families. It hurt that Carly could get more help from her tribe of peers than from me, but I understood it.

Acid swirled in my belly like something that bubbled and popped in a Yellowstone caldera. I hadn't eaten since noon the day before, and even though I hated the thought, I heated a can of soup and forced it down, sitting at the old table in the kitchen. My own frazzled reflection in the window kept me company.

I rinsed my bowl and reached for the phone just as the cat shrieked. Damn, I had to change that ringtone. Another reason I needed to find Carly.

Susan's name appeared in the ID window. When I answered, she said, "Carly is here."

Oh. I let out a pent-up breath. Safe, but so far away. "Let me talk to her."

Susan hesitated. "She said to tell you she's fine. She doesn't want to talk to anyone. She'll call later."

"That's not okay." Maybe she didn't want to talk to me, but I needed to talk to her. "Give her the phone."

I knew better than to tell Susan what to do. If you grow up with eight older brothers and sisters, you either become compliant or contrary. Susan chose rebellion. She and Carly were a lot alike that way.

Her tone toughened. "She asked to be left alone. I'm going to respect that."

I backed up a few paces. "Eldon's passing is a big blow, but she can't run from it."

"Just give her a little time, okay?"

I didn't want to alarm Susan by telling her Milo might suspect Carly of the shooting. "Family is the best thing for Carly right now." Oh God, I sounded like Louise.

"Look, it's really not up to you. Carly's been through enough shit. Back off."

The thought of Carly's pain serrated my heart. What harm would it do to let her alone for tonight? Milo could go hang for another few hours. "Okay. Only for a little while."

Susan's silence was the equivalent of a disdainful stare. She was still a teen and knew everything. I sighed. "Then tell her I love her. That we all love her."

Susan sounded sad. "I already told her that. I'm not sure it helped."

Carly might be in the best hands right now. At any rate, she'd chosen, and I'd give her peace. For one day. Then she'd either talk to me or I'd drive to Lincoln and haul her home myself.

I leaned on the kitchen counter, tired of the battering thoughts of Ted and Roxy. I forced my mind to Carly. When had Carly started acting strange? There was one night a few weeks ago.

Carly had whirled into the kitchen like a tornado as I sealed foil over the dinner plate I'd filled for Ted. He'd said he would be home later, because he had to finish some paperwork at the courthouse. I'd stopped myself from questioning why he had to work past eight o'clock.

Breathless, she stood in her gym shorts and hoodie. "Shit. I forgot. I have to bring six pictures of me, growing up, to school tomorrow."

I imitated her, hoping to point out her constant cursing without nagging. "Shit. Okay."

As I expected, she rolled her eyes. "It's for the graduation program. Ms. Parker jumped my ass today. They were supposed to be in last week."

I guess hinting about cleaning up her vocabulary wasn't working. I slipped the plate into the fridge. "There's a box of your parents' stuff in the office closet. There's got to be pictures in that."

We dug out a lidded cardboard orange crate from behind Ted's old shotgun and three years of tax records and plopped it on the living room floor. Carly yanked off the lid and sat back as if a snake might jump out.

Tentatively, she reached to the top and pulled out an envelope of snapshots. "This is so old-school."

"We had a whole different way of doing things before smartphones. Even when we had digital cameras we still made prints." I took out another envelope and flipped through the dozen or so prints. "Look! This is you with Susan and Ruth. I'm guessing you're about four years old." The three little girls sat in the sandbox in back of Mom's house. There was a whole series of them in their matching pink-and-yellow bikinis, pouring sand on each other, racing in the green grass, holding Kool-Aid cups, and sporting red-stained grins.

Bittersweet memories brightened in my mind. "Ruthie was staying with Mom because Louise was in labor with Esther. Your mother brought you in to play, and you three girls ran like wild animals."

Carly smiled. "Ruthie still gets crazy when her mom's not around."

"I'd just turned eighteen, and Mom let me share the margaritas she'd made for her and Glenda."

Carly stared at the photos as if transporting herself back to the sunny backyard. "That doesn't sound like the kind of day Louise would approve of."

I laughed. "We paid for it. When Louise showed up the next morning and found the three of you snuggled into one bed, with grass clinging to your feet and the Kool-Aid mustaches still on your faces, she pitched a fit about irresponsible child care."

Carly considered it. "I can see how she wouldn't take to three drunks minding her kid."

I brushed that off. "We weren't drunk. And even if we had been, the twins were thirteen and plenty old enough to babysit."

She set that packet aside and pulled out another. "This must be me and Dad." She handed me a picture of Brian, asleep on the couch with a two month-old Carly snuggled on his chest, thumb in her mouth.

We shuffled through the stacks of photo envelopes. Carly sat on the floor, her back propped against the couch. I perched on a rocker. Carly probably didn't remember most of what she saw in the photos, but here was proof she'd had a mother and a father and they'd loved her. She didn't cry, but her face looked brittle.

I told her story after story about Glenda as a child. Fearless, rebellious Glenda, always organizing the Fox kids on one adventure after another. She had us building tree houses that fell from the branches, bike races that ended in blazing crashes, safaris involving a thermos of milk and peanut butter sandwiches eaten in the pasture behind our house. It's a wonder any of us survived childhood.

I listened as Carly took her turn describing the world Glenda had created for her on the ranch. The same sort of fun, only safer and more controlled. "Dad was really different when he was around Mom. Sort of relaxed and easy."

None of the Foxes saw what Glenda did—general opinion of the clan being that Brian lacked brains and confidence and needed someone to tell him what to do. Before Glenda, I suppose it had been Eldon directing Brian's life. Even if I saw them as ill-suited, Glenda and Brian seemed devoted to each other. I chalked it up to a mystical match only they understood. After Glenda died, Brian became edgy. Marrying Roxy only added to the scent of desperation that clung to him, as if he had to work every moment to live up to her expectations.

Way past when Carly and I both should have been in bed, I said, "You want something to drink?"

She nodded and dug back into the box. I headed into the kitchen, hoping to find something without caffeine.

Why wasn't Ted home? I hadn't expected he'd be out this long. He probably stopped at the Long Branch after he finished the paperwork, and got sidetracked. Unlike me and Carly, he didn't have to be up at dawn.

I heated milk in the microwave. As far as I knew, Carly and I were the only people on the planet who actually liked warm milk. I thought we could both use the comfort.

I started into the living room with the mugs. Carly studied the contents of a dark-blue file folder. When she heard me, she slammed the file closed and looked up, a strained smile on her face.

I handed her a cup. "What was that?"

She didn't look at me. "Dunno. What do you think of these?" She laid out a half dozen photos, ranging from her as a newborn to her in early grade school. All of the shots showed Carly with either Glenda or Brian or both.

"Those should work." I plopped onto the couch beside her and traced my fingers along the top of her head, messing her blonde ponytail.

She dropped her head forward and encouraged me to keep massaging. We sipped our milk in silence. After a while she set her mug on the carpet. "Did Ted hang out much with Dad?"

I thought a minute. "Brian was a little older than Ted. They knew each other, but I don't think they were close friends. Brian went to

Kilner, so he didn't really have the same friendships he'd have had if he'd gone to high school here." Brian always acted as if he was a cut above the folks around here, and I assumed he felt more educated and worldly for his time at the military school. At any rate, he kept in touch with some of his old classmates and liked to drop details about their wealth and accomplishments into his conversations.

Carly pushed away from me and stretched her legs out. "So weird that Granddad would send Dad to a private high school. He's such a cheapskate."

I'd wondered that, too. "You ought to ask him about it."

She frowned at the box. "I did. Granddad said he'd gone there, and his dad too. So it was a legacy thing." She let that sit a moment. "Ted was sheriff when Dad died, wasn't he?"

"Yep."

She bent over her legs to stretch her back. "Did he investigate the accident?"

Carly watched too much TV, with all the cop shows. "It wasn't the kind of accident that needed investigating. Your father flew into the hill." On a beautiful spring morning with no wind, in a Cessna 182 that he'd been flying for four years.

Her eyes strayed to the folder. "They said he probably got distracted or confused and made a mistake, but did they check the plane to make sure it hadn't malfunctioned or something?"

I didn't want to think about the pile of twisted metal and charred plastic, the mangled body. "I doubt they could tell much from what was left. As I recall, he'd just had the plane in for its annual, so somebody must have checked that, at least."

"Yeah." Her eyes lost their sharp focus. Did she relive that afternoon often? Thankfully, she hadn't seen the plane go down, but she'd arrived in time to see Harold Graham and Eunice Fleenor load the gurney into the back of the ambulance. She'd missed

Brian's face, of course. They'd zipped the black body bag before she arrived.

My eyes drooped, but I didn't want to leave her alone with all the memories and loss.

Finally she stirred and pushed herself up. "See you tomorrow."

I staggered to my room and she made her way upstairs. The creaking of the ceiling, from Carly's restlessness, drew me out of sleep from time to time. Late in the night, I heard her talking to Ted. Content that he was home, I drifted off.

Carly took the photos to school the next day and, as expected, left the rest of the box's contents strewn around the living room floor. I put it all away. Curious about the blue file folder, I saved it out to read. But before I even opened it, one of my sisters called, and then it was time to check cows and get dinner going.

I pushed back from the counter. It seemed like I'd grabbed the folder with a pile of bookwork and had shoved it into the file cabinet, in a section marked "After Calving." My filing system might not be the most advanced, but I hated clutter. I had learned to keep my life as simple as possible during the weeks of calving. Stashing paperwork out of sight helped my psyche. Now, though, I'd take a cluttered office over a missing niece and cheating, bullet-riddled husband.

My house felt like a vacuum. No wind to buffet against the walls and windows, no one to turn on the TV or music, no conversation. I usually relished this kind of silence, but I wouldn't mind a little Carly bedlam about now. I headed to the office. The drawer where I kept the After Calving material was half open, and papers struggled out the top as if someone had yanked something out of the folders. I rifled through it. No blue file.

Up the steep attic steps, I snapped on the light. Carly's room took up one half of the attic, with storage on the other side. As always,

I drew in a breath to steady myself. With Ted's approval, and even his help, Carly had painted the plaster walls a startling chartreuse, outlining the windows in tangerine and lime. It was like being trapped in a Skittles bag. Clothes, books, makeup, shoes—the life of a teenager littered the floor, and a muffled odor of ripe workout clothes hung over it all.

I stood amid the wreckage and let my eyes travel over every surface. No blue file. I didn't expect to make a dent in the mess, but without much thought I grabbed a few jeans and shirts from the floor and dropped them on an overstuffed chair Carly had insisted on bringing from the Bar J. Not that I'd know if anything were missing, but I didn't see Birdy Bird anywhere. Seemed odd that a seventeen-year-old would take a stuffed animal with her for an overnight, or even two nights. Guess she was feeling pretty bad. I sighed. If she'd brought the file up here, it could be buried under . . . What was that? A plate of mummified Christmas cookies?

I backed down the stairs. I'd ask her about the file later. As soon as I had her home, we'd discuss how cleanliness might not be next to godliness but could go a far piece in preventing disease or insect infestation.

I checked the cows once more, set my alarm for two hours, and climbed under the comforter. In my bed. All alone. When I wondered if Ted would ever share my bed again, I finally broke apart and bawled into the emptiness. But not as long as I'd have thought, before I dropped down to sleep.

The alarm jangled me awake twice in the night to check the cows. I'd expected to stay awake fretting both times, but some self-preservation instinct allowed me to crash again. Good thing, because my phone started ringing before five a.m. and that was it for me.

9

With a gasp, I fumbled for the phone on the table next to the bed. The cat shriek had to go before I keeled over with a heart attack. In the time it took to punch on and bring it to my ear, I'd already run through the disaster possibilities. Ted had taken a bad turn. Carly in any manner of trouble. And that didn't count the random accidents my eight brothers or sisters and their families might be in.

"What?" I nearly shouted into the phone.

"Uh, sorry." Douglas's calm voice cooled my panic. The gentlest of the Fox kids, Douglas seeped unnoticed among the others, usually on hand to lend gentle support. Unlike his twin, Michael, who always popped and sizzled with energy.

I brought my own voice down to his kind level. "What's up?"

A cow's moo floated to me. Douglas managed the university research ranch at the far northeastern corner of Grand County. Sounded as if he was already at work. "Didn't mean to wake you up. We heard about Eldon and Ted and I wondered if you knew anything."

I plopped back on my pillow and closed my eyes. I gave him the scant information I knew about Ted's condition, the dull throb in my gut flaring when I avoided telling him about Roxy. I'd let Ted recover before one of my brothers killed him. The good citizens of Grand County had done an amazing job of keeping news of Ted's affair from the sibs. If any of them had known, Ted wouldn't have survived long enough to let an outsider shoot him.

Douglas projected away from the phone in a commanding voice. "Her. I need blood and fecal samples." He came back on the line. "What about who shot them? I hear Milo is investigating, and they say the state patrol sent an officer. But I figured you'd know more than any of them."

I barely finished explaining what I didn't know and where and how Carly was taking it when the call waiting beeped. I checked it. "Michael's on the line. Can you fill him in? I need to check the cows."

"Sure. Take care of yourself." With Douglas, that wasn't a throwaway phrase.

I padded to the kitchen, ignoring a call from Louise and two from other local folks. The last thing I wanted was to talk to people. One of our own had been gunned down in his home and the sheriff lay in the hospital. People were upset and concerned. Of course they'd call. Most of them would know about Ted's affair. I needed some time to temper myself to be in public. Besides, I didn't know anything about the shooting, and as sheriff's wife—not sheriff—I didn't have to talk to them.

I choked down some toast. I had to eat, but the simmering thought of Ted's betrayal seemed lodged in my gullet. When I added real grief over Eldon and what it must be doing to Carly, and the general stress of calving, it's a wonder I wasn't puking every thirty seconds.

I set my phone to vibrate and went about morning chores, knowing work would quell my agitation. While loading a round bale on the hay sled of the tractor and using the hydro-fork to deposit it in mini stacks in the calving lot, feeding the horses and bulls, checking the stock tanks for ice, and pairing up the new calves and cows and kicking them to the adjoining pasture, I checked each vibration. Since none of the calls came from Susan's phone—Carly's phone still sat in the house—and none from the Lincoln area code, I let them all go. Including the dozen from Ted's phone.

The sun climbed higher but didn't offer much heat. Knowing what surprises April often dishes up, the chilly, dry, and still day suited me fine.

I'd just pulled a heifer's calf and was on my way to the house to change my blood- and mud-smeared jeans and maybe force a little lunch down my throat when the purr of an engine alerted me to someone approaching. The nose of Sarah's green Dodge pickup poked around the gap and hurried toward the house.

That was the best sight I'd seen in a while, and I waited for her to pull up behind the house. With her thick chestnut hair tied in a bouncy ponytail, she slid from the tall four-wheel-drive and landed on the dirt driveway. Her outfit matched mine—Carhartt barn coat, faded jeans, flannel shirt—except she didn't sport the stylish cow manure and blood I was rocking.

She draped her arm over my shoulder and pulled a bottle of Jack Daniel's from her coat pocket. "It was only a matter of time before that shit-heel showed his true colors." She twisted the top off the bottle and handed it to me.

My fingers closed on the cool glass and my heart sank further. "You knew?"

She grabbed the bottle back and took a slug. With eyes blazing in fury she swallowed. "Not until this morning. Louise called and said you weren't answering."

I took the bottle. "How did she—"

Sarah flicked her fingers in a drink-up gesture. "Aunt Tutti or something."

"Doesn't matter. I'm pretty sure we're the last to know." I tipped back the bottle and let a dose of fire burn its way to my empty gut.

The Jack tradition started senior year in high school. Neither of us had dates for prom but, thanks to Jack, we'd had a great time anyway. Throughout college and until now, we'd tipped the bottle at our graduations, engagements, another month when one of us found out she wasn't pregnant—first in celebration, then in commiseration. Richard and Sarah had been trying for a baby for over a year. Ted and I knew we wanted kids, just hadn't decided when. Sarah and I didn't always mark the highs and lows of life with bourbon, but often enough.

Other women might hug me or want me to cry. But Sarah and I understood each other better than that. She tilted her head and assessed me. "What are you going to do?"

I passed her the bottle. "I ought to leave him."

Always my staunchest defender, Sarah gave me a halfhearted nod. "Is that what you want?"

Walk away from the only man I'd ever really loved? The only man who'd ever loved me? Leave Frog Creek without a backward glance? Fire up the chain saw and lop off both my arms; it wouldn't hurt any worse. I reached for Jack and slugged it back. It burned like acid and erupted in my stomach. "You never liked Ted. Robert hates him."

Sarah grabbed the bottle and took a swig. "So? You love him. That didn't stop, yesterday, when you found out."

She sounded suspiciously like Dahlia. "You think I should stay?"

She held up a hand. "Whoa. I didn't say that."

"Then, what?" I clutched the bottle, but my stomach lurched, so I didn't drink.

She folded her arms, calm flowing from her, as usual. "Take some time to think before you react. Right now you've got emotions running rampant. Let it settle, then make a decision."

My eyes weren't red-rimmed and puffy from crying. I was taking care of business as usual. Growing up in the middle of nine kids had taught me how to keep a stone face. If you let someone know you're ticklish, they'd be sure to tickle you. But Sarah was tuned into my silent distress. She might not know exactly what I was feeling, but she knew I felt it a lot.

My phone vibrated in my pocket and I pulled it out, not so much because I wanted to talk but more to change the conversation. I didn't recognize the local number, but I answered it anyway.

A booming voice identified himself. "This is Clete." Clete Rasmussen was county commissioner, with a million years seniority. He probably wanted to know Ted's condition. "I understand Ted is in the hospital and won't be able to make it to tonight's debate."

Ha. Pretty casual comment, considering everything it meant. "I don't suppose he's up to it right now," I said.

Clete cleared his throat; the sound blasted a pathway straight to my brain. I switched the phone to my other ear. "We still plan to have the debate for the school board and whatnot," he said. "But somebody suggested it's not fair to Rich Hamner if he don't get to speak his mind in public."

Rich Hamner, Ted's only opponent, didn't have trouble speaking his mind most Saturday nights in the Long Branch.

"So I was thinking," Clete rambled on. "Maybe you could fill in for Ted. Come to the debate and sort of . . . be Ted's mouthpiece."

Someone suggested? Someone named Dahlia? I'd have to sit in front of a roomful of my friends and neighbors and even a few not-so-friendly neighbors and try to sound halfway intelligent. There wouldn't be a soul in the room that hadn't heard about Ted and Roxy, and they'd scrutinize me. I'd be like a plucked chicken turning over an open flame, the fat popping and sizzling in the fire. "I don't think so."

Sarah frowned at me. She couldn't help but hear Clete's thunderous dialogue.

He cleared his throat again, but this time I was ready and had the phone a couple of inches from my head. "I understand. But it really ain't fair to Rich Hamner. And you know Ted's platform, and it seems like the neighborly thing to do."

Sure. Neighborly. I opened my mouth to say no again, but then I glanced at Sarah's stern face. One reason for Ted's popularity at the polls was the backing of the Fox clan. If I turned away from him, he might not fare so well.

I didn't care. He deserved to lose the election. His going to prison for Eldon's murder would even be sweeter.

Probably.

Sarah raised her eyebrows and tilted her head.

Damn it. She was right. The only way to buy myself decision time was to hold it all together. My stomach did a barrel roll and splashed into the inky ocean. "Fine. I'll be there."

When I punched off, Sarah clapped me on the back and offered me the bottle. "What doesn't kill you makes you stronger."

I shook my head. "You hate Ted."

She knocked back a gulp and twisted the lid on the bottle. "But I love you."

She had made the first moves to leave, when Aunt Twyla's Jeep Wagoneer puttered over the AutoGate, followed sixty seconds later by my neighbor, Doris Cleveland, in her dark-blue, twenty-year-old Lincoln Continental.

Sarah raised her eyebrows in a question.

I thought about the sixteen missed calls on my cell. "Guess I should have answered the phone. I never thought anyone would drive all the way out here to gossip."

Dick Fleenor, the EMT Eunice's rancher husband, followed the two women in his beater ranch truck.

Sarah scooted to her Dodge. "I'd love to stick around, but if I have to go to town tonight for the debate, I need get some work done."

She drove ahead and around the ranch yard in a circle and waited for the caravan to file behind the house. She stuck an arm out her window and waved as she accelerated away, leaving me to deal with the gossip patrol.

My nose was used to the manure and calving fluids, my own work-strained body, and the bits of straw and mud that clung to me. I wondered how offensive I'd be to civilized people. If they'd held off for a few more minutes, or at least given me some warning, I might have had time to clean up.

Twyla hit the ground with her mouth running full speed. "I tried to call but you didn't answer. People have been stopping by the Long Branch all morning." She opened the back door of the Wagoneer and hefted out a grocery bag.

I hurried over to help.

Doris Cleveland crept to a halt behind Twyla and lugged her basset hound face toward us, two loaves of bread clutched to her chest. She wore her husband's oversize work coat with the logo of Hodgekiss Feed and Grain embroidered across the back. The Clevelands owned the ranch farther down the road from Frog Creek. We shared fence lines and two-track trail roads.

Twyla settled one paper grocery sack in my arms. A Tupperware dish, probably containing the obligatory green-Jell-O salad, sat atop a five-pound can of coffee. "No one knows where to take the food. Your father must have gone somewheres, because no one's answering the door." Her disapproval of Mom's capriciousness about opening the door to uninvited guests was a given.

Dick Fleenor, potbellied and slow moving, joined us, toting a plastic grocery bag with two sleeves of paper cups towering out the top. "Eunice sent me over with supplies. She didn't know where folks were gathering and said you'd know what to do with this."

For Sandhillers, bringing food and paper plates to grieving families was like washing your hands after using the bathroom. You might survive if you didn't, but you wouldn't feel right about yourself.

Despite my growing nerves about the debate and falling behind on my ranch chores, as well as worrying that I smelled like a floating garbage barge, I invited them in for coffee.

"Only a quick cup," Twyla said. "With the debate tonight, we'll probably be packed for supper, and then that damned news crew tromping in and out at all hours."

"I can toast up some of this cinnamon swirl loaf to go with it." Doris pointed her doughy chin at the bread she held.

Dick grinned and held the porch door open while we trudged inside.

I set the coffee to drip and directed Doris where to find the knives and cutting board. "I think I'm out of butter. Sorry."

Dick rummaged in the bag with the cups. He pulled out a tub of margarine. "Here's the goose grease. Eunice thinks of everything."

I excused myself to change out of my gunk-caked clothes. By the time I returned, Twyla was pouring coffee and Doris had filled a plate with warm cinnamon swirl toast, dripping with margarine.

Dick sat at the Formica table and talked around the bread in his mouth. "Eunice said Rope and Nat looked pretty torn up."

Twyla blew on her coffee. "I can see where Rope would be wrecked. He and Eldon have been close since they were pups. But that Nat, I'd say they was more crocodile tears."

I picked up a slice of toast. It smelled good, and it might be smart to let it soak up the Jack in my empty belly.

Dick warmed his hand on his coffee mug. "I always liked Nat. She was full of spit and vinegar when we were in school."

Nat? She seemed like a tangle of anxiety now.

Doris busied herself putting the cold groceries, a casserole dish, and the Tupperware bowl in my bare refrigerator. "All that trouble with Mick took it out of her."

Mick was Danny's father, Rope and Nat's only son. He'd got on the wrong side of the law in Omaha and was locked up. That's why Danny lived with Rope and Nat.

Twyla sipped noisily. "I wouldn't wish that hellion on anyone, but Nat was a bitch well before Mick went bad."

Doris looked affronted. "I don't think that's right."

I nibbled at the bread.

Twyla shrugged. "She's a slippery one. You knew she told Rope she was pregnant to get him to marry her, and there wasn't a baby for eight more years. I wouldn't be surprised if she didn't shoot Eldon and Ted herself."

Dick frowned. "No reason for her to do that."

Twyla had a cagey look to her. "Folks liked Eldon because he was generous and helped people out. Like loaning Tuff Henderson money to buy the Stewarts' place."

Doris reached for the bread. "I didn't know that."

Satisfaction that she'd produced new information seeped across Twyla's face. "Course, Tuff spends all his time bellied up to the bar, so he's bound to lose it all. But Eldon, he did all sorts of things like that."

"That don't say why Nat should hold a grudge against him," Dick said.

Twyla leaned forward. "Well, see, that's just it. He helped out everyone else but never helped Rope out."

"Did Rope want help?" Doris asked. She'd finished another slice and reached for the last one on the plate.

Twyla set her nearly full cup in the sink. "Don't know if he cared, but I heard Nat and Roxy complaining about it one time."

I perked up. Tending bar, Twyla was privy to all kinds of unguarded conversations, and her insight could be helpful. In such a small town, everyone in the county mingled together, drawing interaction between unlikely partners.

Dick pushed back from the table. "I don't believe Nat would shoot anybody."

Doris pushed her finger on the bottom of the bread plate to catch the last crumbs. "But she might know who did."

Trying not to show my impatience, I ushered them out, and then stood for another fifteen minutes while we indulged the Sandhills custom of saying good-bye, starting another bit of conversation, saying good-bye again, and repeating the process a few more times. It was as expected as an encore at a rock concert.

It was already early afternoon. I hurried to the calving lot to make sure the cows were okay. Since I'd moved to the ranch, I'd never been this distracted in calving season. Then again, I'd never had a hailstorm of problems like this beat down on me. I thanked whatever good luck had brought the mild weather. In fact, it was better than mild, which probably meant a surprise storm on the way. Though an April storm could hardly be called a surprise.

With any luck, everything in the calving lot would be copacetic. I'd do a little boning up on Grand County, in anticipation of questions Clete Rasmussen was likely to ask, then get myself cleaned up and presentable.

All my plans disappeared in a puff of toxic fumes when Louise's Suburban charged toward the house. I'd rather hook my foot in a stirrup and be dragged through mud than discuss my wrecked marriage with Louise.

I kept hiking to the calving lot. "Hi, Louise," I said, when she threw herself from the Suburban and barked my name.

"We need to talk." She actually stomped her foot.

I considered ignoring her, but that would only keep her at Frog Creek longer. Best take the beating and get it over. I plodded down the hill. "You can talk while I do some stuff." I passed her on my way to the back porch.

She stayed on my heels. "I know you've been through a lot. It can feel like the end of the world when you find out your husband has been unfaithful."

Did she know from experience? I spun around. "You?"

She raised both hands and waved them. "No, oh no. Norm would never."

"Right." Norman probably wouldn't change underwear without her approval. I stopped on the back porch and pulled off the ragged hoodie that could use either a wash or a burial.

"This is just like you to bottle everything up. Glenda was the only one who could ever coax you into letting it out. Lord knows, Mother never even tried."

"Mother—'Mom' to the rest of us—doesn't believe in prying." And Dad didn't believe in gossip. Neither trait had stuck with Louise.

Louise huffed. "Or doesn't care. I'm concerned. You need to talk about your pain or it will fester."

I maneuvered around Louise, into the kitchen. "I'm really busy today. I'll stop in for coffee next week and we'll hash out every feeling I've ever had."

She shoved around me to keep me from going into the living room, popping me against the refrigerator.

I pushed her, not enough to bounce her on the counter, but enough to emphasize my words. "Back off."

She braced for battle. "You're not putting me off this time."

I really wasn't up for this after all. I spun around to escape out the back door.

Before I got there, she wrangled by me—she had a definite weight advantage—and deposited herself in front of the door, phone in hand, punching furiously.

"What are you doing?"

She held the phone up to her ear. "Staging an intervention."

"What?"

She used her pudgy palm for a stop sign and talked into the phone. "Ready? She's here."

I waited to see what came next.

My sister Diane's exasperation shot through the speaker. "What the hell are you going to do about Ted?"

Louise looked annoyed. "We're supposed to be giving her support." Louise loved conference calls in equal measure to how much we all hated them. She cast sad eyes toward me. "As your loving family, we want to give you some guidance through this difficult time." She sounded as though she was reading from a script.

"I'm good. Thanks."

Louise lurched toward me, but I dodged before she could smother me in one of her flesh-eating hugs. "That's only the pain putting up walls. You need to trust us. We're older and have seen more of this sinful world."

Why, oh why hadn't she been a missionary in Botswana and left the rest of us alone?

"Hello-o-o." Diane sounded impatient. "I've got a meeting in about two minutes. I want to know what you plan to do about that shit you married."

Louise's gasp of disapproval was predictable. "Diane, please."

I pivoted away and shot through the living room, aiming for the front door. Louise surprised me by passing me and getting there first.

Diane's voice drilled from the phone. "Look, I know you think you love him and all that bullshit."

Louise propped herself against the front door. “I’m sure you don’t use that dirty talk in board meetings.”

At times like these I longed for a few comic books and a bed to crawl under. Let my sisters hash it out.

Diane kept talking. “Ted’s been using you for years, making you work the ranch while he plays Marshall Dillon. I hope now you at least see what a misogynistic pig he really is.”

I switched directions and popped into the office. Maybe I could dig out something from Ted’s files to help me in the debate. Bad idea, because Louise moved to barricade the office doorway.

“This is not about your divorce, Diane,” Louise said. “We need to let Kate talk.”

I didn’t.

Louise began the conversation for me. “I’ve never trusted Roxy. From the time you and Ted first got together I’ve had a feeling she had her eye on him. Is that how you felt?”

Maybe. Okay, yeah. I should have trusted my instincts.

“Of course she didn’t trust that bitch Roxy,” Diane said. “But she did the ostrich, head-in-the-sand thing she always does. The issue is not what Roxy did or didn’t do. It’s what her bastard husband did.”

And they were off to the races, as usual. I could let them rant while going about my business and entering their arguments on my mental *t* graph: one side for staying, one side for leaving.

I opened a drawer in Ted’s file cabinet. I had no idea what I might need to know for the debate. I tried to imagine the questions Clete would come up with and what the audience might ask. He’d want to know Ted’s plan for keeping kids from drinking and driving. He’d ask about patrolling during the county fair. He might even ask if and when Ted proposed to hire a deputy, which had been in the budget for three years.

Louise countered. “Her husband is in the hospital, not knowing whether he'll walk again. He's made mistakes, sure. But that doesn't mean she should shirk her responsibility to him. She married him for better or worse. Just because he faltered, she doesn't have to compromise her character. Even more so if he's a paraplegic."

Louise earned a point for her side.

I found a file of this year's county commissioner meeting minutes. Maybe there was a log of trending crimes for the last few years. That way, I could remark on Ted's strategy for preventing those, which I'd make up, of course.

Diane sounded breathless, and I assumed she was rushing toward her meeting. "So, let Roxy take care of him. She wanted him when he *walked* into her house; see how she likes it when he *crawls*."

Score one for Diane.

Louise seemed to have forgotten about me. "He's only a man. She wouldn't leave him if he developed cancer or some other disease. They'd fight it together. Is this different?"

Sleeping with an ex-girlfriend versus ALS. Louise didn't score that point.

"Oh, for God's sake, Louise. Even your Bible says it's okay to dump the prick."

Louise dove into her favorite topic. I had no trouble moving around her. "The Lord says you *may* divorce in the case of infidelity, but you don't *have* to."

I hit the back door when I heard Diane say, "I've got to go." As an aside, she said, "Katie, you know I love you, but you've got to grow a pair and boot that prick to the curb."

Ah. The sound of a gentle breeze through new leaves soothed my ears. Diane and Louise had laid out the pros and cons of sticking by my man. All I had to do was decide.

The county debate hovered over my shoulders, breathing down my neck. Despite the early afternoon sun, dark clouds of worry blotted out the cheer. As with so much of my life, everything hinged on Ted.

So, instead of chores and boning up on Grand County details or making sure I had an ironed shirt, I tumbled into Elvis and took off for the hospital again.

About halfway to Broken Butte my stomach did swirls that Van Gogh would have appreciated. My mouth flooded, and I had only a few seconds to slam on the brakes and pull over. I didn't even get out of the car before cinnamon swirl loaf splattered onto the pavement. I heaved until there was nothing left.

A windmill pumped clear water only a few paces into the pasture, so I climbed out, shimmied through the wires of the fence, and made my way there. I rinsed my mouth with water pumping from the pipe and drank a few sips, worried that a gulp would hit my gut and start the whole process again. Some people have panic attacks, some slip into depression. I guess I handle emotional upheaval in a lumpier way.

I climbed back into Elvis and headed down the highway, letting my mind float. Full awareness flashed with a sudden jolt. A washing machine agitated inside. I clamped my lips against the threat. What if my nausea and food aversion weren't symptoms of emotional distress? Three of my sisters were mothers. Glenda, Louise, and Diane. All three had suffered morning sickness.

10

An hour of pointless worry later, I made my way to Ted's room on feet heavy as a Clydesdale's. I didn't see Sid, but Dahlia held a plastic pitcher and watered an arrangement of lilies and daisies.

Her chatter sounded overly chipper. She started when I entered. "Kate! Why aren't you getting ready for the debate?"

Ted, still pale, didn't say anything. He smelled a little fresher than yesterday, and it looked like his blood circulated, even if it wasn't enough to give him a rosy glow.

"I'm heading that way soon." I gave Dahlia an assessing study. "You probably want to get cleaned up yourself, so you'd better get going."

She rewarded me with an uncertain look, wondering what shortcoming I'd noticed and how extensive the repairs would be. She set the pitcher on the radiator next to the flowers and leaned close to Ted, rubbing his arm. "I do need to wash my hair and make sure Sid wears something clean. Will you be okay?"

He manufactured a weak smile and patted her hand. "Thanks for staying with me all afternoon."

She kissed his forehead. “That’s what you do when you love someone.”

Subtle, Dahlia. I waited while they exchanged a few more admiring and loving words, and dodged the daggers Dahlia shot at me as she sashayed out of the room.

I leaned on the radiator that ran the length of the room, underneath the window, and placed my open palm on my belly. If my curdling stomach wasn’t caused by emotional turmoil but by a baby growing inside me, then Ted and I would be attached forever, even if we weren’t married.

“It’s good to see you,” Ted said. The buttery feel of his tone and sincere affection in his eyes smothered me.

I resisted the urge to step closer and touch him, the physical need to bend down and put my lips against his. “Okay.” I cleared my throat. “What do you suppose Clete will ask?”

His face fell. “I was hoping you were here to forgive me.”

I pushed off from the radiator and walked to the foot of his bed. Sarah said to give myself time, and that’s what I intended to do. “Let’s concentrate on the debate first.”

If his eyes were fingers, they’d be stroking my hair. “I love you, Kate. Ever since you threw that punch at me on New Year’s Eve. I need to know there’s a chance for us.”

Ted hated anyone to be mad at him. He’d charm and cajole until he softened the toughest resistor, not because he cared for them but because he wanted them to love him. He was trying to break me down. And even knowing this, the memory of that night fluttered inside me, ripe with the excitement of romance.

I’d been in the Long Branch on New Year’s Eve, closing on midnight. Dickie Halstead had brought his slick college roommate home for the weekend, and the dude thought he was all that and a bag of chips. He’d been dogging me, trying to buy me drinks, putting his hands where they oughtn’t be, and promising we’d seal the new year with a kiss. When the countdown started, I spotted him shoving his way toward me. I wound through the herd of drunks, trying to get away. When the shout of "Two! . . . One!" rose, someone grabbed my shoulder. By that time, I'd had enough folderol from the dude, and without looking first, I whirled around and drove my fist into his chin.

The chin belonged to Ted, and I hadn't done much damage. But the incident tickled him and we'd started dating. It was like someone clicked a light on in a gloomy room. When Ted shined on me, the whole world brightened. Within months we were married. I'd never regretted it. Not a lot, anyway. I wasn't sure even now that I'd do it differently.

Ted's skin had the dry, pale look of plaster. His eyes filled enough that a tear fell from each. I tried to predict which would reach his chin first and what route it would take through his stubble. He sniffed. "I'm so sorry."

"Hey, I've got a new rule for you."

His bloodshot eyes appeared worried. "Rules?"

I watched closely to see his reaction. "No Roxy. If you want me to stay, you can have no contact with her. No calls, no visits."

Was that sorrow? "I can't stop her from coming in here or calling me."

"If she shows up, you send her away. If she calls, hang up."

He shook his head. "But I can't be mean to her."

My skin burned, sending heat all the way through me. Very slowly, as if talking to a two-year-old, I said, "You're married."

He looked chastened. "I know. And I love you. But she's all alone. I can't just cut her off."

Unbelievable. Even for Ted. I leaned forward and glared at him. "Your choice. You hurt her or you hurt me."

"I just need some time." He sounded as though he believed the request was reasonable.

Maybe I'd harbored this secret idea that I'd walk into the room and butterflies and bluebirds would swirl around us. We'd fall into each other's arms, all the past vanishing in our declarations of true love. Disappointment dropped, heavy and blue.

We didn't speak for a moment. "Are you mad at me?" he asked.

Didn't I have a right to be? I stood at the foot of his bed, feeling untethered. Screaming, crying, pounding his chest—while it might feel great—would accomplish nothing. Words couldn't come close to solving anything. So I stayed silent.

His pathetic smile was probably calculated to elicit my sympathy. "I don't have any feeling yet. Doc says he's not worried, but I think he's hiding his concern."

A thousand words of support and encouragement stayed fenced inside of me. He didn't deserve my care. I walked to the window to shed the urge to say something nice.

A long, uneasy silence followed. The afternoon was dying as quickly as my hope. I hadn't really come here to talk about the debate. Whatever I'd wanted, I wasn't getting. I turned to leave.

"No. Wait!" Ted sounded desperate. "I didn't kill Eldon. I didn't."

Wow. He'd shifted from the I-love-you-please-don't-leave-me track with a jolt. "What did Milo say?"

Ted grasped the rails. "He says it looks like I did it."

I shrugged. "Did you?"

"You know I didn't. But I can't prove anything in this hospital bed. You've got to help me."

No. I didn't have to help him. I stopped at the foot of his bed. "Why should I believe you didn't kill him? Seems like you're pretty good at lying to me."

His face mottled like a tomato left on the vine during a heavy freeze. "I know. I'm sorry. But this is different. I didn't do it."

Yeah. That didn't mean I wouldn't be happy to see him hang for it.

But that wasn't true. Sarah was right. With this much confusion, I needed to stay steady.

Ted probably knew everything going through my head. Hope lit his eyes. "Help me with this. Like we've done before. We're good at figuring out the puzzle."

Back and forth, the Louise and Diane battle waged in my head. The Sarah Solution felt like the safest course. I let out a sigh. "Okay. But let me ask you something first."

Trepidation slowed his response. He probably thought I wanted to know about Roxy or something affair-related. "Sure."

I turned back to the room and leaned against the window. "Did Carly know about you and Roxy?"

He shook his head. "I'm sure she didn't. Why?"

I scowled at him. "Because she's been acting weird lately, and if she found out about you and Roxy, that might explain it."

His eyes flicked away and back to me. "I didn't notice she's been any different."

Carly's world was under attack and I needed to know on how many fronts she was fighting. "Is that what you were talking about a couple of weeks ago when you came home really late and Carly was still up?"

"What? When?" He sounded rattled.

"Were there so many nights you were with Roxy that you can't figure this out?" At most, I would only be a couple of weeks along. Was that too soon for nausea? Should I tell him I might be pregnant? No. I should not.

He acted as if he was concentrating hard to remember. It was probably a delaying tactic while he considered how his answer might help or harm him. "When Carly was up? Recently?"

I waited. "What did you talk about?"

He paused. "I don't know."

I pushed away from the window, impatient with his stalling. "You want me to help you but you can't answer one question for me?"

Again, silence. He inhaled. "A few weeks ago she wanted to know if I knew where the wreckage from her dad's plane was taken."

It wasn't a healthy obsession. "What else?"

"She asked a bunch of questions about when Roxy and Brian decided to build the new house, and how much I thought it had cost. It seemed off the wall, but you know how Carly is."

I knew how Ted was, too. At any questions about Roxy, he'd backpedal and avoid answering. I stared at the rippling wheat for what seemed like an hour. Several times I was on the verge of telling him I might be pregnant. Instead, I did what I do. I got down to business. "Let's see if we can figure out who killed Eldon. What do you remember from that night?"

He wrinkled his forehead in concentration. "I can't remember being in Eldon's house."

I hated to even think this. "Going to the Bar J. Maybe we ought to start there."

He quit moving. "You don't want me to do that."

True. "Okay. Let's start with you leaving Roxy's house."

Another lump traveled down his whiskery throat. "She had the extension club meeting and she was running late. But I was sleepy because . . . Well, you know how I get after . . ."

I clenched my fists. "Then what?"

"I decided to take a quick nap before I came home, because I knew you'd be calving and dinner would be late."

I considered shooting him myself. "So Roxy left you. She wasn't at the ranch at all?"

He nodded with effort. "I woke up about an hour later and got dressed."

Another detail he could have deleted. Yet, the events seem to be coming back to him.

"The wind was blowing and I thought it might start snowing. I was thinking about how miserable it would be for you, night calving, and I thought I heard arguing, but then figured it was just the wind."

His tongue ventured out and traveled along dry lips. A sweating pitcher of ice water sat on the bedside table, with a bendy straw in it. I didn't offer it to him.

Perspiration smeared his pasty face, showing his fatigue. "Then I heard it again. I looked over at Eldon's house and saw someone on the front porch. I thought maybe he was hollering at me and I didn't want to go over there. He wouldn't be happy to see me there with Roxy."

Yeah, I knew how he might feel.

His eyes drooped closed and he rested a beat before going on. "I kept walking to the cruiser. But decided I'd better go deal with it."

He smacked his dry tongue in his desert of a mouth. "No one was on the porch when I got there, so I let myself in. I . . ."

He stopped talking and his eyes lost some focus.

"Who was in the office?" I prompted.

He concentrated on the memory I couldn't see.

I pushed him. "What made you go into the office?"

He let out a pent-up breath. "I can't remember."

"You don't know who was on the porch?"

Frustration, and maybe a twinge of fear, hazed his words. "No. But we know the motives for murder are money or love."

Here we go again. "I've heard that."

"Right. So, they say May Keller has a thing for Eldon. Maybe she got tired of being rejected."

Really?

He warmed to the subject. "Or maybe Jack found out about Eldon's affair with Aileen Carson."

Again with Aileen and Eldon. "Do you have any proof of that?"

"No." He paused. "What if Eldon refused to loan someone money?"

Twyla had mentioned something about this. "How do you know about Eldon lending money?"

His excitement disappeared in a puff and I had my answer. "He wouldn't loan Roxy money—is that what you're saying?"

Ted raised a hand as if to ward me off. "She doesn't need money. I'm saying maybe someone else was desperate for his help. When he refused them, they might be mad enough to kill him."

I paced at the foot of the bed. So far we hadn't come up with anything. I slapped a hand on his bedrail and he jumped. "Why can't you remember?"

We caught each other's eyes and held. This is the weird bit of love I'll never understand. Chemicals, subconscious, pheromones, whatever it is, jumped between us like energy waves in a Tesla tube. It's the way we'd always been together. Just me and Ted in our own world.

I did not want to love this man.

"I need you, Kate." His whisper slid over my skin like a caress.

I made myself picture Roxy. Funny how that brought the arctic freeze back in a hurry. "If you'd think about that night, maybe something would come back to you."

He shifted his glance out the window to the wheat field, the green blades undulating in April's never-ending breeze. Something subtle flitted across his face.

"What?" I urged him.

It took him a single second to hide the alarm mounting in his eyes, and he yawned. It had to be fake fatigue. He brought his attention back to me. "You need to get back for the debate and I'm really tired."

"You remember something."

He raised his eyebrows in innocence. "Nope. No. All this thinking wore me out."

I glared at him for a moment, but he was right. I needed to take off. "Okay. But I'm coming back and we're going over this again."

I could have lived forever without seeing the true caring in his eyes. "You're a good woman, Kate. I promise to do right by you."

It was a little late for that.

I skedaddled back to Frog Creek, no further ahead as far as suspects or debate prep and lots further behind as far as time. I made a quick pass through the calving lot, craving more of the peace I felt in the quiet of the herd.

I had less than an hour to get cleaned up and make the drive to town. Instead of leaping up the steps at a run, I plopped down and watched the cows on the hill. One cow kinked her tail.

I closed my hand around the phone in my pocket. I needed to talk to Carly, as much for me as for her. But Susan wouldn't let me, and calling would harden them both. I ground my teeth in frustration. A stupid debate loomed, which I had to ace to keep Ted in office, so I could keep my options open to live at the one place on earth I'd made my own, with the man who'd sworn to love me forever. Chores mounted up with feeding, tagging, pairing up, doctoring, and fencing. Maybe it was time to admit I couldn't do everything.

I padded inside and dialed the Choker County sheriff's number.

"Have you found Carly?" Milo asked, as soon as I said hello.

"She's in Lincoln with Susan." I braced for more of his accusations.

"Huh." He umphed as if he had settled himself and his gut in a chair. "I hear you're gonna fill in for Ted at the Legion."

"Have you found out anything about Eldon's murder?" I didn't ask what I really wanted to know: Did he still suspect Carly?

"What say I catch up with you after the debate?"

Milo refused to tell me more and I had to promise to meet him at the debate. It seemed like there would be yet another new twist in the crazy maze called my life.

11

What do you wear to a debate to represent your cheating, lying, shot-in-the-line-of-duty, perhaps paralyzed, repentant, but still maybe-not-faithful husband? I chose a black broomstick skirt, in case I needed to invoke the powers of the witch in me; polished black-and-turquoise tooled cowboy boots, in a pretense that I had taste and flair; and a short soft buff leather jacket, just because I liked the way it felt and it might relax me. I surveyed myself in the mirror and focused on my flat belly.

That was a situation for another day.

I'd give Ted's left nut to be able to stay home and watch my cows. How insane was it to put myself through this to defend Ted's position? But I didn't feel I had a choice. If I let it all crash now, out of spite or a knee-jerk reaction, and Ted and I later decided to commit to each other, what would we have left?

I could always bail out downstream.

I looked out the bedroom window while I stuck a sterling silver concho earring into the seldom-used hole in my ear. I squinted up at the sky and eyed some dark clouds in the gathering dusk. If anything fell from the heavens tonight it would likely be rain and not snow, so the cows would probably be okay. Still, I hated leaving them on their own. I grabbed my phone and hurried toward the back door. I punched the speed dial.

Jeremy, Fox number eight, panted into the phone. “Yeah?”

I tried to sound breezy. “What’re you doing?”

“Now?”

“Yeah.” Friendly, not bossy big sisterly. “Or right away. Soon, anyway.”

“Right now,” he grunted, “I’m in the middle of someone.”

A high-pitched giggle made me cringe. It didn’t surprise me, not much anyway. “Never mind.”

More giggling.

I heard the grin leave his voice. “No. Wait. What is it?”

“Nothing.”

“I heard about Ted and stuff.”

Of course he did. It had been almost two whole days; why wouldn’t someone fill in my twenty-one-year-old brother? “I just wondered, if you weren’t busy, if you could run out and keep an eye on my cows.”

“Dad said I should be at the debate, but if you need me at the ranch, I’m on it.”

There was nothing that kid wouldn’t do for anyone. That’s probably why he never had two bits to rub together, since he’d loan or give money to anyone who needed it. He had a son, little red-headed Mason. The only surprise is that more of his kids hadn’t popped up. Hands down, Jeremy was the most loveable of all the Foxes.

“Thanks. I don’t know when I’ll be home.”

“No worries,” he said. “I’ll bring someone to keep me occupied.” More giggling.

Great. I gave him a list of chores I hadn’t been able to get after.

That eased my mind considerably, and in short order the debate would be history and maybe my hands would quit shaking. I needed to handle one crisis at a time, and right now it was the debate's turn at bat. My conversation with Milo waited in the bull pen.

I started down the back steps, and then realized I was wearing only one earring. I sprinted back to the house for its match.

Back on the road. One of the biggest advantages of living at Frog Creek is that I stayed isolated. With Ted and Carly going to town every day, I hardly ever left the place. In the last few days, though, I'd spent more time driving than ranching.

Fifteen minutes later I swung onto Main Street, angle parked toward the top of the hill, and climbed out of Elvis to hike up to the Legion hall. Wind buffeted the trees and sent a chill over the darkening sky.

Heavy feet carried me toward the hall, which sat like a flat-roofed castle centered on the top of the hill. Too bad I couldn't climb on my sled, as I'd done on snow days as a child. I'd slide down Main Street, the straight line that ran from the front door down the middle of the street, bisecting the post office, Burnett's Tack Shop, Hodgekiss Farm and Ranch Supply, and the Long Branch on one side of the street, and the First State Bank, Dutch's Grocery, the Methodists' Jumble Shop, and a rickety fourplex known as the Apartments, on the other.

I lingered at the windmill that the Grand County Commercial Club erected sometime in the nineties, smack in the middle of the road, halfway from the Legion to the highway. They thought it would bring to mind the bygone days of the 1880s, when Hodgekiss was a railroad stop for loading cattle for the Chicago stockyards. The windmill hadn't drawn tourists, as was intended, but it did give teenagers something to light on fire at Halloween.

I approached the pride of Hodgekiss, the Legion hall. It played host to wedding receptions, funeral meals, important meetings, card parties, anniversaries, and any birthday ending with zero. It's where Dahlia and Sid had arranged an all-county barbecue when Ted and I were married. Dad pulled for a big wedding, but I didn't want one, and Mom backed me that time. Dahlia insisted on what Dad called a big whoop-de-do. I figured, if she wanted to pay for it, I could dress up and be nice. I did and I was, even though Roxy showed up and got stinking drunk and had to be dragged outside when she erupted in a geyser of tears.

The locals gave the Legion such high priority that the cash-strapped county paid someone to maintain the lush grass and attached playground. It was the only city park we had. If a crowd was involved and it didn't have to take place in a church, the Legion was the spot.

I stepped from the street to the curb and a greeting floated to me from behind a dying elm at the edge of the street. I squinted in the dusk to focus on a tall figure stepping toward me. It took a moment for me to place him. Glenn Baxter. He had several inches on me, and his dark hair showed a bit of salt in the pepper at his temples. He looked younger, with more life in his face, than he appeared on TV. Who knew how old he was? Vast amounts of wealth could buy vats of Grecian Formula, and more than a facial twice a year.

"You're Kate Conner." His voice sounded like corn husks in a breeze. I wasn't surprised that he knew me. He probably had people who could find my picture or give him a description. But why did I matter to him?

A stranger lurking in the growing evening shadows unsettled me, even if the guy had more money than God. "I didn't realize you were in the Sandhills," I said.

His too-new jeans and scuff-free cowboy boots didn't help him blend with the surroundings. "I told you earlier: I'm here working a deal with Eldon."

He hadn't mentioned his location. "Are you going to the debate?"

He eyed the Legion hall. "The media is on hand. I avoid them when possible. They've even chased me away from the Long Branch."

I didn't wish him luck finding lodging. I took a step toward the building. "I'm running late, so I need to get going."

He lurched in front of me, blocking my way. "I've been waiting to talk to you."

Why wasn't anyone else on the street? Normally, people straggled in, not feeling great urgency to catch every word of a local electoral debate. Not tonight. With Eldon's murder and Ted's condition, people must have arrived early to get in on all the latest news.

Baxter's pale face loomed in front of me. "What about your niece? Have you discussed her selling the Bar J?"

I smelled urgency, maybe even desperation. "The last thing she needs to think about right now is selling her land. Please respect that."

He spoke with a raspy wheeze, sort of like threatening voices on telephones in the movies. "This buffalo-common issue means a great deal to me. I'm very anxious to speak to your niece."

Sinister. That's the word that popped into my mind. "She doesn't need to think about this now."

He leaned toward me, maybe about to argue his case, but the door of the Legion opened. A bearded hulk in jeans and a faded T-shirt, with a camera hoisted on his shoulder, walked out, followed by a pudgy woman, probably fresh from journalism school, with a microphone clutched in her hand.

"Who did that guy say he was?" The woman would never make it far in television with that screechy voice.

The guy dropped the camera from his shoulder, letting it dangle from his hand. "County commissioner."

"He can't chase us out of the debate." She gave a petulant shake of her head.

They pounded down the sidewalk toward us. The guy sounded bored. "We've got interviews about the rancher's murder. Nobody cares about politics in this no-place."

In a gravelly whisper, Baxter said, "I need to talk to Carly

Edwards. As soon as possible." He swiveled on his boot heel and hurried toward the shadow of the elm.

His pale, thin weirdness left a ghoulish taste in my mouth. I hadn't seen the last of him; that seemed plain. But tonight Baxter and his creepiness dropped to the bottom of my mind as I climbed the rest of the way up the front yard.

With sweating palms, I entered the Legion hall. I squinted in the gloom created by iffy fluorescent lights against the dark fake-wood paneling. Voices boomeranged against each other and the scuffed, probably asbestos-laden tile floor. The panels between the kitchen and the hall were pushed up and Jim Lee, a veteran of the Korean conflict, and Bud Simms, my uncle and owner of the Long Branch, tended bar. That amounted to distributing Coors and Coors Light, and Pepsi products the bottler in Broken Butte sold at a discount, and making sure the coffeepot didn't run dry.

The smell of scorched coffee, stale beer, and warm bodies pressed together, topped by a layer of Old Spice and English Leather and the cheap perfume carried by Kmart, greeted me, as it had for every social gathering since I could remember. It didn't make me feel the acceptance and support it normally did. I wasn't Kate, one of the Fox kids, cousin, aunt, lifelong friend. Even though I'd been all those things. Tonight I was the buzz of gossip and speculation.

Folks had probably already decided how they'd vote for commissioner and school board. Until yesterday, voting for Ted was a given for most of them. Even if Eldon hadn't been murdered, a debate was a good excuse to head to town to have a few drinks and gather the latest news with Grand County's finest. And some of its less than fine.

But something big had happened at the Bar J. Like Carly wanting to be around her friends to process her loss, the good citizens of Grand County naturally drew together over this latest tragedy.

Knots of people filled the hall, and a heavy mood flattened what would normally be boisterous exchanges. Serious faces and low tones told me they were probably discussing Eldon and Ted's shootings. There would be no end to speculation about who did it. My empty stomach turned a few somersaults at the thought of Carly on that list. I searched the room for Milo but didn't find his brown uniform among the crowd.

Dahlia held court with a group of ranch wives that included her two sisters, Rose and Violet. It was the over-fifty version of the cool kids' cafeteria table. Her radar alerted her to me, and though her lips smiled, her eyes sliced me like razors. She wore jeans with some kind of shiny bling sprinkled down one thigh, as if Tinker Bell had ralphed on her leg.

Just forty-six hours since Ted and Eldon had been shot. Plenty of time for word to travel around Grand County two and a half times. No telling how jumbled the story was by now. They'd know about Eldon's death. You couldn't mask the fact of Ted lying in the hospital. The rest was up for interpretation. Maybe "they" had a theory about Roxy and Ted.

I might have been paranoid, but it seemed like a hundred and forty-seven eyes drilled into me. Merle Doak accounted for the odd eye, since he'd fallen while running with scissors and had poked the other out. Really. They wanted to know how I was holding up after finding out about Ted and Roxy. Without appearing as panicked as I felt, I scanned the room for allies.

Sarah and Robert wound through the milling bodies, making their slow progress toward me. Sarah had her usual easy smile, masking whatever she felt. Robert's eyebrows forced that worried column into his forehead.

Sarah and I had shared a desk in kindergarten, and pretty much everything else all along, including rooming together in college. I couldn't say, between Sarah and Robert, who was my best friend. Maybe in family issues Robert took the lead and in the woman department Sarah edged ahead. Either way, they both knew everything there was to know about me. Or as much as anyone. For me, their being married seemed about perfect.

Sarah closed her warm fingers around my hand. "You look fabulous," she whispered.

"A fabulously hot mess," I said.

Robert frowned at Dahlia. "I can go out to your house right now and toss Ted's crap to the road."

If I didn't perform to Dahlia's expectations, the crap in the road would be mine.

Clete Rasmussen towered behind me. He had the look of a gnarled cottonwood, exhausted by reaching its roots toward the aquifer. "Good," he drawled. "We can get started. We're only fifteen minutes late."

I mumbled an apology about calving. Without warning, someone grabbed both my arms, jerked me from the floor, and spirited me toward the door. I tilted my head to see Douglas and Michael, the twins, five years my junior, grinning as they kidnapped me.

Clete stuttered and Sarah reassured him I'd return in one piece. The door banged shut behind the boys. A brisk wind bit at my cheeks while they whisked me to the side of the building away from the playground and plopped me down in deepening shadows.

They'd started out identical, but I'd never had any trouble keeping them straight. Michael had all the vinegar of Louise, and Douglas was a sugar bear. They both had the dark, wavy hair and Mom's blue eyes, but where Douglas had grown wide and welcoming, Michael had hardened into granite. Together they created mischief, if given half a chance.

Michael shed his grin. "Why are you standing in for that son of a bitch?"

Douglas threw a thick arm around me and pulled me to him. I appreciated his heat, as well as his affection. I leaned into him and his hold tightened.

"I talked to Diane," Michael continued. "She said you weren't leaving him."

Interesting how she came up with that, when I hadn't decided yet.

The door of the Legion opened and Louise stormed out. "Everyone is waiting for you."

While Douglas hugged tighter, Michael spun around to Louise. He didn't get a word out before fury in the form of Dahlia billowed from the Legion hall.

She waved her hands as if swatting flies. "Go on back inside. I've got to talk to Kate."

Brave Foxes, every one. They stood their ground less than one second before retreating inside. I shivered at the absence of Douglas's warmth.

Dahlia hugged her arms against the cold and looked me up and down. "At least you've put on a skirt."

"I don't know what you're so worried about. It's a debate with Rich Hamner. He runs every four years and never comes close to winning."

She pursed her lips. I had to admit, for a woman on the downside of her fifties she'd held up well. Rocklike abs with no middle-age pooch, and skin like cream. Even with the advantage of a couple of decades, I never looked that good. "Did it occur to you that if people sense any weakness in Ted's position, they might run against him?"

Didn't make any difference. "It's too late to file."

Her expression told me how stupid she thought I was. "For the primary, yes. But someone could run a write-in campaign for the general election. You must look committed and loving and make Ted out to be strong and competent to keep anyone from thinking they might have a chance. Even if . . . if he doesn't . . ."

As if my life hadn't turned strange enough, Mom wafted out the front door, spotted me, and floated our way. She drew her turquoise cashmere shawl close against the chilly evening. "Dahlia. You look pretty." Mom never lied.

Dahlia often did. "How nice to see you out and about, Marge."

Mom didn't cringe at the ugly nickname Dahlia insisted on substituting for "Marguerite," which she claimed was too formal for people who were practically family.

"I understand Ted's injuries might be serious." Mom's voice was smooth and sweet as custard, a tone I knew to be wary of.

Dahlia's mouth twisted. "Did Kate tell you that? I only ask because she has been so busy she's hardly been to see him."

Her gray waves rustling in the near-dark, Mom smiled like an angel. "And yet, here she is, taking heroic measures to help him."

Dahlia opened her mouth, but before words tumbled out, Clete burst from the Legion.

He bellowed at us from the walk. "I can't hold off any longer. We need to start this debate now."

Dahlia grabbed at my arm to propel me forward, but I shrugged away. She opened the door and disappeared inside. Before I followed, Mom put her arm around me, draping cashmere across my shoulders. She leaned close and murmured in my ear, "Go placidly amid the noise and haste." The opening line of "Desiderata."

Mom's faint scent of Lily of the Valley calmed me.

"I would normally avoid Dahlia," she said, "as she's a vexation of the spirit if ever there was." Another "Desiderata" reference. It was Mom's guide to life. "However, in this case I felt compelled to do a little vexing of my own."

If Mom wanted to vex, Dahlia had no clue how lucky she'd been with Clete Rasmussen's interruption.

I, on the other hand, understood perfectly that I was heading for destruction.

12

I wanted to saddle up and ride to a shady spot on the bank of Frog Creek, lean my back against an old cottonwood that a forgotten homesteader had planted there in hope of a prosperous ranch life, and cry until the pressure in my chest eased. My husband had betrayed me, leaving shreds of bloody flesh lumped where my heart used to beat. And now I had to put myself in front of the community and act as though nothing had changed.

I stepped into the noisy Legion hall. I might have been projecting my angst, but it seemed to me that even the air had an edge to it. Faces appeared strained, voices tighter than usual. Mom drifted off, taking her soft cashmere shawl and Lily of the Valley with her. Dahlia herded Sid and the rest of her contingent toward the front.

Clete ushered me in and pointed toward the long cafeteria-style table along the wall. "You can sit next to Rich."

Without warning, Clete tilted his head back and bellowed above the noise. "Take your seats. We'll get started."

The glow from one of Hodgekiss's four streetlamps beckoned from beyond the windows in the door.

Rich Hamner sat at the table with his hands folded in front of him, a nervous grin plastered on his face. He ran for sheriff because he believed that sheriffing was easier than working as a ranch hand—and paid better, too.

I couldn't disagree. Ted spent most of his time cruising around, gossiping with the coffee bunch every morning at the Long Branch, driving the patrol car in the Grand County Fair parade, and occasionally busting an underage drinking party or issuing a speeding ticket. Not much marred the tranquility of Grand County, but when it did, I'd often helped Ted untangle the mystery.

I smoothed my windblown hair, pulled a barrette from my skirt pocket, and tried to tie down the riotous mop. Several people smiled or nodded at me. Normally I'd have exchanged words with a dozen people before now. They were appraising me, seeing how I held up under the strain of the Roxy/Ted situation. Some people didn't even venture eye contact, just gave me a side-eye. Or else I was paranoid. I stepped to the front.

Rich had combed his hair and slicked it with nasty-smelling gel. It was the campaign look he pulled out every four years for the debate. While at the Long Branch or working, he either wore a stained and sagging felt cowboy hat, gray with age, or sported greasy hat-hair.

I nodded to him and slid onto the cold metal folding chair. With the bare table, I was glad I'd worn the broomstick skirt to drape well below my knees.

Clete stood to the side of the table. He had the presence of Moses as played by Charlton Heston—before Moses grew the white beard but when he was still a fun-hater. My family took up the first three rows of folding chairs, on my left side.

Uncle Bud and Aunt Twyla crowded in. Twyla grinned at me from beneath her dark hair. Dad stood next to Jack Carson by the bar, Coors bottle in hand. Jack Carson had a face like a cement wall, if walls had intense eyes. He had about the same sense of humor, too. Jack stared at the chairs halfway down from the speakers' table. I followed his line of vision to see his wife, Aileen, sandwiched between Bill Hardy and Shorty Cally.

Bill and Shorty were always on the outs, but Aileen's wide smile seemed to bring them together. Aileen was one of those cheerful types, ready with a tease. She freely handed out hugs and pats. Slightly overweight, with unremarkable hair or facial features, she had that attraction that drew friends like flies to a carcass. She was the flip side of dour Jack, but I couldn't credit Louise's speculation that she'd been carrying on with Eldon.

Clete started talking before the stragglers found their seats and the conversations drifted to murmurs. "The primary's in two weeks, and along with the state ballot, we've got some seats to fill here in Grand County. Clerk of the District Court Ethel Bender is running unopposed for her eighth term. So, obviously, we won't be debating that. One commissioner seat is open, and we have four candidates. Three school board seats are up, and eight folks tossed their hats into that tiger cage." A few people laughed. "That will be the last debate of the night so we don't have to round you back up when you spill out the doors for your brawls." More chuckles. School board fights sometimes caused feuds that lasted for generations.

"We're starting the agenda with the race for Grand County sheriff. As you're all aware, there was a shooting last night at the Bar J. We lost one of our finest citizens, Eldon Edwards, and we all grieve for his family." He paused for respect. "Sheriff Ted Conner was injured in the incident. So Kate here, his wife"—as if anyone didn't know—"will be sitting in for him."

He waited for a smattering of applause. "Running against Sheriff

Conner is Rich Hamner." More noncommittal clapping. "We'll begin by having the candidates introduce theirselves and say a little about their qualifications for the job."

Rich nattered on about how the county needed fresh blood, a point he made every election. This time he added a new plank about not being related to half the people of the county. I'm sure that was inspired by me sitting next to him. Rich might be an unambitious cowboy with marginal hygiene and one year of junior college but, surprisingly, those experiences did not make him a great speaker. He mumbled and stumbled and sprinkled it all with so many "ums" that if they'd been salt we'd all have died of stroke.

Qualifying to run for a Nebraska county sheriff wasn't difficult. Basically, you had to win the votes. After that, you had one year to complete and pass a twelve-week course at the police academy in Grand Island. Until being certified, a sheriff couldn't perform anything official, so the state patrol and neighboring county law enforcement filled in. It's fortunate the good people of Nebraska are so law-abiding.

When my turn came I sat up straight and pretended Ted loved me exclusively. I addressed Ted's experience, mentioned that, due to his efforts at the high school, teen drunk driving had been virtually eliminated on prom and graduation nights. I concluded with Ted's dedication to the people of Grand County, as demonstrated by him taking a bullet in the line of duty.

Dahlia and Sid watched me from directly behind my kin. Violet, Rose, and their husbands filled out the row. Dahlia nodded with every point I made on Ted's behalf.

Clete opened up the floor for questions, and hands shot up.

"What do you know about what happened at the Bar J?"

This was a perfect opening. I needed to show Ted's assertive action while I studied the audience to gather clues about who killed

Eldon, to clear Carly of suspicion. "Not much. But Ted is keeping abreast of the investigation from his hospital room."

More hands popped up and Clete pointed. Yes, I answered, the shooting happened at the main house. Yes, Milo Ferguson from Choker County was handling the investigation. No, there hadn't been any arrests. Yes, Ted responded quickly. Thank goodness Grand County rescue arrived so fast, and yes, we're all thankful for the expertise of Harold Graham and Eunice Fleenor, since they surely saved Ted's life.

Aileen dropped her head, and her shoulders heaved. Both Bill and Shorty put a hand on her back, double-teaming the sympathy. Jack scowled, and I was sure his Pepsi can dented under his clenched fingers.

I answered the onslaught for ten minutes while poor Rich's spine softened and his knees thrust farther under the table as he slouched deeper into his chair.

Nat and Rope sat in the last row. It surprised me they had attended the debate, because they stuck close to home most of the time, but it worked out well for me. I'd try to talk to Nat. If she had the savvy Twyla suggested, she might know if someone had a grudge against Eldon. As the questions about Eldon droned on, Rope and Nat looked more and more uneasy.

Clete called on Dahlia's older sister, Rose. The three Flower sisters were notoriously competitive. They spent every holiday together, socialized on Saturday nights, joined the same clubs and church, and even vacationed together. My theory is they believed the old adage about keeping your enemies close.

Rose, the spitting image of Dahlia, if Dahlia gained twenty pounds and grew another chin, leaned back in her chair and folded her arms. "The story I heard is that Ted charged into Eldon's house, intending to save the old man. My question for him, and you, since you're his proxy, is this: As a trained officer of the law, isn't it foolish to run headlong into a dangerous situation? I mean, folks are making him out to be some kind of hero, but it just seems plain stupid to me. And he's lucky to still be alive, let alone a cripple."

A universal gasp rose from the crowd. Dahlia glared at Rose.

I'd been careful to keep to the line that Ted was recovering. Rose had succeeded in her probable goals of (1) showing she was on the inside with all the information, and (2) getting in a stab at one of the favored grandchildren.

The Foxes may not always be polite to one another, but by God we stick together against outsiders. "Ted's not a cripple," I said. "The bullet caused some swelling in his spine, but Doc Kennedy thinks he'll be fine." Might be a lie, might not be. I'll settle that with the Almighty on Judgment Day. "As to Ted's training, he attended the twelve-week law enforcement course in Grand Island when he was elected the first time, eight years ago." See how I cleverly inserted his experience in there? "He returns every year for a refresher. Since we weren't at the Bar J, it doesn't seem productive to second-guess his informed choices, does it?"

Clete called on May Keller. She stood from somewhere in the back. "If elected sheriff, what do you propose to do about Glenn Baxter buying up all the ranches around here?"

The room went quiet.

Clete addressed Rich. "Since Kate's been fielding most of the questions so far, why don't we give you a chance to speak?"

The look of panic in Rich's eyes made me wonder if we'd need to get Harold and Eunice up here for resuscitation. He stammered. "Well, I. Um. You know. It's a bad deal. But some folks. Well, the economy and all. They need. We all need. I think, you know. I heard he's offering good money. But, then. You know. The big ranches, they kind of need to keep going so that people, you know, have a place to work. Even though they don't pay a fair wage for the work the hired men do."

Rich stopped talking, apparently believing he'd answered May's concerns.

Clete raised his eyebrows, inviting me to speak.

Glad to respond to something besides Eldon's murder and Ted's condition, I relaxed. "Well, May. We might all have opinions about whether it's a good idea to create a buffalo commons or not. But we're a land of laws. The sheriff's job is to uphold the law. If a citizen wants to sell land he owns, and there's no problem with fraud or deceit, there's no call for the sheriff to interfere."

Several people nodded. Mom winked at me. Dad lifted his beer bottle. I glanced at the back row. Rope sat alone. Maybe Nat couldn't take the conflict. I'd bet she was hiding in Rope's pickup.

May, her voice like a bow across a loose fiddle string, shouted, "That's bullshit! Pardon my French." Her lack of decorum didn't faze me. I allowed leeway for her oxygen-deprived brain.

Bill Hardy jumped up. "If Glenn Baxter succeeds in buying out these ranchers and they turn this place into buffalo common, those burly bastards will tear through the fences. Us little guys will end up with trampled pastures and cattle strung from here to eternity. We can't afford to hire the help it'd take to keep up with that rodeo."

"Yeah." Shorty Cally pointed his finger at Bill, nearly poking Aileen in the eye. "But you can't tell a person what they can or can't sell, if they own it."

Clete held up his hand. "Let's all just save the fighting until the school board debate."

This issue trumped even Eldon's murder. I studied the audience for guilty faces.

Bill Hardy paid no attention to Clete. "When all's said and done, I think Milo's gonna find out Eldon was shot on account of him getting ready to take the buyout."

May's violin screech rose higher. "Milo Ferguson don't know his butt from a hole in the ground if he figures Eldon was gonna sell. No one shot Eldon on account of land. There's reasons besides real estate to shoot a body."

That's the kind of remark that made the likes of Ted and Louise suspect May. I didn't put her on the list, though. She'd never be able to climb the stairs to Eldon's office.

Dwayne and Kasey Weber, a couple in their late thirties and relative newcomers to Hodgekiss, seemed to agree with May. Dwayne even said, "Yeah, Eldon wasn't the great guy people made him out to be."

"Tighter than a tick," Shorty Cally said.

"Wouldn't walk across the street to save a drowning cat." Bill Hardy agreed with Shorty, maybe for the first time.

Aileen patted both men on their arms. "That's not true. He was a saint. Helped more folks than anyone will ever know."

Even from across the room I could see crimson slashes flare on Jack's cheeks. It looked like jealousy to me, but was it because Aileen had touched Bill and Shorty or because she had defended her lover?

Kasey and Dwayne Weber turned to each other with irritated expressions. Kasey rolled her eyes and Dwayne sneered. He might have mumbled "Asshole" to Kasey, but I'm not the best lip-reader of cowboys who don't enunciate well.

A group of older women in the front row, to my right, leaned forward over their knees and drew their heads together. I was sure I heard Carly's name whispered, then all four of their heads popped up and they studied me. Damn it. Gossip and suspicion were creeping.

The situation was running amok, and I thought I ought to pull it back onto the Ted track. I raised my voice. "We're all concerned about who killed Eldon and why. Let me go on record to say that Ted will get to the bottom of the crime. And if he isn't fully recovered and able to move around, I guarantee to help him, and we will find Eldon's killer."

That might all be a load of horsefeathers, but weren't all campaign promises? It sounded impressive, anyway.

Clete raised both his arms, Moses ready to shatter the tablets. "That's enough. Time's run out for this debate. We're gonna move right on to the county commissioners. Everyone, just stay in your seats while we play musical chairs up here. Thanks to Kate and Rich."

Polite but unenthusiastic applause filled the room as we pushed back from the table. At the same time, the scraping of chairs and volume of voices increased, showing how much control Clete wielded. Tyler Krug and Bill Hardy met in the aisle between the folding chairs. Their argument devolved to shouts and fingers pointing into chests, while May complained to people sitting around her. Other knots of people formed to cuss and discuss. Jack Carson plodded purposefully to Aileen and put an arm around her shoulders.

The Webers, still with sour expressions, hurried out the door. The subdued tone of earlier shifted to a higher decibel as Grand County voters struggled to convince their neighbors one way or the other about the buffalo common issue.

Whether you were for pulling up the fences and letting buffalo roam freely over the hills, as they'd done two hundred years ago, or were against relocating families and closing down already dwindling communities, it didn't seem to me to be a practical plan.

White settlers came late to the Sandhills. It is an inhospitable place with unique geographical features. The massive area is like a grass-covered Sahara. Except, before the fences and caretakers had shown up, the hills had been scarred with sandy blowouts. Responsible grazing had allowed the empty patches to heal and grow back. That knowledge put me on the side against the common.

Free-ranging buffalo might be the natural way, but those beasts were hard on the delicate land out here.

My main concern right now was zeroing in on a suspect to hand to Milo so he'd leave Carly alone.

I spotted Rope with a group close to the bar, so I booked it for the door, hoping to find Nat. Milo hadn't put in an appearance, and that gave me time to pick any nits Nat might have about Eldon's enemies. A hand grabbed mine and started shaking. May Keller's cracked face beamed at me. "Fine speechifying. I see where you'd have to walk that line about setting policy and enforcing the law. You got my vote."

I gave her hand a squeeze and tried to extricate it from her grip. "Thanks, but I'm not running."

May reluctantly let go of my hand. "Well, honey, you ought to be."

I ducked out the front in pursuit of Nat.

13

A cold blast met me when I rocketed from the Legion. The leather jacket didn't offer much protection. I spotted Rope's pickup parked in an angled space halfway down the block, under one of the streetlights. Nat's silhouette stayed motionless as I approached and knocked lightly on the passenger window.

She jerked and coiled into herself. She acted reluctant to roll down the window.

I felt bad for giving her a scare. She didn't seem like a barracuda, as Twyla accused. "Can I talk to you about Eldon?"

Her eyes shifted from me to the street behind, giving off a whiff of nerves. "Not now. I really—"

"You probably knew him better than most people."

She started to wring her hands. "We're put on this earth to endure trial and hardship. Eldon's heartbreak is over."

That was a whole pile of nothing. "Do you have any idea who might have wanted to hurt him?"

She dropped her hands into her lap and turned red-rimmed eyes to me. “How is sweet Carly?”

If I answered her question, maybe she’d get back to mine. “She’s in Lincoln with my sister.”

Nat seemed surprised. “That’s odd.”

“She and Susan are close. Susan will help her.”

Nat shook her head. “Your family.” She clucked her tongue. “You know, I wanted children like your folks. Nine—imagine. But I had trouble. I lost so many before Mick. I took care of him. Watched over him.”

I tried for another angle. “Mick grew up on the Bar J. Eldon was probably pretty good to him, huh?”

Nat didn’t seem to hear me. “And Hank and Marguerite kept having children and letting them grow like weeds, no tending.”

She had a point. It’s not that I ever felt neglected, as Louise obviously did, but I often wondered why Mom had a flock of children when she seemed so detached. That was a mystery for another day.

Nat stared out the front of the truck. “And yet they all grew up, except Glenda, who was the best of the lot.”

I might have been shocked or hurt if this were the first time I’d heard this opinion. People idolize those who die young. I also thought it might be true. Wind bit through my jacket, and I drew it closer around me.

Nat jerked back to the moment. “I’m sorry, Kate. It’s all too much for me. Eldon’s passing, and today is the tenth anniversary of Mick’s trial. I’m not myself.”

Since I didn’t know Nat well, I couldn’t vouch for her state. “I suppose Milo talked to you already, but I wondered if you’d seen anyone at the Bar J the day Eldon died.”

Her hands worked in her lap again. “Yes. I did tell Milo. Carly was there.”

I couldn't hide my surprise. Carly was at the Bar J? "What was—"

"Nat." Rope's low rumble cut her off.

A squeak of distress escaped from Nat's lips.

I turned to Rope. "I was asking Nat if she remembered anyone out at the Bar J—"

He cut me off. "Me, Danny, and Nat were in the calving shed. Didn't see nothing."

Pick any old-time stoic cowboy character, from Clint Eastwood to John Wayne, add a dollop of restrained wrath, and you have Rope Hayward.

"Did you ever hear him argue with anyone on the phone?" I asked. "Or see someone at his house?"

Rope retreated to the driver's side of the pickup. "You did a fine job," he said through tight lips. "We've got to get back to our cows. You know how it is."

I placed a hand on Nat's open window frame, as if trying to reach in and grab more words. It didn't take a psychiatrist to see that Nat was afraid of Rope. The last thing I wanted was to cause Nat any trouble. I strove for a casual tone. "Sure. Glad you could make it in for the debate."

"You'll let us know about Eldon's services?" Rope said.

Eldon's next of kin was Carly. As her guardian, did that mean that planning the funeral fell to me? I'd have to talk to Dad; he'd know what to do. "Absolutely."

The sound of Rope's door opening masked Nat's voice. "I have the morning shift at Hardee's. I can talk then."

Hardee's? In Broken Butte. Another long drive. I nodded.

I backed up and watched as Rope eased the pickup from the parking space and rode the brakes down the hill to the highway.

With my mind on finding Dad to ask about Eldon's funeral, I hurried back toward the Legion. Milo still hadn't appeared, and that was eating at me too. Before I got to the door, a figure stepped from the shadows at the side of the building, right at the spot where Michael and Douglas had dropped me before the debate.

"Kate."

Despite the cold spring night, flames leaped into my eyes. I stood paralyzed between rational behavior and emotional reaction. One said be calm, the other said kill.

Roxy stepped closer. The outline of her coiffed hair caught light from the streetlamp. She probably used waterproof mascara, but dark smudges still showed under her eyes. Her tight jeans puddled over high-heel cowboy boots, and she stuffed her hands into a puffy down coat. "I came to apologize." She swayed slightly.

Perfect. "Okay, then." I reached for the door handle.

"Please, just listen to what I have to say."

"Thing is, I'm really not interested." An empty branch banged on the roof of the Legion hall in applause for my response.

She planted her feet as if readying for a shootout. "If you go in there, I'll follow you. I'll make a scene so loud and big you'll never live it down."

Although I didn't think any more public humiliation would faze me, I wasn't the only one to consider. Dad stood in the Legion, surrounded by his family and friends, and he cared what they thought. The sibs were in there on account of me. I wouldn't subject them to a Roxy performance. "What do you want?"

She flexed her finger for me to join her at the side of the building. "I'm sorry you got caught up in this and got hurt."

She and Ted with their trite lines. I had to listen, but I hadn't agreed to talk.

Her whiskey-stained breath came at me. "But I love Ted. I've always loved him." She started to cry. "He may never walk again. And I don't know if I can be the kind of woman to care for a cripple. I keep thinking of that song 'Ruby.' Will I be the kind that takes my love to town?"

"You have been so far," I said, but she didn't seem to hear.

"It's easy for you. You grew up with this big, loving family, always helping you and supporting you and on your side. I never had that. I got the shaft all along. I married two losers. They both promised to love me and provide for me and they both lied. Then I fell in love with Brian."

"Fell in love or found a mark?"

"It was all perfect. Except Carly, she always hated me." She swiped at tears. "And Eldon, he hated me even more."

Headlights illuminated the lawn. The outline of a light bar on top of the car showed in the streetlamp.

She slumped against the side of the building and gave into sobs.

The car slid into a parking place, and Milo climbed out.

Roxy pushed herself upright. "But I'm done with all of that now."

Milo lumbered up the hill toward the Legion.

"This time, it's coming my way. Before he died, Brian made me secretary of the Bar J Corporation. That means I'm a signatory on the Bar J checks. Eldon wouldn't allow me near the checkbook, but he's not around anymore."

She'd slept with my husband, and I'd have to figure out how to deal with that, but she better not screw with Carly or she'd be in real trouble. "Nice try. I'm pretty sure Carly inherits the ranch."

Roxy must have been saturated with whiskey to utter her next line. "I don't need her permission to write checks."

"I can see you're grieved."

She didn't pay any attention. "If that place was mine I'd sell to Baxter and be out of there so fast fire would fly from my heels. But I'll be doing the next best thing. I'm going to have the biggest horse barn, with a giant indoor arena, and I'll breed the finest cutting horses this country has ever seen. It'll make Eldon turn in his grave to see how I spend that money he hoarded."

She broke down into sobs again, and I figured she'd told me

about all she was fixing to say. I thought about rolling her for the down jacket, but in light of the Choker County sheriff making his way toward me, I decided against it. I walked away from her to meet Milo.

Milo spotted me and found a dually pickup, parked near the front walk, to lean his bulk against. "Howdy, Kate."

I wanted to shake off my brush with Roxy like a dog shakes off water, so I plunged into my conversation with Milo. "You don't still suspect Carly?"

He shook his head and went down another path. "Carly's got a birthday coming up, doesn't she?"

Would it change the way they handled the investigation if she were no longer a minor? "She turns eighteen in two weeks."

Milo fished a toothpick from his breast pocket. "Eldon's lawyer told me that if Eldon dies after she turns eighteen, Carly inherits the ranch."

If you're a sheriff, it pays to have well-placed relatives. My kin had assisted Ted—well, me—in some of his investigations. "Doesn't she inherit the ranch no matter how old she is?"

Milo nodded. "Yep. But according to the will, until she's eighteen, she's not named manager, so she doesn't get to make decisions."

Milo poked the toothpick between two teeth and prodded a bit. "I wonder. I figured Eldon held ownership of the whole ranch until he passed. Then Roxy would get a parcel of the Bar J but the bulk of the ranch would go to Carly. If Eldon sold out to Glenn Baxter, would he be willing to split that big pile of cash with Roxy?"

I snorted. "Not likely. He didn't care much for Roxy, and besides that, he was tightfisted."

Milo nodded. "That's kind of what I thought."

I followed Milo down that track. If Eldon sold to Baxter, Roxy wasn't apt to get much for her few years of living at the Bar J. If Eldon didn't sell and Carly inherited the Bar J, Roxy was due to get even less. But if Eldon died before Carly grasped the Bar J's reins, Roxy could sell to Baxter and walk away with a bundle of cash, free and clear.

Carly would get a much bigger pile of dough from the sale, but as a shareholder in the Bar J, Roxy would probably have enough to set her up in style. With her share, Carly would never have to worry about money. But she'd lose the ranch forever.

I leaned forward. "You think Roxy killed Eldon?" Maybe she wasn't even drunk, and all that talk just now was a sham to cover her tracks.

If so, that meant she'd shot Ted, too. Maybe Ted tried to stop Roxy from killing Eldon and she fought him. Maybe they weren't having an affair.

Right. And maybe I can fly.

Milo pulled the toothpick out and sucked his teeth. "She's got a tight alibi."

Balls.

He ran his tongue across his teeth, apparently satisfied with his grooming. "Given the time of death and of Ted's injury, Roxy's whereabouts are accounted for by five ladies, at least. I couldn't get ahold of Tina Barnes, probably because her cat ate her hearing aids and she was sleeping. But the others said Roxy was at the schoolhouse for the extension club meeting, for about three hours. She even brought the dessert they all claim was a store-bought cake."

A gust boxed my ears, but not so much that I didn't hear Milo.

"My theory is that Ted, on behalf of Roxy, tried to convince Eldon to sell the Bar J. With that chunk of change, he and Roxy could move to Tahiti and spend their days drinking mai tais."

I didn't have to think that over for long. "That's crazy. It doesn't account for Ted's injury. Someone shot them both."

Milo worried a back tooth with his tongue and reached into his shirt pocket for another toothpick. "See, that's the thing that was so curious about the crime scene."

I waited while he inserted the toothpick, feeling like I wanted to jam it down his throat to get him to speed up.

"There were two guns. Eldon and Ted were shot with different weapons."

I couldn't make sense of that.

"The bullet in Ted looks like one that came from Eldon's gun. The one Rope says Eldon kept in a drawer in his office. The same gun we found in Eldon's hand."

"And what about who shot Eldon?"

He sucked his teeth again. "That one looks like a little ol' bullet from a thirty-six. The kind found on the floor next to Ted. That gun"—he clicked his tongue on his teeth—"belongs to Roxy."

You could have knocked me over with a feather.

"I figure Ted and Eldon had a discussion about selling the ranch. Maybe Eldon wouldn't sell. Or maybe he wasn't gonna give Roxy a dime. Things went south. Eldon shot first, didn't kill Ted, so Ted pulled his trigger."

My voice sounded like it came from a dry well. "You think Ted killed Eldon?"

"Yep."

Ted was lots of things, but not a killer. "You're wrong."

Milo pushed himself from the pickup with an *umph*. "I just came from his hospital room. He confessed."

A scream knifed through the air, and I feared it had come from me. But Milo's attention jumped toward the Legion.

Roxy stood with her hand to her mouth.

14

Forget about Eldon's funeral, Ted's infidelity, and the debate. I sprinted to Elvis and dove inside, searching for my phone. I needed to call Ted. He didn't kill Eldon, so why did he confess?

I tore through the passenger seat, the floor, even under the mats. No phone. Sitting in front of the wheel I closed my eyes and steadied my breathing. When had I last seen the damned phone?

On my way out of the house I'd called Jeremy. Then I ran back for the other earring. I must have set the phone down and forgotten it. Elvis's tires squealed as we backed out of the parking slot and I goosed him out of town.

I ground my teeth and tapped the wheel, but it didn't make the drive go any faster. How did we ever survive without cell phones? Not being able to call Ted made me itchier than a heifer in a bull pen.

As the miles dragged, my head swirled with anxiety. If Ted killed Eldon—which he didn't, so why did he confess?—then Carly was no longer a suspect.

Once Roxy calmed down, after hearing Milo's shocker, she'd understand that for the next two weeks the fate of the Bar J was in her hands. She'd be counting millions by the opening bell of business tomorrow. I needed a plan to stall her.

I finally slid around the last curve to the house.

Lights spilled from every window, reflecting on the grass. Jeremy's beater Ford pickup sat behind the house and I was thankful he was still here. But acid bit into my gut at the other vehicle parked in front.

Dahlia's tricked-out Dodge dually.

I parked behind Jeremy and hopped out. I had to call Ted, but I needed to collect my wits before facing Dahlia. I couldn't feature why she was here, and if I let on about Ted's confession she'd go berserk—not something I wanted to witness. To give myself time to cool down, I took the well-worn dirt path up the hill and into the calving lot. Not much of a moon, and no flashlight, so I couldn't inspect the back ends of the cows to see if any had started labor. But I paced through the drowsy herd, counting and seeing if any were in distress. I gave no thought to manure gathering on my dress boots or worrying about being in my skirt. Even the cold didn't penetrate.

The cows paid little attention as I prowled the lot. I counted ten fewer than I had this morning. Jeremy must have kicked the pairs to the south pasture, as I'd asked. Another week and we'd be done. Time to start thinking about our branding.

What would happen this year? Would Ted be in jail? Would I even be living at Frog Creek? I retraced my steps, wishing I could hang out up here with the cows. But I couldn't let Jeremy deal with Dahlia alone.

An owl hooted a low and lonely call. Hooves scuffed on the cool sand of the lot. Night air dampened the hay strewn around, and the tangy smell teased of summer. Would I still be on Frog Creek come summer?

I sucked in a fortifying breath, descended the path, and made my way to the house. After removing my boots and placing them under the bench, I stopped on the back porch, my hand on the glass knob, and listened. No screaming or breaking glass. Always best to check, when approaching Dahlia.

I eased open the door and padded into the kitchen. The overhead light shone on dirty dishes filling the sink. Jeremy had found some of the food Twyla had brought. My phone nestled among the crumbs on the Formica table. I picked it up.

Dahlia and Jeremy were talking in the living room. Whatever the reason for her visit, it wasn't because of Ted's confession, or dishes would be broken, the roof blown off the house. They knew I was inside, from the sound of the pickup arriving and the back door opening. There was no sneaking in. I took a few extra seconds to wipe the frazzle from my face.

Jeremy sat on the couch, arms crossed at the back of his head, ankle resting on his knee, the picture of ease. Not all Foxes oozed charm, probably because Jeremy got our whole allotment. I'd never felt comfortable enough around Dahlia that my shoulders didn't hug my ears.

Maybe I ought to greet her with the opening sally of "Grandma!" Then again, even if it were true, I wanted to keep that information to myself.

Jeremy pulled a hand from behind his head and gave me a peace sign. I nodded a greeting to him. "Hi, Dahlia." So far so good. I hadn't said anything yet to set her off. "I didn't expect you out here. You must not have stuck around for the rest of the debates."

She rotated her head slowly in my direction. I half expected it to keep spinning all the way around, à la *The Exorcist*. Black streaks damped her cheeks. "You don't even seem upset."

I can never remember what you're supposed to do when a bear

attacks. Wave your arms and appear bigger or back up slowly? "You heard about Ted?"

"I was already on my way out here when Roxy called." Her eyes filled and tears washed more black down her cheeks. "My son needs a pair of pajamas. He can't wear that hospital gown. But someone will have to help him put them on, because his legs . . ." Her words dissolved in watery slur. "What was he thinking, to tell Milo that?"

Jeremy patted her hand. "I'm sure there's an explanation."

I'd like to hear that explanation. The hospital switchboard probably wouldn't put a call through to Ted's room this late, so I dialed his cell. It went straight to voice mail.

Jeremy dashed from the room and returned with a toilet paper roll. He handed it to Dahlia, and after thanking him like he'd brought her frankincense and myrrh, she tore off a line and dabbed her face. A full box of Kleenex perched on a bookshelf not five feet from where Dahlia sat, but I didn't offer it.

She sniffed in her transition from femme fatale to dragon. "He wouldn't answer my calls, either."

I shrugged out of my leather jacket.

Dahlia crossed her legs and one foot started bouncing. With those high-heel, pointy-toed cowboy boots, it seemed like a threat. "You need to go see him tonight. Now. There's no restriction on spousal visits."

"It's after ten o'clock. I think it's best if we get some sleep and take a running start at this tomorrow."

She sat, I stood, and yet she managed to look down her nose. "You're supposed to be helping him get reelected, remember?"

Silent as snow, Jeremy retreated to the dining room.

I pulled an earring free. "You'll probably get to the hospital before I do in the morning, so I'll send the pajamas with you now."

Jeremy lunged from the dining room. "I can get them. Tell me where."

Dahlia teared up, and her voice wound through the tragedy lodged in her throat. "He's such a good boy. He didn't deserve any of this."

Being in Roxy's bed might be a contributing factor to his bad luck. There was always the possibility that Milo's theory was correct. "Let me get those pajamas."

"Stay." Jeremy held up his hand. "I'm on my way."

I might have been blind to Ted's affair with Roxy, but my eyes were wide open with Jeremy. Something was up. "I'll do it."

He hurried toward the small hallway that led to the bedroom, attic stairs, and bathroom.

Dahlia rose from the chair. "Are you purposely sabotaging his campaign?"

Excuse me? "I thought I did pretty well at the debate."

"The posters. You promised to set them out." Why would she care about posters when it looked as if Ted had just bought a one-way ticket to jail?

She clicked her tongue. "When do you plan to post them?"

The twelfth of Never, as Dad would say. "I'm a little busy."

Dahlia added a tremble to the words she directed at Jeremy. "Maybe you could put them up tomorrow?"

What a suck-up. "I'd love to," he said

"Except I could really use you here again." A growl backed my voice, and I glared at Dahlia.

Jeremy was all helpful to Dahlia, but for me . . . ? "I have stuff I need to do tomorrow."

I couldn't watch the cows, talk to Nat at Hardee's, convince Roxy not to sell the Bar J, and witness Ted's full descent into craziness all at the same time. First, I had to send Dahlia home. "I'll get Ted's pajamas." I spun around and Jeremy stepped into my way. He stood there for a beat, as if he meant to block me.

I put a hand on his arm and nudged him aside. I walked into the dark hallway, noticing that the bedroom door I usually keep open was closed. I pushed it open and snapped on the light. Not surprisingly, the bed was occupied.

Alexis Manning lay with my comforter pulled up to her chin. If she'd been a cockroach she'd have scuttled under the bed. I stepped into the room, shut the door behind me, and considered her for a few seconds. I went to the bureau and found a pair of Ted's pajamas. Not his favorites, though.

I shut the light off before leaving the bedroom and snicking the door closed.

Jeremy tensed when I emerged from the hallway and studied me as if planning his defense. I walked past him without eye contact.

Dahlia stood near the front door with her coat on and snatched the pajamas from me.

"Tell Ted I'll be there as soon as I can in the morning," I said.

She tucked the pajamas into the crook of her arm. "Suit yourself. I'm driving back to Broken Butte tonight." She laid it down like a challenge. Of course, when she finished her hour-and-a-half drive, she'd be home. After I got to Broken Butte and pried an explanation out of Ted, I'd still have to drive back.

I held the door open and congratulated myself on not slamming it behind her. I watched out the front window as she drove away.

Jeremy clasped his hands in front of him and rocked on his heels. "I'm sorry about Alexis. I was just getting ready to take her to town when Dahlia showed up."

Alexis was only a year older than Carly. "Does Alexis's father know she's here?"

He looked at the ground. "He thinks she's watching movies at Brittany Ostrander's."

Tonight, someone else's rebellious teen was not my problem. "Thank you for not letting Dahlia know about your extracurricular activity." I walked to the kitchen. If I was eating for two I ought to choke something down.

He followed me. "Sorry about the dishes. We were going to clean up before you got home but—"

"Dahlia. I know. She's messed up my plans plenty of times." I pulled a peanut butter jar from the cupboard and dug in a drawer for a spoon. "Alexis is too young for you. I don't care what she says: if you continue this relationship, you're taking advantage of her."

"You're not going to tell Alexis's father, are you?"

I gave him a stern look, as if considering it. "You're night calving tonight and staying here all day tomorrow. Before you leave, make sure you wash my sheets and remake the bed." I dug up a spoonful of peanut butter and brought it halfway to my mouth. My stomach flipped and hit like the time I belly flopped off the high dive. "Take her home. Break up with her gently."

He nodded vigorously. "Right. Right. Thanks."

I swallowed the lump of peanut butter and shoved the jar back in the cupboard. I cut off a slab of the cinnamon bread and carried it with me. "I'm going to sleep in Carly's room. Do not wake me up."

He trailed me to the stairs. "Thanks. You're the best."

Gross as I felt about him and Alexis using my bed, having him in my debt and therefore obligated to take care of the cows seemed like a fair trade-off.

My superpower of falling asleep no matter how bad my world was crumbling didn't fail me, but it wasn't strong enough to ward off dreams. Nat leered at me from behind the counter of Hardee's while Roxy and Ted shared an old-fashioned milk shake and tossed hundred-dollar bills at dancing hamburgers. I chased Carly out the door and into glaring sunshine, where she faded away, arms outstretched toward me.

15

Robins and kingfishers raised a ruckus while I made my way through the calving lot. The sun hadn't yet sent its first blast over the hills across the valley in front of the house, and the morning chill hung heavy as my mood. Looked like two or three more cows dropped their calves in the night. All must be well or Jeremy would have left a note. I'd heard him bang onto the back porch around four in the morning from his last check. When I dressed and tiptoed out the back door, he still had an hour before he'd head out again.

For all his good-timing and frivolous ways, Jeremy never shirked work. If he said he'd take care of the cows or kids or do a chore for Mom, by God, it'd be done. Sometimes, when he didn't want to be tied down or was set on having fun, Jeremy was hard to locate. I had him today, though, and that left me free to find out what Ted was up to. But first I had to talk to Nat. After that, much as I hated the thought, I'd need to ask Ted's help to keep Roxy from selling the Bar J.

I left a note for Jeremy to run to Hodgekiss and get some groceries at Dutch's and to be sure to charge them to Frog Creek. For all the help he gave me, I didn't care if he shot my carefully planned grocery budget. Jeremy and Alexis had left one serving of the corned beef casserole Twyla had brought, and I forced myself to eat breakfast.

I slowed at the outskirts of Hodgekiss. The sun stretched and yawned, not in full morning mode, so it seemed odd to see someone walking along the highway, hidden by a hoodie pulled low on his head. It took me a minute to recognize Danny Hayward. What was he doing in town this early on a Tuesday morning?

He'd probably partied all night with one of his friends. It wouldn't surprise me if he'd sneaked away from the Bar J after his grandparents were in bed.

Danny Hayward was a problem. Maybe Carly didn't need Danny to find trouble, but he always seemed to make it worse.

A year ago, the slate clouds had pressed on Carly and me as we cranked Elvis's heat and drove up I-25 from Denver in silence. I debated introductions to the conversation. My first thought was *What the hell is wrong with you?*. That seemed counterproductive.

After about two hours of silence, she squeaked, "I'm sorry." And started to cry. It had taken a year for her to cry after Glenda's death, and she hadn't done much since.

I whipped off the interstate, into an abandoned gas station, rammed Elvis into park, and leaned over the console to put my arms around her. "I love you, Bird."

She bawled for a while and I let the heater blow while I held her, the box of the console biting into my ribs and my lower spine twisting.

When the sobs tapered off, I sat back in my bucket seat and tried not to look relieved. "Tell me what happened."

She wiped her face on the cuffs of the flannel shirt I'd given her when I discovered she had only the tank top she wore. Her backpack contained nothing but a few bags of Cheetos she'd probably bought from a gas station, and Birdy Bird. This was April, the month of sixty-five degrees one day and a blizzard the next. "I had that fight with Louise and she made me so mad I called Danny to come get me."

After Brian's death, Louise had been named Carly's guardian. The fight—epic, by both Louise's and Carly's accounts—had started over an insignificant disagreement about Carly wearing a tank top to school.

I wished Carly could learn to be like water and flow out of the way. But she was more like her mother, Glenda, and had to Cool-Hand-Luke Louise's authority. When we were growing up, Glenda and Louise punched, pulled hair, and yelled at each other while I hid with a comic book under the bed and Diane took the opportunity to help herself to whatever the older two fought over.

Having already advised Carly of better ways to deal with authority, I didn't waste my breath. "I thought you and Danny broke up."

She swiped at her face again, removing some of the black mascara and eyeliner she favored these days. "We did. But I knew he was in town and he'd come get me."

"So, you left with Danny."

She nodded.

"And he had beer."

She nodded again.

I started Elvis and pulled back onto the interstate, still two hours from Frog Creek. "When did you decide it would be a good idea to run away?"

She offered the universal adolescent shrug. The one that makes adults want to knock the kid's block off.

"Don't make me drag this out of you."

She exhaled. “We drove around awhile. Danny kept bringing up all the good times we had, growing up at the ranch.”

She stopped and drew in a shaky breath. “He’s the only one of my friends who remembers Mom. And he gets what a total bitch Roxy is.”

I waited while she paused.

“He’s got all kinds of bullshit with Nat and Rope. They try to control him.”

I felt like I had to defend my team. “Danny’s lucky to have grandparents who love him.”

“I know Rope and Nat are nice people. Louise probably is, too.”

Point made; we could move on.

“We got drunk and convinced each other we’d be better on our own and decided to live in Denver.”

Again I bit back my first thoughts, starting with *What kind of idiot are you to drive drunk?* and moving on to *How did you think two sixteen-year-olds would support yourselves?* Instead, I tried to sound calm and sensitive. “Then what happened?”

“We got the hotel room and Danny found somebody to buy him beer and he had some pot.”

She stopped, probably waiting for me to gasp and lecture her on premarital sex, substance abuse, and generally skanky behavior. I didn’t.

“Every time I tried to talk about making a plan and getting jobs, Danny got mad, so I let it drop. But then we ran out of money.”

“And that’s when you called me?” Diane lived in Denver. She’d have been at Carly’s side in a heartbeat.

“Not until he got scary.”

I clenched my hands on the steering wheel. I wanted to brain that asshole kid. “Did he hit you?”

She shook her head. “No. But he was getting close. He shoved me against the wall. I thought he was one beer away from putting his fist in my eye."

Carly was no one's fool.

"So I walked to the Denny's and called you."

"He didn't come after you?"

"The pencil dick probably kept drinking beer and smoking until he ran out or passed out or both."

We drove several miles while I tried to get my temper under control. "I'm glad you called me. Louise is pretty worried." I paused. "And really torqued off."

Carly looked ashamed. "I'm sorry. But I shouldn't have to live with someone like her. I know she's got five kids and looks stable and all that shit. But she's a fascist."

Her voice rose in frustration. "I don't need someone hovering over me all the time, making me eat breakfast and checking my goddamned homework."

She swiveled in her bucket seat and faced me. "And having to talk like I'm six years old or Louise stops every conversation and says, 'Carly, language.' Like I'm going to fucking be a nun or something."

Louise did it to me, too. "She gets that from Dad. Still, a teenager is a kid, and there's nothing wrong with having a few rules."

Carly flopped back in the seat and stared out the windshield at the fat raindrops popping on the glass. "Why can't I live with you?"

We drifted into our own schemes for the rest of the drive, commenting from time to time on the weather or mundane topics.

Because Frog Creek was south of town, off the highway we were traveling, I pulled in to the ranch before taking Carly to Louise's. After dropping our coats on the back porch, we walked into the kitchen to find Ted chopping onions and browning hamburger for spaghetti.

"Hope you're hungry." He smiled and invited me to kiss his cheek.

I obliged, then stepped back, trying to keep trepidation from my voice. “Carly’s going to stay with us.”

He nodded at Carly. “Great. I’ve got plenty. It’s my special sauce. You’ll love it.”

“Not just for supper.” I took a deep breath, lining up my arguments and appeasements. “Probably until she graduates.”

He never hesitated. The staccato of his knife on the cutting board kept its pace. “Be careful with that space heater in the attic. It’s fine to run it while you’re in your room, but turn it off when you leave. Don’t want it overheating and starting a fire.”

From that moment, there was never any question of Carly not being welcome. I’m not sure I ever loved Ted more.

I shook my head to clear it of kind thoughts about Ted. He was a lying, cheating scumbag. Damn. He was both: generous and loving, diabolical and dishonest.

Danny looked pathetic, huddled in the hoodie. He might be a no-good cuss, but he was a kid. Alone, sad, and cold. If I saw a stray dog, I’d try to lend a hand.

I braked Elvis, pulled a U-turn, and headed back to see if I could give Danny a ride someplace. As I eased Elvis onto the shoulder in front of him, he craned his head up. He hesitated a split second, then wheeled around and bolted across the highway.

What the . . . ? I slammed Elvis into Park and launched after Danny. I didn’t have to chase him far. He’d crossed the highway and barreled down the embankment toward the railroad tracks. By the time I got to the top of the ditch, he’d stumbled on the steep bank, probably because he wore his baggy pants too low. He rolled to the railroad right-of-way and lay on his back, panting and ashen.

I picked my way down the ditch and stood above him. “Morning.”

Even from where I stood I could smell sour body odor. He struggled to his hands and knees and scrambled away.

I lunged for him and grabbed fistfuls of his hoodie. "Hold on there, cowboy. Where are you going?"

He bucked but I held on. He yelled, "Leave me alone. Get away from me."

"Wait!" I planted my hands on his shoulders and pushed him to sit. "What's the matter with you? I'm not going to hurt you." Unless he'd hurt Carly; then he needed to worry. But since she was in Lincoln, he was probably safe from me.

Puffs of breath rose in the chilly air. "What do you want?"

I squatted to look into his face. His pupils swallowed most of his iris. Whatever he saw, I'd bet it wasn't real sharp. I let go. "What are you on?"

He pulled back. "What? Nothing. I just came to town early. Gonna lift weights before school."

"That right?" I studied him a minute. "Rope and Nat know you're here?"

A lump rolled down his Adam's apple. He breathed harder. "Carly asked me to meet her before school."

I grabbed the front of his hoodie and yanked him toward me. "Don't use Carly for your excuses."

Life stirred in his dull eyes. "Why don't you and all your bullshit family leave her—leave us—alone? I'm what she needs. I can take care of her."

Weaselly, smelly, jerk. He seemed pretty far from death, and probably couldn't get into too much trouble this time of day, so I'd leave him alone. "Want me to give you a lift to the school?"

"Fuck you."

That let me off the hook with poetic finality. I'd do my part by letting Nat know I'd seen him.

Elvis waited for me like the trusty mount he was and we hi-yo-Silvered down the road, leaving Danny to his morning workout.

Dad's pickup sat outside the house, so I pulled in behind it and let myself into the kitchen.

"Morning, sugar." Dad stood at the sink, filling his thermos with coffee. He wore his steel-toe boots. "You did a mighty fine job at the debate last night."

I poured a cup of coffee. "We need to do something about Eldon's funeral."

He screwed the lid tight and wedged the thermos into the oversize backpack he used for a work grip. "Already talked to the funeral home. We decided on Friday. I told 'em to pick some regular hymns. Carly doesn't have any favorites, does she?"

Hymns? "Not that I know of."

He lifted the heavy pack and grunted as it settled on his back. "Eldon wasn't much of a churchgoer.

Carly should have a hand in saying good-bye to Eldon. "Thanks."

"You've got a lot of other deciding to do; guess I can help out with the funeral."

I stared at my coffee, then up at him. "You knew about Ted and Roxy, didn't you?"

No hound ever had sadder eyes. "I'm real sorry, Katie."

I nodded, swallowing the lump. It seemed natural to have him defend his choice to not tell me, but this was Dad. He treated us like wildlife. It'd pain him to watch an elk drown from falling through the ice on a Yellowstone lake, but he accepted the natural order of things. Dad's principles were a little too rigid, to my way of thinking, but I wouldn't change him.

He kissed me on the forehead and left for work. He'd return in two days, give or take.

Mom wandered into the kitchen. She wore her New York getup: black turtleneck and yoga pants. Everyone wore yoga pants these days, but Mom had been wearing them ever since I could remember.

She'd pinned her hair into a French twist and wore makeup. She was stunning in a way Dahlia could only dream about. "You look tired, Katharine."

If tired was all, at least I didn't look as poorly as I felt. "You finished the piece?"

She was pretty when she smiled. "I think it's one of my best." She filled her copper teakettle and settled it on the gas stove. "Your father's right."

"About what?" I set the coffee down, untouched.

She opened a silver canister and spooned out loose tea leaves. "You have decisions to make. Many times in your life you've fallen into things or taken the path of least resistance. This time, you need to make conscious choices."

With more than a touch of defensiveness, I said, "I will."

She stood by the stove, waiting for the water to boil. "It's not enough to let Ted choose. That's what happened when you married."

I settled for the weak defense. "I love Ted."

She considered me. "But not until he picked you. Then it was as if you felt obligated to pick him back."

That wasn't true. Or was it? Did I only start loving Ted after he wanted me?

I preferred it when Mom seemed oblivious.

She tapped the side of the kettle to test the heat. "Even though I'm against interfering, I'm going to give you a teensy bit of advice."

Would it offend her if I pulled my phone out and recorded this? Louise would never believe it.

"Dig deep into your heart. Find out what you love the most. What has driven you from the time you were a child? When you discover it, you'll know what to choose."

With that, she stepped close to me, placed both of her hands on my face, and pulled my head toward her, looking into my eyes. The cool of her palms, roughed from her work, felt like a benediction. Her eyes told me, in a way her words never could. "I do so love you."

I breathed in her Lily of the Valley scent. "I love you, too," I managed to croak.

She brewed her tea and I forced myself out of the sanctuary of home.

Spring decided to throw off her gloomy sweater and strutted out in a sundress. The hills had that sweep of green that would make a cow's mouth water just thinking about tearing into the juicy grass. I wasn't quite that taken with the sunny day and promise of new growth.

I drove along the rolling hills, only noticing the state of the pastures and the weather because, for the last eight years, these details had dictated my days. Today, it could have been blowing or sleeting or blazing under a burning sun.

I tried to cling to the blessing I felt Mom had given. But I kept returning to her advice. What had driven me all my life?

That wasn't hard to define. Glenda and I had talked about it many times. After growing up in the chaos of hand-me-downs, securing solitude only under a bed, never having room and peace to think and be, we'd both found our place in the world. We had homes and purpose and something we called our own.

I believed Glenda loved Brian, and I loved Ted, even if I had fantasies of castrating him right now. But I loved Frog Creek as much as Glenda and Carly loved the Bar J.

The highway stretched in a straight line, with flat pastures on either side. A gravel shoulder and deep barrow ditch lined the roadsides, with a three-strand barbed wire fence a few yards into the prairie.

Lost in retrospection, I topped the last hill just before the long flat into Broken Butte.

Damn!

A stream of black blocked the lane in front of me. Cows. Maybe three cows or a dozen. Holy mother. My insides exploded in fear. I'd smash into one or several of them and we'd all splatter in a rain of gore. I reacted.

I hit Elvis's brakes and jerked the wheel to the right. Thank God no one but me and a million suicidal cows were on the highway. I had little control. No way Elvis could weave through them like a pole-bending mare. My teeth clenched and my eyes squinted while I expected to slam into five hundred pounds of black hide and bone.

Baby. Oh, baby. I had to come through this in one piece in case—

I barreled through the cows, nicking one but not even toppling it.

I wanted to close my eyes and throw my hands over my face, dive to the floor and curl into a ball like an armadillo. It would do as much good as trying to drive this death rocket. But I couldn't give up.

Like a star trooper avoiding all the asteroids, I banged another cow but miraculously made it thought the herd. Not one animal stood between me and the open road. We'd done it! Even though I was cruising in the left lane, the cows and I had survived. I nearly started breathing again as I jerked the wheel to the right to get in my lane. My hands vibrated on the wheel as an ear-bursting *thunk-clank* exploded in the cab.

Elvis didn't alter his direction. I spun the wheel to regain my side of the road. Elvis had his own idea. Whatever that horrific noise was, it meant something busted. The surge of adrenaline tightened every muscle. I was doomed. *We* were, if I was carrying a new life.

Elvis kept veering left. All the while, the tires gave a shriek and Elvis shuddered as if fighting an interior demon. I battled along with him, willing his tires to straighten, for the brakes to slow us safely. My wishing failed. Metal scraped on pavement. I cranked the wheel.

Useless.

I tugged the wheel frantically but we didn't change direction, and the driver's side tire dropped from the pavement with a bounce. Elvis kept racing to the left. The front passenger side tire thudded onto the shoulder.

We were going to fly from the road. We could flip head over wheel. Be crushed under Elvis's steel.

We lurched toward the ditch. With insane expectations, I kept spinning the wheel, even though it was nothing but a useless appendage. It waggled in my hands. I felt like I held air.

Elvis bucked, his back wheels squealing like a dying rabbit. We headed for the left barrow ditch. Too fast. Too damned fast.

I braced myself, with my foot on the brakes and my back pressed into the seat. The cows on the road were nothing compared to this jet into the pasture.

My life depended on blind luck.

The crunching, screeching, roaring of tires mingled with the stench of burning rubber. Green of new grass swirled with brown of winter kill, mixed with yellow wildflowers and blacktop as the world rushed past my window.

We dropped from the pavement to the rocky shoulder. I bounced hard against the seat belt. My hands flew off the wheel. No loss there. I braced myself between the door and the dash. I clenched my jaw, expecting my bones to break, the windshield to shatter in my face, the steel of Elvis to crumple around me, crushing my body. Mashing the little life that might have started inside me. We crashed down from the shoulder into the ditch, plowing sand and weeds in the grill. I bit my tongue and tasted the tang of blood as we slammed into the far side of the ditch.

My forehead banged against the useless steering wheel as we came to an abrupt stop.

Silence. Alive.

I might have sat there two seconds or maybe twenty minutes. When awareness caught up to me, the only sounds were ragged breath, a meadowlark, and Elvis's idling engine. I killed the engine and swallowed blood and fear. Hot rubber, and freshly plowed dirt filled my nose.

Both hands planted on my stomach. "Are you in there?" I whispered. At most I could only be two or three weeks along. Even though my seat belt dug into me, it would take much more trauma to hurt a baby inside all my body's insulation.

With shaky fingers I tried twice to unhook my seat belt. "What did you do?" I asked Elvis, more to hear a voice, as proof of life, than expecting him to answer.

In my rearview mirror, I watched the scattered cows bunch along the side of the road.

I had to throw myself against the door several times before it cracked open. That was probably a good thing to beat some sense into me. I pushed the door against a pile of sand and weeds and climbed out. My knees buckled and I hit the ground. I rested on hands and knees for several seconds before collecting myself. I was alive and unhurt. No need to fall apart.

A cool April breeze chilled the sweat I hadn't realized covered me. I reached back inside and pulled out Ted's old hoodie, which I kept behind the seat. I slipped it over my head and it hung to midthigh. Coaxing my legs and feet to work, I made my way to the front of the car and bent down to look underneath.

Well, what do you know about that? Elvis had a broken tie rod. That's exactly what it had felt like, once I thought back to the clanking noise that had started the terrifying seconds. I had survived and diagnosed the problem, but it didn't make me feel any safer.

The tie rod wasn't just broken. I dropped to the ground, and on my back I scrunched under Elvis to get a better look. My breath bounced against the underside of Elvis, loud and fast with fear.

The bolt holding the tie rod to the driver's side tire was missing. The rod had become detached when I swerved to miss the cows.

Elvis was old and prone to mishaps. It's possible this was an accident, pure and simple. Possible.

Except, I'd stated in front of the Legion hall full of people that I would see to it that Eldon's murderer was found. The person Milo thought had killed Eldon was lying in a hospital bed in Broken Butte, unable to walk, let alone mess with a tie rod.

There was someone else who didn't want me to find the real killer, and they'd gone to some trouble to make sure I didn't.

16

I called Robert and Sarah to my rescue and waited in the ditch for them arrive. Two eighteen-wheelers roared past, and an old rancher pulled off to ask if I needed help. By then, the loose cows had wandered back to their pasture, probably on their way to the windmill. Other than that, it was me, the wind, and a herd of cows keeping watch on the prairie.

Robert and Sarah ranched twenty miles east of Hodgekiss and down a one-lane blacktop road another five miles. They lived farther away than some of my family, but they'd help me out without too many questions. Since they owned a flatbed trailer, they could haul Elvis home. Robert dropped Sarah at Frog Creek so she could bring Ted's pickup for me.

The long wait gave me time to calm the tremors that radiated from my gut. Someone had tried to hurt me. Maybe even kill me to stop me from finding Eldon's murderer. That was enough to send me cowering to Frog Creek and my cows.

Except, now that the hell-ride was a memory, it didn't scare me as much as torque me off.

Thank goodness I'd left home at first light. The wreck set me back more than two hours. How long did the breakfast shift at Hardee's last?

Robert arrived in his working clothes, hair matted and sticking out in forty-five directions from the Elmer Fudd cap he always wore on cold mornings. He leaned under Elvis to inspect the tie rod, even though I'd explained the "accident."

By the time he climbed out, Sarah had joined me, asking if I needed them to take care of anything at the ranch, but also checking me out for injuries and agitation. I was glad for no hugs and are-you-okays.

Robert frowned at me. "Looks like someone removed the bolt."

Sarah spun toward me. "What's going on?"

I tried for a chuckle, which sounded more like a drowning goat. "Elvis is old. Things fall apart."

"Maybe," Robert said. "But what if there's something else?"

I started moving toward the pickup. "There's nothing else. I've got to go."

Sarah took a step after me. "Is this connected to Eldon's and Ted's shootings? You need to be careful."

Robert raised his voice to follow me into the pickup. "Call me if you need anything."

I needed time to go back a few days, but Robert couldn't give me that. "Thank you. I know I seem like a mess, but I promise I'll explain it all to you soon. I'm okay. Really." *Or I will be, anyway.*

I climbed into the luxury of leather seats and automatic windows. Frog Creek purchased a new pickup every other year. It went to Sid and Dahlia. Their two-year-old pickup then went to Ted. And Ted's four-year-old pickup became the official work truck—in other words, mine. Technically, the newer pickup was for both Ted and me to use, but we called it Ted's pickup and I rarely drove it. Ted mostly drove the county cop car, the one I assumed was sitting behind Roxy's house now.

With one last wave and a mouthed thank you to Robert, I pulled onto the highway heading for Broken Butte. My ever-practical mind began to assess. Because the ranch was incorporated, all the equipment, as well as the livestock, the house, and everything in it, belonged to Frog Creek. The corporation shareholders consisted of Sid, with 33 percent; Dahlia, with 34 percent; and Ted, with 33 percent. If I divorced Ted, the best I could do would be 16.5 percent of the home and business I'd poured myself into.

That train of thought chugged to nowhere. I turned my attention to Hardee's and Nat. I needed to find out what she knew about Carly being at the Bar J that day.

Old cars and pickups filled the Hardee's lot. I parked and walked into a circus of high-schoolers. Not only sprayed with the nectar of a sunny spring morning and the end of the school year looming, they also were wired on the last bit of freedom before first bell. Noise and laughter and a few flying hash browns pounded on the nerves of the war-weary counter help. The smell of fryer grease and burned coffee assaulted me.

I dodged a sailing straw wrapper and sidled up to the counter. Nat Hayward stood with her back to me, pulling sandwiches out of the warming bin and stuffing them into a bag. She turned and saw me and her eyes flew open in surprise. She'd asked me to come here, and yet she still acted like Peter Rabbit caught in Mr. McGregor's garden.

She dropped the sandwiches in the bag, zipped her fingers along the top to seal the fold, and barely projected above a whisper, "Eight thirty-five." A strutting six-foot-two, acne-faced boy with flopping bangs grabbed the bag. Nat stepped back to the order area.

"How long have you been working here?" I asked.

She poised her fingers above the computer register and didn't look me in the eye. "I took a job as a maid at the Rodeo Inn three days a week. As long as I'm in Broken Butte, I might as well get a few more hours in."

"It's a long way to drive." I cut it off before I finished with "for a minimum wage job." I was sure Eldon paid them a decent salary. I know he supplied them their house and all the beef they could eat. He probably paid for their groceries and utilities as well.

Three girls giggled and flirted behind me. A kid with a breaking voice answered their teases.

Nat raised her gaze to mine. "Danny's got some lawyer bills from when he and Carly ran away to Denver."

Ouch. When Carly had called me, I'd picked her up and brought her home, leaving Danny on his own. I'd called Nat and Rope, of course, and told them the hotel where Danny was staying. Before they could get him home, he was picked up for trying to hold up a gas station and for minor in possession of alcohol. Nat and Rope had never made mention of it. Maybe they blamed me or Carly for Danny's trouble.

"Do you know why Carly was at the Bar J the day Eldon died?" I asked.

She glanced around, eyes jumping from customers to the other workers. "I shouldn't have told you to come. I've got nothing to say."

"Did Rope tell you not to talk to me?"

Her hands wound around each other. In a stilted voice, she said, "Sausage, egg, and cheese Texas toast breakfast sandwich?"

I nearly threw up at the mention of it. "Come on, Nat. Talk to me."

Her fingers trembled as she stabbed at the order kiosk. "And a country-fried chicken and gravy breakfast platter."

A crew of teens pushed through the doors, heading for the counter. I leaned across to Nat. "Look, I barely survived a car wreck just now and I think someone doesn't want me to look into Eldon's murder. I don't know if it has anything to do with Carly or not, but if you know something, you need to tell me."

Her hand flew to her mouth. "Oh. Oh, no."

I grabbed her arm. "What is it? I won't tell Rope you talked to me."

She gasped and leaped back, whipping her head from side to side to see if anyone was watching us. She took a split second to steady herself, then stepped up to the order line. "Eleven dollars and twenty-three cents," she said.

I pulled out my credit card and handed it to her for food I didn't want. "Please. Talk to me."

Her hand stopped midswipe, then she had to put the card through again. "I was afraid he'd do something to stop you."

"Who?"

She handed the card back. "Glenn." Her words were so low I had to read her lips.

"Baxter? Why would he want to hurt me?"

She zeroed in on my face and bit her thin upper lip. "He thinks you'll tell Carly not to sell the ranch."

A whole herd of questions popped into my head. "You talked to Glenn Baxter?"

Nat's hands kept working. "He came out to the ranch yesterday. He asked a bunch of questions about Carly. Rope told him how close you are."

The object of the girls' attention poked his head around me. He addressed Nat politely. "Sorry. But we're gonna be late for school. Can I get six breakfast burritos?"

Nat acted flustered to be confronted by the teenager. It must be terrible to be so timid.

I waited while she totaled up his order and took his money. He stepped over to the pickup counter and I crowded as close to Nat as possible.

Her perpetual look of worry cranked up about ten degrees. "He wanted us to talk to Carly and convince her to sell to him. He seems desperate to own that land."

"Hey, Nat." A bone of a woman with few teeth and bad skin leaned against the back counter. Proof the meth trade was alive and well in rural Nebraska. "Order up."

Like a sparrow, Nat flew to the warming bins and extracted boxes and wrapped food. She filled two bags and scurried to the pickup area. I met her there.

The burrito kid took his bag.

"Do you think Baxter and Eldon really had a deal?"

She shoved food in a bag and thrust it at me. I picked it up, the warmth of the container uncomfortable on my palm. I followed her back to the order line.

Her eyes flitted to the rancher waiting to give his order. She stopped before she reached the computer, and leaned toward me. In a voice like a horsefly close to the ear, she said, "I think Eldon backed out of the deal and now he's dead."

She hurried to take the rancher's order.

I bumped in front of him. He was too polite to do anything but give me space. Whether it was interfering or not, I'd better do the responsible-parent thing. "Do you know where Danny is?"

Her hands trembled and she stared at the cash register. "Yes."

She was lying to protect him. "I saw him in Hodgekiss early this morning," I said.

Watery eyes turned up to mine and she squeaked, "Was he alone?"

Interesting question for her to ask. “Seemed like it.” I leaned closer to her. “I hate to tell you this, but he looked drunk or high.”

She gave her head a violent wag. “No. He’s not doing that stuff anymore.”

There was no sense in arguing. “He was pretty miserable and wouldn’t let me take him home.”

Nat avoided eye contact, and she bobbed her head several times. “Okay. Yes. Fine. Yes. I’ll collect him after my shift.”

I hated what I was about to say, but the kid needed help. “Maybe I can have Carly give him a call.”

For the first time, I caught a glimpse of what Aunt Twyla had talked about. The tiniest bit of animosity flickered deep in Nat’s eyes before she lowered them again. “No. Don’t do that.” She waved me away. “I gotta get to work.”

“Can we talk later?”

“I got nothing more to say.” She leaned to her right to look around me at the rancher. “Can I take your order?”

I hesitated a moment, but I shouldn’t harass her anymore in the middle of Hardee’s, so I left. On the way out I off-loaded my order to a bottomless pit of a teenage boy, who acted as though he’d won the lottery.

Next stop, Ted. Why did he confess and what did he remember? Plus, there was the issue of leashing Roxy.

Buds brushed the old elms and cottonwoods with a pale green. Cheerful daffodils poked through the flower beds that highlighted the center median along Main Street. Here, in the big city of Broken Butte, they employed a full-time maintenance person who plowed snow in the winter and tended to the medians in the summer. Many of the people who lived in Broken Butte took the time to water and mow their grass, and more than half even planted flowers and had some landscaping. On a bright April morning such as this, the town looked welcoming and spiffy, as if it wore a new Easter bonnet.

I pulled into the hospital parking lot and slid from the pickup. My boots on the concrete reminded me how much I'd rather be shuffling through the ranch's sand than chasing murderers. A shiver ran over me and I clenched my fists. Did someone really tamper with Elvis? Did they mean to hurt me?

The hospital office staffers were settling in, chatting with one another, getting cups of coffee. I recognized a few and nodded hello as I strode past. On the wing outside Ted's room, the orderly loaded breakfast trays onto a cart. Even if I weren't put off by food, it would have smelled as appetizing as wet silage. I almost felt sorry for Ted.

I made my way to Ted's room, pausing outside to listen. Al Roker blasted good cheer about the unseasonable spring weather in New York City. I poked my head in and surveyed the room, looking for the enemy.

Propped on pillows, Ted's fresh-shaved face appeared tense as he frowned at the sign-waving crowds outside 30 Rockefeller Center. The pajamas I'd picked out for him lay on the bedside table.

"No Dahlia?" I eased my way inside.

Ted turned his face to me and grimaced. "I asked her to go after she shaved me this morning. She was pretty upset."

Maybe I'm touchy, but I thought letting his mother shave him, when it was his legs that couldn't move, not his arms, was kind of weird. Big difference between me and Ted: it'd take a broken tie rod and threats to my niece's well-being to make me ask for help, and even then I hated doing it. Ted seemed to enjoy having other people do for him, especially if he could do it himself.

He reached for a button on the handle of the bed and a mechanical groan played while the head raised him to a sitting position. He pointed the remote control toward the overhead television and silenced Savannah Guthrie midsentence.

"God, it's good to see you," Ted said.

I hated that it felt good to see him, too.

He narrowed his eyes. "Are you okay? You look pale."

Possible pregnancy, mixed with a car wreck that might have been intentional, could drain a little color from my face. "Has Doc Kennedy been in?"

His hands clenched the blanket. "Yeah. He didn't say much. I still can't move my toes."

Weird how I could almost forget that he had destroyed the foundations of my life. "It's early yet. Doc said it could take a while for the swelling to go down. And your nerves could take months to rejuvenate."

I didn't want to recall all the things I loved about Ted. But there they were, running past me like the feed on the bottom of the CNN screen. He gave me back rubs more often than I gave them to him. He not only tolerated the tidal wave of Foxes, he seemed to love them. He made me laugh. He could focus on me and make me feel like the only person in the world. He loved me.

But I wasn't his one and only.

He worked his jaws back and forth. If he'd had ice in his pitcher, he'd be crunching away. "You're going to leave me."

Was I? My hand snaked to my belly before I realized it, and I pulled it away. "We need to talk about what happened that night."

His eyes glistened. "You should find another man, someone better than me."

I felt like crunching on something myself. "Did you shoot Eldon?"

He didn't look at me. "Yes."

Why was my heart thudding, my lungs feeling crushed? "I don't believe you."

Like water turning to ice, Ted seemed to harden in front of my eyes. “I did it. It was self-defense. I burst into the office and startled him and he shot me. I reacted. It’s a tragic mistake I’ll have to live with the rest of my life.”

“Oh, come on. That sounds like you’re an actor in the junior-class play.”

That accusation didn’t sit well with him. “I heard you announced to the whole county that we’re going to find Eldon’s killer. Well, now you know I did it, so you can stop searching.”

“Maybe Milo can’t see through this, but you’re full of malarkey.”

Anger settled into lines around his eyes. “You’re always so sure of yourself, aren’t you? Well, we aren’t all perfect. Sometimes I make mistakes.”

Did he consider his affair with Roxy a mistake? Or our marriage? “Confessing to a crime you didn’t commit is a pretty big blunder.” I shrugged. “I don’t care if you want to go to jail. Maybe Roxy’s alibi isn’t as tight as Milo thinks and you’re taking the fall for her.”

His jaw twitched, but whatever he thought to say he kept to himself.

“What I do care about is Carly,” I said.

There was no faking the alarm that flashed in his eyes. “Have you talked to her?”

I quashed that tenderness I felt when he showed kindness toward my family. “Roxy has the power to sell the Bar J to Glenn Baxter. You can’t let her do it.”

Fatigued dragged at his face. “I can’t do anything about Roxy. You told me I’m not even allowed talk to her.”

“This is serious.” I didn’t need his childish reaction.

He closed his eyes for a moment. “Okay. I’ll make you a deal. If you promise not to investigate Eldon’s murder, I promise to do what I can to stop Roxy.”

I saw no reason to tell him I'd do what I darn well pleased about the investigation. "Deal."

We remained silent for a few moments. Finally, Ted said, "I'm sorry about cheating. You didn't deserve that."

My hands fisted. Pressure pushed behind my eyes. "No, Ted. I surely did not."

He fought back tears. "I wish I could take it back."

"Take what back?" I waited to see what he regretted.

He blinked the moisture from his eyes. "I wish you didn't hurt so much."

Wrong answer. He wasn't sorry he'd been with Roxy; he was sorry he got caught. "Yeah. Roxy's sorry, too."

He frowned at me. "She's not a monster. She's had some tough breaks in her life."

"Tough, sure," I muttered. "Big new house, leather seats and climate control in her spanking new Expedition."

"You've never liked Roxy. But she's not that different from you."

By the grace of God I kept from choking him. "We're nothing alike."

He raised his eyebrows and shrugged as if to say he knew better.

The law might frown on assault and battery of a hospital patient. I didn't want to spend time in jail on account of Ted. "See ya," I said.

"Wait." He grabbed my arm.

I stared at his hand and sent a deadly warning with my eyes when I shifted them to his.

He released me. "I want you to know I love you. I've always loved you and I always will."

"That sounds about as true as your murder confession."

I left him looking like a barn after a tornado had ripped through it. I think Aunt Tutti said hi to me on my way out, but with the steam spewing from my head I couldn't be sure. I hit the front doors and shot out of the hospital into the parking lot.

Like me, April had her dander up. The wind nearly tore my hair out by its roots as I walked back to the pickup. I bowed my head, keeping my eyes on the pavement until I closed my hand on the latch, jerked the door open, hurled myself inside, and slammed it shut before the wind could wrench it from my hands.

"Hi."

"Aah!" I threw myself against the door as if a giant, hairy skunk had spoken from the passenger seat. That might have been preferable to what actually faced me.

"What the hell are you doing here?" I asked Roxy.

17

"It's too windy to wait outside," Roxy said.

"I ought to start locking the doors." No one in Grand County ever locked a car or house door. In fact, our house didn't even have locks.

She lowered the visor and grimaced in the mirror. She probably didn't want to face me with lipstick on her teeth. "Where are we going?"

"I'm heading back to Hodgekiss. I'm pretty sure you're going straight to hell." Her perfume wound around my head like a boa constrictor. If I knew about such things, I'd probably be able to tell what designer fragrance she wore. To me, it smelled like slut.

She slapped the visor up and turned to me. "Did Ted tell you why he confessed?"

What evil magic made her look so fresh? "I'll have to get your hangover remedy. You don't even have a headache, do you?"

She reached into a silver lamé bag that could have held the Mormon Tabernacle Choir and their little brothers. Out came a pair of sunglasses with so many rhinestones on the frame I risked being blinded. "I don't remember everything I said to you last night. I was understandably upset. My lover had been shot and I don't know if he'll ever walk again."

Unbelievable. "And how are you holding up today?"

"I allowed myself one small breakdown, but I'm ready to fight now. I'm a strong woman determined to save my man." She paused. "Our man. You're going to help me."

"No, I'm not."

She jumped at me. "You know he didn't kill Eldon."

"Probably not."

"So you can't let him take the blame."

I inserted the key into the ignition. "I've got some things to do today. Get out of my pickup."

She let out an impatient sigh. "It's my fault Ted's in this trouble."

I agreed with her up to a point. "No one forced Ted to sleep with you. He had a choice."

She considered that. "I'm not sure that's true. I really think we're meant to be together and there's no fighting that destiny."

"Like I said. Get out of my pickup."

She held up her hands. "Okay, okay. I get that you're mad at me. But maybe I should be mad at you, too."

"At me?" The words clogged in my throat.

She smoothed her tight pink sweater over her breasts—those breasts so much more impressive than mine. "Sure. If Ted and I are meant to be together, you're the one who is the interloper."

Her ten-dollar word stopped me for a second. "Is there something about the concept of marriage you don't understand?"

She wagged her head. "What is it, really? A quasi-religious institution requiring a certificate handed out by the government. Based on what? Those two organizations' interpretation of a love relationship? How does that even make sense? Is it a legal partnership to share assets and children or is it a mashup of church and state standardizing morality? Whatever it is, church or government, I say they have no right to dictate to me who I love and how that relationship should work."

That was a whole lot more analytical thinking and use of polysyllabic words than I'd have thought possible for Roxy. "What you're saying is that marriage means nothing and you can do what you want, including sleeping with a married man."

"I think that's a pretty rudimentary way to state it, but basically, yes."

Where did this vocabulary spring from? "Okay, *now* you can get out."

A gust rocked the pickup and we bounced together for a moment.

"I'm not leaving. We have to find Eldon's killer to free Ted."

I'd had enough of this game. "You run along and find the killer. But be careful, because someone doesn't want the killer found."

She tore off her glasses. "Ted was right. You are the most stubborn person!"

I wasn't stubborn. He just wanted his way all the time.

She sounded matter-of-fact. "People are talking about you. They know you're investigating, and you seem sort of professional because of the speech and being married to Ted. People like you and they'll talk to you."

Translation: people didn't like Roxy. I hadn't realized she was capable of honest self-awareness.

I tilted my head back and moaned. "Will you please leave me alone?"

"You're going to help me, and here's why: I control the Bar J. I can call Glenn Baxter at any moment and start negotiations."

I whipped my head toward her.

"But I won't. *If* . . ."

I waited.

"If you help me figure out who killed Eldon."

If I hadn't lost my sense of humor two days ago, I might laugh at this twisted "Gift of the Magi." Ted promised to get Roxy not to sell if I didn't investigate. Roxy promised not to sell if I helped *her* investigate. "If Ted goes free, you might not end up together."

She lifted an eyebrow at me.

"He told me he wants us to work it out," I said. Even though I wasn't convinced of his sincerity.

The other eyebrow poked up. "Is that what you want?"

I didn't like Roxy. I didn't like her at all. I channeled Mom and gave Roxy an unvexed, serene look.

She folded her arms, smug all up in her face. "Start the pickup. We're going to Hodgekiss."

18

I wasn't sure how much I'd compromise to keep living at Frog Creek, but I'd do just about anything to save the Bar J for Carly. Even if it meant helping Roxy.

Neither of us spoke for an hour and twenty minutes. I normally would have turned on the radio and listened to the midday livestock reports, but I didn't want to diminish whatever discomfort Roxy might experience in the silence.

I pulled into Hodgekiss. "Okay, Sherlock," I said. "Got any good ideas?"

She flipped one spiral curl with her index finger. "Yes. How about you?"

I didn't want to collaborate but I had to. "Nope. Who do you think did it?"

"Oh, come on. Make a guess."

Gah! She was itching for a knuckle sandwich. "Don't make me kill you."

She stuck out her lower lip. "Spoil sport. I think it was Dwayne and Kasey Weber."

They hadn't been happy about the discussion at the debate and had zipped away at the first chance. That didn't mean they were murderers, but it was as good a place as any to start. "Why do you think they did it?" I asked.

My guess is that Roxy harbored jealousy of Kasey Weber. They were both leggy, some might say pretty, women who took pride in their sex appeal. They hung out together and acted as if they considered themselves the social stars of Hodgekiss. Like most frenemies—a word I cringed to use, but one that Roxy probably loved—they both were competitive.

I don't like a "they say," but that didn't stop me from my internal mixing of fact and conjecture. Roxy married Brian about a year after Glenda passed. They'd only been married two years before he died. But in that short time, he'd provided her with the resources to be the queen she probably felt she was meant to be. She had money, prestige, and a handsome husband.

But then Kasey appeared on the arm of Dwayne Weber, not a year after Roxy and Brian married. Dwayne's divorce wasn't final when Kasey moved in with him, a sure sign they'd been having an affair. The two of them launched into a business, raising rough stock for the rodeo.

Brian's accident left Roxy with an unfinished horse barn and a tight budget doled out by her skinflint father-in-law. Kasey and Dwayne had earned a stellar reputation and were driving new pickups, hauling fancy stock trailers, and sitting with rodeo royalty at the National Finals Rodeo in Las Vegas. That placed Kasey well above Roxy on whatever diva scale they used.

Roxy tapped the dash and gave me that smug smile. "Let's go out to their place and find out."

"Tell me now. I don't like playing games."

She resigned herself to me being a stick-in-the-mud. "I was visiting with Kasey at the Top T bull sale last fall."

Roxy kept talking, but my ears quit listening as a white-hot poker jabbed me. Ted had gone to the Top T bull sale last fall. I'd had the flyer sitting on the kitchen table and mentioned I thought we ought to bring in some new blood for our herd. The Top T is outside of Billings and is known for its easy-calving Angus bulls. We'd been buying bulls from local producers for years. That's not a bad thing, and we could still get good genetics, but I'd wanted to take a few days off with Ted. Just him and me on a road trip to Montana. At the end, we could buy a bull or two and charge all the expense to the ranch.

Ted had thought it a grand idea. He ran it by Sid and Dahlia at one of our interminable Sunday dinners—one of the dinners Dahlia insisted we drive to Broken Butte to attend, every other weekend. She'd assign me something like a salad or dessert, for which she always had a comment. Things like "You say you used nutmeg in this apple salad? Huh. I've never tasted anything like it before." Or "I understand how sometimes the eggs just don't beat up enough to make a decent meringue. It doesn't taste that bad."

Sid thought new genetics was a good idea, too, and we got the go-ahead. But Ted planned the trip during the weekend of Mom and Dad's fortieth wedding anniversary, a party my sibs and I had on the calendar for months. He pled forgetfulness, but even back then I'd wondered about it.

Now it made sense. He'd taken Roxy. A tiny ice pick stabbed into my temple.

Roxy didn't notice my silence. "Kasey and I have been friends for around five years. We know things about each other no else knows."

And yet, compadres that they were, Roxy didn't hesitate to rat her out.

We headed east out of town to the Webers' parcel. If it sat outside a city, it'd be called a ranchette. In Hodgekiss, where medium-size ranches measured in the five-thousand-acre range, the Webers' one section didn't amount to much.

April had stopped pitching her hormonal fit and the wind had died down, but she was fixing to drop into her melancholy stage as a bank of dark clouds scooted toward the sun. After a short drive we pulled off the highway and rolled up in front of the Webers' manufactured home. By Grand County housing standards, it ranked toward the top—mostly because it was only a few years old. In another ten years, it would look like any number of double-wide trailers plopped in the middle of pastures.

A newer metal barn and several corrals perched directly in back of the house. A group of pens held bucking horses. Bulls of various breeds dozed in other pens. Some with horns, some brockled, black, dun, or even striated, they looked nothing like the menacing monsters they'd become in a rodeo arena. Portable panels ran in every direction, as if the Webers used whatever means they could to create more space for the stock.

The whole operation had the feel of too much squeezed into too little space.

"Ready?" Roxy nudged my arm.

On principle, I shot her a contemptuous glance, then climbed from the cab. A feedlot smell whacked me in the face.

Roxy met me in front of the pickup. She was all graceful, long-limbed giraffe next to my squat toad.

I slapped myself upside the head. Not literally, but on the inside. Ted picked me. And he wasn't the first one who had ever wanted me. I had left a string of broken hearts in my wake. Okay, two—and admittedly they were both even more flawed than Ted, if that was possible. Still, it would do me no good to denigrate myself.

Why the hell was I even thinking about this? I needed to

concentrate on finding Eldon's killer so that Roxy wouldn't sell the ranch. My priority had to be Carly.

Roxy strutted ahead of me like a runway model in her fashionable cowboy boots, up the packed dirt path toward the redwood deck, and I followed in my scuffed and muddy ropers. The front door swung open before we could knock.

Kasey pushed the screen out and slipped from the house to the deck in her stocking feet. "Oh my God! What are you doing here?" She threw her arms around Roxy. "I'm so sorry to hear about Eldon."

Roxy produced not one but a whole passel of tears. Like a miracle fountain, they gushed out of her eyes. "It's a tragedy."

Even Kasey seemed taken aback. She patted Roxy's shoulder and her glance drifted to me. She had to be wondering what Roxy and I were doing together.

Like Roxy, Kasey had long, lean lines. When she'd shown up in Hodgekiss a few years ago, people took to calling her High Pockets. She wore faded Wranglers and a T-shirt. Her thick blonde hair, usually worn free, was held hostage in a braid today. She must hate not having her sexy on with Roxy looking all dolled up.

Kasey waited until Roxy gained control and pushed away. With a devilish gleam in the back of her eye, she said, "How is Ted? I heard he was shot."

Roxy's tears started all over again. "He's so brave."

I resisted rolling my eyes. "He'll be all right."

Kasey put an arm around Roxy again. "How are you? I've been so worried."

Roxy brushed away a tear. "I must have missed your call. You know how spotty cell service is between here and Broken Butte. I've been on the road almost constantly."

Kasey didn't miss a beat. "I didn't call. I knew you'd call me when you were ready to talk, and I didn't want to interrupt if you were"—her eyes shifted to me, then back to Roxy—"busy."

Roxy flipped her hair, apparently finished with the mourning portion of the visit. "It's okay. She knows."

Kasey's eyes widened in surprise. I was pretty darned surprised to be traipsing around the countryside with Roxy, myself.

A gust sent the overpowering odor of manure whirling around our heads. The sun dimmed, and we looked up to see gray elephant clouds lumbering close. Kasey swung the screen open and gestured inside. "Come on in. I put the coffee on." Of course she did. If you were in the house and someone drove up, you made coffee. It was Sandhills law.

We stepped into the faux foyer, a square of tastefully patterned linoleum to mark the area before the Berber carpet began covering the living and dining room. That ended with more of the same linoleum, in the open kitchen visible through the breakfast bar. The whole house had a sterile feel, as though they'd bought it furnished in the drab earth tones and hadn't added any of their own touches.

Either Dwayne and Kasey maintained the modest home because they hoped to move to a bigger, better place soon and didn't want to put too much into it, or they'd grown up in rural poverty and a new house decorated by the manufacturers passed for elegance.

We followed Kasey into the kitchen. "Where's Dwayne?" Roxy asked.

Even without makeup, Kasey's vivid blue eyes and long, dark lashes gave her a finished look. "One of the mares is foaling and he's got her in the barn. He's been babysitting since four this morning."

Kasey grabbed three matching ceramic mugs, with the Weber Roughstock logo, from a cupboard and filled them. I took a sip and felt the hair growing on my chest.

Roxy and I perched on barstools, looking into the kitchen. Kasey leaned against the counter, facing us. From where she stood, she had a clear view of the road heading into her place from the highway and of the lane leading to the barn, where Dwayne held vigil.

Roxy took a sip and set her cup down. “I brought Kate along because she’s sort of filling in for Ted. Did you go to the debate last night? I hear she did a great job representing him.”

Kasey wore a suitably grave expression and drew her cup to her face. I wanted to spit my coffee at Roxy. “We did. Kate is a natural. I’ll bet everyone there would vote for you.”

Roxy frowned. “Vote for Ted, you mean. Kate did well because standing in for Ted is so easy.”

A wicked light flashed in Kasey’s eyes. “Of course. That’s what I mean.”

Roxy acted insulted, but continued. “It’s terrible that Eldon was murdered, of course. As sheriff, Ted needs to figure out who did it.”

Kasey’s jaw tightened.

Roxy nudged me with her eyes. “Yes,” I said. “So, I always thought Eldon was respected by everyone, but last night it seemed to me there were people not very happy with him.”

I should have asked a real question, because Kasey didn’t seem inclined to pick up the conversation. I tried again. “Did you and Dwayne have any reason not to like Eldon?”

The kitchen darkened as the clouds gained on us. Kasey looked into her cup. “No. Not really.”

The first fat drops smacked the kitchen window like tiny liquid cluster bombs. Kasey remained serious.

Roxy toyed with the handle on her mug. “What about that thing.”

Kasey wore a totally fake expression of confusion. “What thing?”

Rain rattled on the roof and thwacked the windows. Roxy looked apologetic. “You know, that land deal with Jack Carson.”

Kasey’s smile looked strained. “Oh. Yeah. I’d almost forgotten.” She didn’t play amnesia well.

I sipped at the acidic brew, which was boring holes in my stomach lining. What was the rule about pregnancy and caffeine? “What happened?”

The kitchen darkened more, so Kasey snapped on the overhead light. “Last summer, Dwayne and me were looking to expand. We’ve got some stock contracts we made from winning Breeder of the Year last year. So we’re sitting in the Long Branch one night, talking to Jack Carson, and he mentions this parcel. He’s got three pivots of alfalfa and doesn’t want to bother with the natural hay meadow anymore. One thing leads to another, and me and Dwayne make him an offer.”

The worst of the rain moved on and left a few pecking remnants.

“So Jack says yes and we go to the bank, but because of the economy and all that, they won’t give us the cash. Then we hear Eldon Edwards sometimes loans money to young people starting out. So we go to him and he acts like he likes the whole idea and it’s all easy-peasy.”

She reached for the coffee and poured more rotgut into her cup. She raised the pot to us and we declined.

“We get all the details lined out and Dwayne and I start packing up the panels and equipment. And lo and behold, Eldon shows up and says the deal’s off. No explanation. No nothing. Just no money.”

Kasey’s tone was calm, but her skin had taken on a rosy heat. “I wanted to strangle Eldon for screwing up our deal. I mean, look at us. We’ve outgrown this place.”

Roxy kicked me on our side of the counter.

Kasey sipped her coffee and offered a foxy grin. “It worked out well for us in the end.”

Roxy’s returning smile pulled tight at the corners. “Why?”

Kasey leaned forward. “We haven’t told anyone else yet, but yesterday we signed the papers to buy Justin Calloway’s place over by Danbury.”

“Really?” Roxy squealed with fake delight.

“The best part is that we’re getting more ground and paying less per acre than we would have with Carson’s meadow.”

"Congratulations," I said. She didn't know the real reason I said that was because she'd annoyed Roxy with their good fortune.

Kasey gave us a saucy wink. "Me and Dwayne didn't kill Eldon."

Roxy acted shocked. "What?"

Kasey sniggered. "I know that's why you're here."

Roxy's eyes widened. "I'd never . . ."

Kasey tilted her head. "But I have a pretty good idea who did."

"Who?" Roxy asked.

Kasey leaned in. "Jack Carson."

"Because Eldon scuttled the deal between you?" I asked.

Kasey looked surprised. "No. Because Aileen and Eldon had been having an affair."

19

Damp from sputtering rain of the dying storm, I pulled the pickup out of the Webers' ranch yard and followed the muddy road to the highway.

I don't know if I addressed it to Roxy or was just talking out loud: "So far, we've got the theories that Eldon was shot because he planned to sell the Bar J, because he wouldn't sell, or because he was sleeping with Aileen Carson. None of these seem valid. I don't think anyone would really kill him over a land deal." I thought a moment. "Of course, people fought and died over open range laws in the 1800s."

Roxy had the passenger side visor down and was performing some kind of voodoo on her hair. She pulled what looked to be a miniature cattle prod from her purse and plugged it into the power outlet on the console. "Yeah, but everyone knows about the feud between the Carsons and the Edwardses."

I turned up the heat in the pickup. "What was the feud about, anyway?"

She lowered the heat and scrounged in the silver lamé saddlebag.

She extracted a cosmetic bag made of fake cowhide. "Brian said it started when Eldon's grandparents and Jack's ancestors settled out there. Just land stuff; a few affairs thrown in, because that's what always happens."

"I guess things never change."

She ignored that. "Then the Carsons got religion and the Edwardses didn't and that made it worse."

Hardly the Hatfields and McCoys. "But Eldon offering the loan and then backing out might be a mean trick," I said.

She tilted her chin and studied her face like a painter assesses his canvas. "Eldon didn't play tricks. For fun or anything else."

From the cosmetic bag, she pulled out a tube of skin-tone lipstick. She dabbed it under her eyes and delicately patted it in. "If you ask me, Jack's creepy with his religion. He probably killed Eldon over the Aileen affair more than the land." A little eyeliner followed those remarks, and she ended by brushing on face powder. "Those religious types take infidelity really seriously."

Lucky for her I wasn't a religious type. And when did it become common knowledge that Aileen and Eldon had had an affair? That seemed like a "they said" gathering momentum.

My thoughts jumped the track to what "they" said about me and Ted and Roxy. I forced myself back onto the rails.

She stuffed the potions back into the cowhide bag, zipped it, and dropped it into her purse. Out came a small brush, and she gave her hair a vigorous going-over, taking out almost all the ringlets, which had been decimated by the rain. She grabbed the cattle prod thingy. Aha! A curling iron to go.

It was like watching some kind of horror/magic show. She'd transformed herself from drowned cat to rodeo queen by the time we made it to Hodgekiss.

"Even if Dwayne and Kasey didn't kill Eldon, they're still guilty." She rolled out rosy lipstick and brushed it in small strokes.

"For what?" I swerved to avoid a mud puddle, and her hand jerked. "Sorry."

She rubbed the red smudge with the pad of her pinky. "Who knows? Didn't you smell it on her?"

"Nope." I turned the heat up.

Roxy let out a bray. "You don't know Kasey. She's a climber. She isn't happy with second best. That's why she had the affair with Dwayne in the first place. She was married to a real loser and she thought Dwayne had a ton of money. So she hooked up with him. Turns out the money was all his wife's and he didn't get any because of a prenup his wife's family made him sign. They knew he was a crook, early on."

"You sure about that?"

Roxy nodded. "Oh, yeah. It's a known fact that he stole cattle. A calf here, another one there. Not so much as people could accuse him, because it could just be a lost calf. That happens. But there is a pattern."

Another "they say." Only this time I knew better, because Ted and I had discussed the investigation. Lots of people pointed the finger at Dwayne, but we'd followed the clues that led us to Boon Dempsey's son. The one who'd suffered brain damage in a four-wheeler accident. Boon had since replaced all the stolen cattle and no one pressed charges. It was possible to keep a secret in the Sandhills, though it was not common.

Roxy tilted her head to the right and surveyed herself in the visor mirror. "I'm keeping them on the list."

I lowered my own visor. April decided to dazzle us with a dose of sunshine to end the changeable day. The sky she offered was one of my favorites. Dark clouds to the east, lit by the bright rays. Blue giving promise of warmer days; even a rainbow to shimmer across the greening hills.

"Do you think Jack did it?" she asked.

I hadn't even talked to him, so I didn't know. "I'm not sure about Aileen having an affair with Eldon."

Roxy tilted her head the other way and studied her reflection. "I know, right? I mean, I guess he was old and probably would have been grateful for any attention, but, really, Aileen is kind of a dog, don't you think?"

That was less than kind. "She's a nice person. And Jack seems devoted to her." If his attention at the debate was any indication.

"Oh, look, a rainbow!"

We cruised through town, turned north, and rumbled across the tracks seconds before the crossing arms lowered for the BNSF train.

"Are we going to Carson's?" Amazingly, Roxy had more shoring up to do, because she pulled lip gloss from her bag, ran the shiny goop over her mouth, and smacked.

I couldn't keep my mouth shut. "We're going to ask some questions, not to a ball."

Roxy shifted to give me a puzzled look. "Oh, you mean me fixing up?"

"It was only a little rain. Not like it'd have made the roof leak."

She didn't say anything for a moment or two but looked as if she were arguing with herself. Finally she seemed to come to a decision. "I probably shouldn't say anything. But, even though you might not believe it, I like you."

"Sure. You like me enough to try to steal my life."

She chuckled as if I'd told a joke. "So don't hate me when I tell you this."

"Too late."

"You could stand to do a little fixing up."

I willed a neutral expression, but my innards boiled.

"I mean, you're pretty. Don't get me wrong. In that girl-next-door, simple way. But you could be so much more. And, frankly, you're getting too old to go natural all the time."

Against my will I caught a glimpse of the left half of my face in the side mirror. Curls popped from my ponytail, their dampness creating a wild tangle.

"You should straighten your hair, for one thing. A Brazilian blowout would work wonders. They're kind of expensive, but they last for six weeks. Then you don't have to blow-dry your hair every time. It stays straight and takes out the frizzies."

The fire in my core heated up and stone started to melt. "Ted likes my hair curly."

She looked sad. "That's what he says."

I stared at the road, molten rock boiling in my gut.

"And here . . ." She dug in her bag and pulled out the cowhide pouch again. She unzipped it and brought out mascara. "You should use this to highlight your eyes. The blue is really remarkable. And I'm jealous of your long eyelashes. I've got a product you can use before you put on your makeup, that takes the puffiness out from under your eyes. You really should use it every morning, especially this time of year."

Ha! Who has time for makeup in the morning? I've got cows to feed, horses to take care of, and a million chores before fixing breakfast. Besides, I'm out at the ranch all day; no one sees me.

She must have misinterpreted my expression. "I know! I didn't believe it either, but it really works."

She reached over with the mascara and pointed it toward my eyes. I swatted her away. "Stop that."

"The other thing you should do is quit wearing men's clothes."

This surprised me, so I blurted out, "I don't wear men's clothes."

"Okay, maybe not technically. But you wear baggy T-shirts and flannel shirts and regular Wranglers all the time."

"Not all the time." Getting defensive was plain stupid.

"How often do you dress up when you're home? Do you wear makeup for dinner with just you and Ted, or even if Carly is there?"

My idea of dressing up is a shower and clean sweats, but I wasn't going to tell Roxy that.

She nodded as if she'd read my mind and it confirmed her suspicions. "Didn't your mother teach you about makeup? You've got, what, ten older sisters? They should have taught you something."

"Three."

"Huh?"

"Three older sisters. Glenda, Louise, Diane."

She waved her hand. "There are so many in your family. Even Ted couldn't name them all."

"Actually, he can. And he likes them all."

"How did your mother ever come up with all those names?"

The only reason I answered was because I wanted to keep her off the Kate Improvement agenda. "She had a system."

"Really?"

"We're all named for the Academy Award Best Actor or Actress of the year."

Roxy laughed and clapped her hands. "I love Marguerite! Let me guess. You're Kate—"

"Katharine."

I enjoyed the silence for several miles.

"I give up. Who?"

"Katharine Hepburn, for *On Golden Pond*. Glenda was Glenda Jackson. Louise Fletcher. Diane Keaton."

"Louise Fletcher? Who is that?"

I couldn't resist the tick of a smile. "*One Flew Over the Cuckoo's Nest*. Nurse Ratched."

Roxy hooted with laughter, and the tiniest of chuckles squeezed from my chest. "Mom lucked out the year the twins were born. Michael Douglas won for *Wall Street*."

We rode in silence for a few minutes and I congratulated myself on distracting Roxy.

Celebrating victory was premature. Roxy leaned over the console, as if conspiring with me. "I'm going to tell you something my mother told me. And it's not PC and it's not women-empowering or anything, but it's the simple truth."

I didn't want to hear this.

As solemnly as if reciting a prayer, she said, "Have an affair with your husband or someone else will."

She. Did. Not. Say that. Lava popped and climbed up my throat.

She held up a hand as if I'd started to argue. "No, listen. I know it's not fair. But look at me. I never let Ted see me without makeup. I always dress nice, wear sexy underwear, put a smile on my face. When was the last time you did any of that for him?"

"Stop talking." My voice came out as a warning growl.

"As I said, you've got some good basics to work with, you just need to—"

I slammed on the brakes and we fishtailed before stopping in the middle of the highway. "Get out."

The abrupt halt threw her toward the dash, then popped her into the back of her seat. "My God, what are you doing?"

"We're through with this conversation."

Her pale face was a satisfying sign. "I'm only trying to help."

"Here's what would help me. You leave me alone. You leave Ted alone. You leave Carly alone. You move to Tibet and pursue enlightenment."

With the kind of look you'd give to a three-year-old when you're holding the line on bedtime, she said, "I know you're hurt right now. But when you calm down you'll see I'm right."

I slapped the gearshift into Park and jetted from the pickup. In two seconds I had her door open. "Out!"

"You're crazy!" She clutched the doorframe.

"You get one chance to do this the easy way." With eight siblings,

I knew how to fight. "Get out now or I'll drag you out, and that's gonna hurt."

"Fine." She straightened her pink sweater and stepped out of the pickup onto the road. She reached inside and snatched her bag.

I stomped back to my side and climbed in, shoved the gearshift into Drive, and peeled out.

I hadn't traveled a half mile before Mom's disappointed face loomed in my mind. Mom and her damned "Desiderata." I hadn't acted the least bit placid, and probably it was possible to be on better terms with Roxy than leaving her by the roadside.

What irked me the most was that, when I returned for her, Roxy hadn't taken a step toward town. She stood with her arms folded across her chest and her bag dangling from her shoulder as if she knew I'd be back. I pulled a U-turn in the middle of the road and stopped to pick her up.

She climbed inside, way more placid than I'd thought possible, and settled her bag on the floor.

I exploded with all the heat of the volcano. "If you don't want to find yourself hoofing it back to the Bar J, keep your mouth shut about Ted."

The indulgent smile almost made me stop again. "Sure thing."

Roxy started several conversations, mostly to gossip about this or that. Finally, she gave up, pulled out her phone, and started texting. No doubt sending love notes to my husband. I ignored her soft giggles whenever she received a reply.

She addressed me. "My mother is stuck in a motel bar in Las Vegas, New Mexico. Her car broke down on her way from Phoenix. I know it's not funny, but the way she describes the people in the bar is hysterical."

Oh. She wasn't talking to Ted. I still wanted to swat her.

A set of decaying wood corrals and loading chutes marked the turnoff to the old Carson place. The headquarters squatted over the first hill from the highway. I stopped at a wire gate strung tight across the road and waited for Roxy to get out and open it. Normally the gate draped back along the fence, making the road clear. But during calving season the Carsons' new cow and calf pairs lived in the pasture closest to the house, so the gate stayed latched. Live in this country long enough and you come to know how each rancher runs his place.

Roxy tried to wait me out. She glanced down at her crisp designer jeans and fashion boots with two-inch heels, then meaningfully at my ropers and faded Wranglers. When I didn't budge, she huffed and got out to open the gate and hold it while I drove through. She latched it again.

The Carsons' calving lot sprawled in front of their headquarters, straddling the road. I idled through the milling cattle, ever mindful of sleeping calves. Like any good rancher, I studied his herd, noting the body condition of his cows—good—and the health of his calves—also good.

We pulled up in front of his well-kept brick ranch house, probably built in the sixties. Tall cottonwoods shaded the yard and a wide front porch held a swing and old metal outdoor chairs. The kind that bounce when you sit on them.

Jack walked from the barn about fifty yards south of the house. He wore his usual stern expression but seemed curious to see us there. I couldn't blame him for that. Folks in the Sandhills are friendly but not given to dropping in unannounced. Unless they were a neighbor and you happened to live within access to one of their pastures. If you shared fences and roads with neighbors, you oughtn't mow your grass topless or you might get caught. Just making a hypothetical comment; not as if Tank Cleveland caught me doing that. Twice.

Afternoon was punching its time card while evening waited to take the next shift. A chill threatened, which would turn into frost by morning. Jack would be on his way in for about two hours.

He would likely relax, watch the weather report, eat a hearty supper his wife prepared, put his feet up for an hour or so, then head back out to check the cows and do evening chores. If no cows were calving, he'd grab a few hours' sleep and trudge outside every two hours to check the herd. After about six weeks of this schedule he'd be worn so thin that, if he was given to temper, he'd be a bear, and if he was prone to depression, his wife better hide the guns.

I stepped from the pickup onto the ground, which was damp from the afternoon shower. "Hey, Jack."

He eyed me. "Kate." He raised his chin in a Sandhills wave. "Roxy."

Roxy rounded the pickup to stand next to me. I waited for Jack to make his way to us.

"Did you get a good rain?" I asked.

He rubbed his peppery face, which looked like he hadn't shaved in a few days. "Not more'n two-tenths."

"Any rain is good," I said.

Jack landed in the age range "middling," between my folks and me. His kids were grown and gone, but not by long.

He looked down at his mud- and manure-caked Carhartt coveralls, his feet encased in boots stretched with rubber overshoes. "Sad doings about Eldon." He brought his eyes up to mine. "How's Carly takin' it? She was pretty close to her granddad, wasn't she?"

I wish I knew Carly's state of mind. "She's a tough kid."

He nodded. "Will she move out to the ranch after graduation?"

I didn't have to lie. "We haven't talked about it."

I couldn't come out and ask if he'd killed Eldon. I threw Roxy a panicked look.

"When's the services?" Jack asked after a moment of silence.

I looked toward the house. Enough shadows fell that the light shone from inside, silhouetting a figure looking out a window. It had to be Aileen. I waved. The figure waved back but didn't move away. She must have something on the stove or she'd probably be out here greeting us, too. "Friday." I let that sit, trying to come up with something to say.

Roxy jumped in. "That's why we're here. Carly and I are making some decisions for the funeral. I wanted to ask if you'd consider being a pallbearer."

His forehead crinkled in puzzlement. "You could have called. You didn't need to drive all the way out here."

Roxy sighed. "It's so sad at the ranch, thinking about Eldon and Brian and everything. Kate, bless her heart, came out and insisted fresh air and sunshine would do me good. So I thought we might as well come see you. She was right. I'm feeling better now."

He looked from Roxy to me and I almost saw a dialogue bubble form over his head, which said, "Does Kate know about Ted and Roxy?" Ted and Roxy might have been discreet, but no bag could hold the cat now. Everyone knew.

He rubbed his scruffy face and seemed agitated. "Why me?"

"Well, I know how close you and Eldon were." She sounded sincere to her bones.

His hand traveled from his chin to the back of his neck. "Me and Eldon didn't have much to do with each other." If he raged about an unfaithful wife, he hid it well.

Roxy raised her eyebrows. "Didn't you have a land deal a while back?"

His hand flopped from his neck down to his crusty coveralls. "I thought only us knew about it."

Roxy looked solemn. "Family business."

Jack gazed over our heads.

Clouds had vanished, leaving the sky a deep violet, the exact color of Ted's eyes. Those eyes that used to drink me in and warm with passion for me.

"It was bad business. And I'm sorry I dragged Eldon into it." His vehemence surprised me. I tried to weigh his outburst against the calving season personality disorder. It still seemed over the top.

I waited for him to elaborate.

Finally Jack shook his head. "No, I don't s'pose Eldon would want me as pallbearer."

Since no one seemed inclined to continue, I asked, "Why's that?"

Jack turned his attention to Roxy and gave her a mournful look.

She let her lower lip tremble slightly. "It's not my story to tell."

Jack shoved his hands into the pockets of his coveralls and stared at his muddy boots for several seconds. Without raising his head, he started to speak. "I'm sorry to say that I got myself into some money troubles. This fellow from Mississippi was doing some of God's work. At least, that's what I thought. Still do, as far as that goes."

He glanced up quickly, then down.

"He heard this old Bible prophecy about a perfect red heifer being born in Israel. It's sort of a long story, why there hasn't been one in over two thousand years and why there needs to be one. I can tell it to you, but I suspect you'd laugh at me."

I didn't say anything. Roxy made an *uh* sound, so he knew she was listening.

"Being as how I raise Red Angus and how I'm part of the Christ Almighty church, I heard about this man's mission. He needed someone to help him put together this perfect herd of cows, and a place to keep them until they could be shipped to Israel. He had some backers and it all seemed on the up-and-up. So I started to go to sales and buy up the best of the breeding bulls. And you know, that ain't cheap. This guy, he said the money was coming but it'd been held up. He showed me how the devil was working against us. But I know God is on our side."

I cringed, guessing what was coming next.

"I talked to Aileen about it and we agreed the good Lord was testing our faith. So I got a loan on the ranch and bought the cattle. But the man in Mississippi couldn't get the project going. Not on time, anyway. He's still working on it. But for us, time ran out. We were in debt and about to lose the ranch."

"How does Eldon come into it?" I asked.

He looked up. "I'm gettin' to it. So I figured if I could sell that south piece I could pay down the debt and maybe keep from having to lose the whole place. I'd heard the Webers was looking for a bigger place, so I approached them."

He let out a hiccup that might have been a choked sob. "I felt so desperate. I priced it where I needed it to be, not necessarily what it was worth, and I prayed that if it was God's will that they'd accept the terms. They did."

"But then Eldon pulled the cash and ruined it," Roxy said, as if she'd wrapped it all up.

Jack stared at her. "You know that's not what happened."

Her eyebrows shot up, but she said in a normal voice, "Of course not. But it's what the devil would have wanted."

I could tell he didn't buy her version of things, but he didn't seem to care. "Before the sale was finished, the elders came to me and did a laying-on of hands to bring out the devil. You see, I'd given in to the lies and deceit and tried to take the easy way out. They made me realize that I couldn't sell to the Webers. They are fornicators. They cheated on their spouses and aren't even married to each other to this day. I had to cancel the sale, and that meant I'd lose it all."

He swallowed and paused. "But Eldon come by. He said he'd agreed to loan the Webers the money but he wanted to know why I was selling. I confessed all, and told him I didn't know how to get out of the contract I'd signed."

Roxy made another sound of interest.

"Eldon made it all good. He canceled the loan to the Webers. He bought the land from me, then went on and gave me a loan to pay off the bank."

Roxy's face turned a curious shade, sort of like a rusty nail.

"Wow, that's generous," I said.

"That's not all. He gave me a low rate and all the time I need to pay it back."

Roxy drew in a sharp breath and grew even more colorful.

"I always heard Eldon was a tightwad," I said.

Jack's eyes watered. "There was some bad blood with us Carsons and Edwardses, but Eldon always treated me fair. After he helped me out like that, I heard he put it in his will that meadow goes to Rope Hayward's boy."

"Mick?"

Jack shook his head. "Naw, I think we all know he's a lost cause. It's that other boy, the grandkid. He's been in trouble hisself, but I figure Eldon hoped to stop him before he went the same as his daddy. Kind of give the kid a reason to straighten up."

Roxy spun around and marched to the pickup. She launched herself inside and slammed the door.

Jack looked at her. "Guess she didn't know the particulars. But now she understands why it wouldn't be right for me to carry Eldon's coffin."

"I don't see why not."

"Well, Eldon helped me out, but he was put out with me on account he thought I was being too judgmental about the Webers. He said it wasn't my place."

I had no idea Eldon was such a moral beacon.

Jack shrugged. "Might be he was right. I don't know. What I do know is he helped me out of a tight spot and me and Aileen will be forever grateful."

20

I slammed the pickup door and started the engine. What did we have, so far? A couple who'd felt cheated by Eldon but had come out better off. A grateful rancher who thought of Eldon as the Second Coming. No killer there. Ted was still on the hook.

Next stop: Nat Hayward. It was time to corner her and find out what she knew about Carly and the goings-on at the Bar J.

I used the headlights as I drove through the herd. Roxy didn't say anything, but she jumped out the door when I pulled up in front of the gate. After I'd driven through and she relatched it, she plopped back into the seat and folded her arms. She showed all the signs of a full-blown snit.

Rocks pinged on the underside of the pickup. "I guess Jack didn't shoot Eldon," I said.

"Guess not." She barely moved her lips, and she kept her arms folded across her chest.

"Sounds like Eldon was generous to him and Danny."

She sounded miffed. "What a guy."

I turned left on the highway, heading away from town. "Why are you so upset?"

She faced the windshield. "Eldon never gave Brian a damn thing, but he flat-out gives that bad seed a chunk of land. Danny's not even related."

I didn't offer my opinion, that there was plenty of Bar J to go around for everyone. We rode in silence for a bit. I turned over possibilities. "If Ted shot Eldon—"

Roxy whirled on me, arms unwinding from her chest. "He didn't."

"It would be logical how he got your gun. You'd have given it to him." The steering wheel vibrated in my hands as we crossed an AutoGate.

"I didn't have my gun, so I couldn't give it to anyone."

"Then how did it get into Eldon's office to kill him?"

She shrugged. "I don't know. Well, I do know something about it."

She had no trouble giving me fashion tips, but getting her to cough up important facts proved more difficult. I took my eyes from the road to glare at her. "Tell me what you know."

"Not much."

Back to focusing on my driving, I waited. "How about you tell me anyway."

Her face softened a little. "I'm trying to spare you some hurtful details."

"I'm tough. Go ahead."

She tilted her head in a you-asked-for-it way. "Okay. My gun was stolen."

God, she was exasperating. "How's that hurt me?"

"It was at the meeting Glenn Baxter's lawyer had at the schoolhouse."

This would be District 7. The two-room brick schoolhouse for K through sixth grade took up a corner of a pasture between the Bar J and Carson's ranch. "Why is this so bad for me?"

"Because the only reason I had the gun in the pickup is that Ted and I had been out shooting prairie dogs on the east pivot."

This stuff shouldn't faze me, but it felt like a mule kick to the gut. I'd learned to shoot, since there was cause to take care of certain things on the ranch, but being raised by pacifists left a lingering sense of guilt.

Roxy, on the other hand, shared with Ted a love of guns. When they'd been sweethearts, they'd done a lot of target shooting. After Dahlia and Sid had moved from Hodgekiss to Broken Butte, Dahlia had brought boxes of Ted's childhood possessions to the ranch. She'd specifically handed me the box with all his shooting trophies. Amid the faded blue, red, and white ribbons, the gold-plastic replicas of gun-shooters glued onto marble-colored plastic pedestals, were old Polaroids of Ted and Roxy. They grinned, with their arms around each other, holding up those very trophies and ribbons.

I couldn't be jealous of the past, and for the most part I wasn't. But Roxy and Ted dragged their past right along into the present.

Back to the subject at hand. "How do you know it was stolen?"

It was a stupid question, and her look told me she knew I was just saying anything to deflect my thoughts. "It was in the pickup when we went into the meeting, and it wasn't when we came out."

"Who was at the meeting?"

She raised her voice in frustration. "Who wasn't? Every rancher in northern Grand and southern Choker was there."

We were only a few miles from Carson's, and Roxy restarted her beauty ritual, without the extreme measures of the curling iron.

"Okay. Try to concentrate on something other than your makeup. This is important."

She glared at me for a second, then turned back to the mirror.

"It's just as easy to think while looking good as it is to think when you look like a slob."

I squeezed the steering wheel to keep from smoothing my hair. "Did anyone seem upset with Eldon at the meeting?"

She paused, with her lipstick poised for attack. "Well, yeah. Half the people there were either calling him their best friend or their worst enemy." She finished applying the lipstick and smacked her lips. I really hated that sound. "May Keller and Bill Hardy were both yelling at Eldon about being a true Sandhiller and not selling out. Shorty Cally had a few people red-faced about his wanting to sell because he wanted the cash. I don't know."

"Anyone else there?"

"Ranch help, I guess."

"Who?"

"Dang it, Kate. I don't know. Rope and Nat were there, and Dean from the Spade. Grace and Stewie from Messersmith's. Lots of people; even some kids."

"What kids?"

"Carly and Danny and some of their friends."

"Carly?"

"Of course. She probably rounded up the other kids to protest selling. She gave a speech about the younger generation and how they counted on their heritage. She got emotional and cried about having the 'unique opportunity to experience this lifestyle.'" Roxy used air quotes and I wanted to break her fingers.

We turned off the highway onto the Bar J road. I pictured my blonde niece, full of fire and drive, ready to don her armor and ride fearlessly into battle. For all her bravado, she was still a kid. She needed me, even if she denied it.

Roxy leaned forward and placed one perfectly manicured hand on the dash. "Where is Carly, anyway? Is she okay?"

Red polish, of course. I unsuccessfully tried to block the memory of Ted asking me to wear nail polish. I'd reminded him how I needed to trim horses' hooves and wash dishes and drive the feed wagon. I directed my anger at Roxy. "It's taken this long for you to be concerned?"

I glanced at her and she seemed pensive. She returned my glance. "I know I promised you I wouldn't, but I could sell the Bar J. It would be the best thing for Carly, even if she doesn't understand that now."

What made me think I could trust her? "How do you figure it would be the best thing?"

Roxy looked at me like I was nuts. "Have you taken a good look at that girl? She's gorgeous. It would be a waste to hide her out there on the ranch, working in the elements. Think of her skin!"

Yeah. It might end up looking like mine.

"The ranch would make her old before her time. There's so much work, and the worry about the markets. One blizzard could wipe out a whole year's income. She's too smart and beautiful to live in the dark ages."

I thought about Glenda and me. For us, a ranch was the pot of gold at the end of the rainbow. Did Carly feel the same way? Would she love ranching enough that sacrificing other aspects of her life would be worth it?

My answer came in a memory. Two years ago, on Mother's Day, Carly asked me to go for a ride with her. Dad expected us at the house for a Fox potluck, and I still needed to trail the herd from the south pasture into the Burwell section. At first I hesitated. But Carly begged me. She said she'd hook up the trailer and load the horses. All I had to do was climb in the pickup.

It seemed important to her, so I threw away my to-do list and called Dad to tell him we'd be late. Dad's infrequent potlucks were a Fox family requirement, so begging off was like telling him I'd joined the Apollo mission and would be going to the moon for the next two years.

Carly drove us out to the Bar J, several miles north of the headquarters. We bumped down an old gravel road, toward the line shack where she'd lived with Glenda and Brian. The tiny two-bedroom cabin had suited Glenda fine. She loved the isolation of the home tucked below a hill.

Roxy had Brian build her a garish Taj Mahal at the headquarters, complete with an indoor arena. Glenda had loved this simple cabin, situated at the old cow camp fifteen miles from Eldon's place.

Those last few months of Glenda's life, I'd driven out to the line shack almost daily, and eventually had brought a suitcase and camped out on the couch. With Brian focused on Glenda, managing her pain with morphine injections and staying by her side, I tended to ranch chores, cooking, and Carly.

Dark days.

Carly had parked the trailer about a mile into one of the enormous summer pastures west of the cabin. We saddled up and rode for an hour, not saying much, but listening to the meadowlarks and watching the awkward brown curlews swoop and caw. Yellow buttercups, purple spiderwort, and pink primroses pocked the greening hills. The fresh smell of sunshine and grass perfumed the air. Carly led me up a tall hill.

We dismounted at the top and held loosely to the reins while the horses bent their heads and chomped the juicy spring grass.

"You know this is called Wild Horse Hill?" Carly's hushed tone sounded as if we were sitting in church.

I'd been up here several times with Glenda. She'd asked me to drive her here when she grew too weak to ride.

The soft breeze teased blonde wisps from Carly's ponytail. Her cheeks were pink because, as usual, she'd neglected to put on sunscreen. "I know I've been a real bitch lately."

I didn't argue with her.

"I'm sorry I skipped school."

"And the minor in possession?"

She blew a raspberry. "That was totally bogus. I mean, I wasn't the only one drinking."

"That doesn't matter."

"I wouldn't even have been caught except Bryce didn't run. I couldn't let him stand there all alone."

This was one of those times, as a mother, or a pseudo mother, where you just don't know what to feel, let alone say. Yes, absolutely, a fifteen-year-old should not be at a party drinking beer.

She'd escaped Ted's bust of the party. But her friend Bryce, who hadn't been to any beer bashes before, wasn't clear on the escape plan and had been caught with a beer can in his hand. Carly couldn't bear the thought of him having to face the heat alone, so she'd grabbed a half-empty can and walked out. Ted had to charge her, too. He'd tried to get around it, but I insisted she bear the consequences. I was proud of her compassion, but damn.

"Mom used to bring me here." Her voice, so clear in the warm air, so free of self-pity.

When I started to sob, she spun around in surprise. "I cry too, sometimes." She took a few steps toward me, tethered by her horse. She dropped the reins and put her arms around me. "I like to come here to remember her. She loved this ranch—and being on this hill, especially."

I hadn't been back to the line shack since then, though I suspected Carly visited it from time to time, when she stayed at the Bar J on weekends.

Roxy didn't know the first thing about Carly. Maybe someday Carly would change her mind about running the Bar J. Heaven knows, four years away at college could transform her, though it hadn't done so for me or Glenda. But, for now, Carly's heart belonged here.

My hand clenched in frustration. "You promised me you wouldn't sell."

"Carly is seventeen. She doesn't know what's good for her. Most of us didn't have a clue at her age. . . ." Her voice trailed off, as if wistful and wise. "Some of us wasted so much time and waited until it might be too late."

Roxy was about to say something that would really set me off. "Shut up."

"I love that you're always so authentic."

"If you like me so much, why would you sleep with my husband?"

She waved her hand. "You and Ted are totally separate issues. There isn't any reason why we can't be friends."

"There is that one reason."

"Okay, I get that you're upset now. But you'll fall in love with someone else, someone who suits you better. And then you'll thank me for giving you a reason to leave Ted."

"You really need to shut. Up."

"You have to admit that life with Ted is difficult. You aren't the least bit compatible."

Oh yes, we had a great deal of compatibility when it came to sex. At least, we used to. My stomach hurt to think about what we'd done and shared, how he liked to push me beyond my comfort zone, just a nudge, to do and try things I normally wouldn't. He made me feel safe, so I could experiment. I felt adventurous and sexy. Real pain seized me, to think he'd shared all of that with Roxy. Everything I'd done with Ted, she'd probably done too.

Maybe the pain was the baby voting for a home with a mommy and a daddy. "Life with Ted might be lot easier if you weren't in the picture."

"In his way, Ted loves you. But you're more like a little sister or a business partner. Both. He feels like he needs to protect you, and at the same time, he appreciates your attachment to Frog Creek. But you aren't the great love of his life."

The Bar J headquarters appeared in front of us. “And I suppose you are?”

Her eyes had that glint you see in romantic movies. “We’ve been together since we were kids. We had a foolish fight. But now we know we belong together.”

I had a satisfying vision of leaping across the console and closing my hands around her neck:

I shook her and banged her head against the cold glass and her eyes lost that love-light, started to bug out, and her tongue thrust from her mouth. Then the pickup sprang from the road and crashed into the giant cottonwood, because I hadn’t stopped it before I throttled Roxy.

Even my fantasies were out to get me.

I took the spur in the road, around the main headquarters. The cookhouse sat behind the barn and a row of aging cottonwoods. My phone vibrated in the cup holder between me and Roxy. I reached for the glow and noticed twelve missed calls. Since I’d heard no “cat-erwauling,” I must have accidentally set it to vibrate.

I punched Answer. “Hi, Louise.”

“Ruth! Ruthie!”

I waited.

“Hi, Kate. Where have you been? I called out to the ranch and Jeremy answered. Who does he have out there? He better be careful. He doesn’t need any more wild seeds running around.”

The one-story, clapboard cookhouse sat a hundred paces from the barn. Pristine windows reflected my headlights.

“Ruthie! I swear, she disappears when I need her.” The sound of Louise’s furious chopping told me she was cooking supper. “There you are. Run down to the basement and get me a quart of tomatoes.”

Roxy studied her nails in light from the dash.

“Pastor Steve called. Today, please, Ruth. He can’t get ahold of Roxy. Get me an onion while you’re down there. Oh, and see if there's any peaches. I told him to go ahead and have the Lutherans bring the desserts, and the Catholics will do salads. The UCC can bring finger sandwiches."

A person had to run gate on Louise's phone conversations. You opened the gate to let some sentences in, closed it to let others out, and when all was done, you studied the bits you had caught in the corral and tried to make sense of it.

Louise chopped and chattered. "I'll end up in the loony bin. Dad's on the train. Mom wants them to play Gregorian chants and recite the 'Desiderata.' I can't get in touch with Carly, and you're not much better. I suspect you're avoiding me."

Nothing got by Louise. "I'm talking to you now."

"Thanks, Ruth." To me: "I'm making authentic Hungarian goulash from a recipe I found in *Cooking Light*. But I don't have paprika. You think I can substitute a touch of chili powder? It calls for celery, but Dutch's didn't have any. I didn't have time to thaw a roast, so I'm using hamburger. But it ought to turn out yummy. I'll freeze some for you."

Delicious. "Thanks."

"Anyhoo, the funeral home called me and needs the suit to bury him. They want someone to pick out the illustration for the pamphlet. I didn't know what to tell him."

"Just a sec." I lowered the phone. "The funeral home needs a suit and decisions on the pamphlet."

Roxy gave me a stricken look. "No. I can't do that. It takes me back to Brian." Her voice tipped toward that hysterical scale I hated.

"Who's there? Who are you t— Is that Roxy? Oh, no. Do not tell me you're with Roxy."

I wished I could see Louise's face. "Yeah, Roxy is here."

The chopping stopped. "Don't do anything stupid. She's not worth it. I mean it. She's the kind that will sue if you break her nose."

If I thought breaking her nose would help, I'd take the chance. "Don't worry. We're working together to find Eldon's killer."

It sounded like she dropped a pan on the stove. "What?"

I made fake static noise, not expecting to deceive her. "Bad signal. Bye." I punched off her tinny protest.

With that out of the way, I scanned through my missed calls. Ted, Sarah, Diane, Sarah again. Several local numbers I assumed were people trying to get the latest scoop. Ted, Ted.

Roxy reached for the door handle and I held up my hand to indicate one minute. I called Jeremy and got a quick update. We'd had four calves, one cow was in labor now, and all was well.

Roxy and I climbed from the pickup, and I walked around the grill to stand with her, looking at Rope's house. The yard light on the barn pushed back full night. Smells of roasting meat mingled with the calving lot odor.

She patted her flat stomach. "I'm starving."

Yeah. Starving. She'd probably wolf down two saltines and a whole carrot stick. My stomach turned over.

I glanced at the barn. The old-fashioned wooden structure had the typical barn roof. Painted red, with white trim at the hay loft and doors and the Bar J brand outlined neatly above the double doors into the main section, the barn acted as a divider between the headquarters and the cookhouse.

Nat and Rope had lived in the cookhouse since they were married. Nat kept the yard green, if not lush. A chain-link fence separated it from the dirt and gravel where ranch pickups and trailers lined up next to the fuel tanks on their stilts. A gate and a door gave access to the corral and the barn, respectively, so Rope could make his way as easily to the barn as anyone at the headquarters. The corral at the end of the barn opened into the calving lot behind Eldon's house, as it did at Frog Creek. A two-lane road looped to the outside of the calving lot, linking the two houses.

I'd been in the Bar J cookhouse during brandings, when Glenda was alive. The front room looked like a miniature version of an old church basement. A long cafeteria-style table filled the center, with a collection of old, mismatched chairs lining it. This is where Nat would feed the hay crew and ranch help on cattle-working days. The kitchen and the family's living room were through the open doorway at the back of the house. I assumed bedrooms were down a short hall.

We started across the dirt ranch yard toward the house. A country song erupted from Roxy's purse. It was one of those whiny women singing about true love. I avoided country music—not easy in Nebraska—so I couldn't identify the song. In one movement, Roxy jerked her purse from her shoulder, located the phone in a pouch, and had it to her ear before it rang twice. "Yes."

She pulled the phone away from her ear. "I'll be there in a second," she whispered to me.

It didn't take a genius to figure out who was on the phone. I didn't want to hear her sweet-talk my husband, using some kind of code so I wouldn't know what they meant. I planted my feet and put my hands on my hips, sending a threat I fully intended to carry through.

Roxy rattled, "Can't talk." She slid the phone back into her bag.

We continued up the walk.

If Eldon was reluctant to spend money on the headquarters house, he seemed even stingier with the cookhouse. It needed a coat of paint, and several of the spindles on the porch railing needed replacing.

I banged on the front door. It was one of those century-old wood frames that didn't seal completely, with glass panels in the front, the caulking chipped and falling out. Paint peeled from the metal knob and from the plate that held the old-time keyhole, which had probably never felt the turn of a key. A frilly fake-lace curtain on the inside blocked all but the outline of Nat approaching.

Roxy's phone sang again. She glanced at the display, frowned, and turned her back to me. "This is Roxy."

Nat opened the door. She stood squarely in the doorway, blocking most of my view of the inside. She bit her lower lip and shot nervous glances beyond me, taking in Roxy and the pickup. "Oh, my. Kate Conner."

She said it loud, as if announcing it. Maybe Rope lurked in the living room at the back of the house.

"Is Danny here?" I asked.

The question rattled Nat further. "No. It's a . . . He's in town. Play rehearsal."

I strained to see behind her and she wiggled into my way. "You picked him up this morning?" I went on.

She hesitated, as if trying to remember. "Yes. No. He was already in school when I got back to town. Everything is fine. It's okay."

I doubted anything was ever okay for this nervous wreck. "Can I come in? I need to ask you about the land Eldon gave to Danny."

Behind me, Roxy added a definite tease to her voice. "I'm surprised to hear from you."

Nat shifted from foot to foot, her eyes constantly scanning behind me. "I don't . . . I can't really . . ." She let out a long breath. "Leave us alone. Please."

She must really be afraid. It wasn't fair to put her in a dicey situation. "Can you tell me where Rope is? I'll go talk to him."

Her hand shot up to her mouth. "No."

Roxy startled me by putting a hand on my arm. She frowned and listened intently, then answered, "You're on your way now?"

Nat and I watched her.

After a few seconds, Roxy responded, "Of course. That's perfect."

More male rumbling from the phone, then she hung up and looked at me. "Change of plans." She pulled me away from the door.

Without waiting, Nat pushed the door closed. The curtains ruffled, then stopped moving.

I let Roxy tug me down the sidewalk. "What change?"

"You have to take me home."

"I what? No. I'm not your chauffer."

"The wind will wreck my hair, and I don't want to get mud and cow poop on my boots."

"That's not my problem."

"You'll want to be there, anyway. This is part of the investigation."

Everything she did chapped me. "Who was on the phone?"

"That was Glenn Baxter. He's on his way to my house."

21

I carried the smell of roasting meat with me even after we'd loaded into the pickup and backed out of Rope's yard.

Roxy yanked down the visor and fluffed her hair. "It'll have to do. I won't have time to curl it."

Ted should see Roxy all flustered in anticipation of meeting another man. A prospect who could provide her with more than Ted ever would. Financial potential beyond her dreams. Ted should know the depths of her shallowness.

Ted loved me. I believed that. Last Sunday, I was stacking the dinner dishes in the strainer. We don't have a dishwasher. It's just another of the luxuries my siblings take for granted. I try not to covet their appliances, but I hate doing dishes by hand. I especially loathe drying. I played a Jenga game with the glasses, plates, and bowls; if I lost, all the dishes would tumble from the counter and smash on the floor. That wouldn't be a big loss to anyone, since I was still using the hand-me-down Corelle with the little green flower border I'd inherited from Aunt Twyla.

I had balanced a saucepan between the sink and the dish strainer. The back porch door swung open and footsteps behind me announced Ted's arrival. I concentrated on creating my tower of ice cream bowls on the edge of the dinner plates.

Ted wound his arms around my middle, pulling me into his warm body. "It's Sunday and we've got the whole place to ourselves. Let's find a sunny spot and see what comes up."

I was embarrassed that my immediate response was to catalog when I'd last checked the pregnant cows, whether any were calving, what I should get done before sundown. To my credit, I didn't say any of that out loud. But I didn't respond with immediate enthusiasm.

He nuzzled my neck. "It's a day of rest, but we don't have to rest all day." He pulled me closer and rubbed against my backside, just in case his reference had been too subtle.

It hadn't been. I pushed against him, feeling that tingle, even after eight years and the exhaustion of calving season. I glanced out the window. It was one of those amazing early spring days that, for a few hours in the high afternoon, can feel like summer. No wind, bright sunshine.

I set the bowl in the sink and turned into his embrace. "Let's go."

I wasn't surprised when he led me to a grove—well, it was a windbreak of cedar trees—where he'd spread a thick, soft blanket. He'd picked a handful of wildflowers and even opened a bottle of chardonnay.

Last Sunday. Damn it. Only a week later, he was lying in Roxy's bed.

I shot Roxy a crusty look, but she was still busy primping in the mirror. It took a minute to drive to the back of the barn so I could take the trail road to Eldon's house. This path, barely big enough for a motorized vehicle, was a shortcut between the two yards and ran along the calving lot.

"Don't go through there. It's bumpy and muddy. We're trying to let it heal over, and no one is supposed to drive on it. But Danny uses it all the time." She lowered her voice conspiratorially. "He's a delinquent."

At least we agreed on one thing. I turned the wheel and pointed us back up the road between the headquarters and the cookhouse, heading toward Roxy's castle. I slowed when we passed Eldon's house. It hadn't changed in the two days since he'd been shot, but somehow it looked abandoned and haunted. Tracks led from the side of the house to the calving lot.

We continued the hundred yards to Roxy's obscene monstrosity. It was two stories but seemed bigger, with the first floor's cathedral ceilings. Giant logs acted as porch pillars, contrasting with a red brick facade. Windows covered most of the walls, some with arches. Several steps led to the spacious front porch, where a half dozen willow branch rockers and chairs invited nonexistent visitors.

It rivaled any house in Diane's upscale Denver suburb. Diane pulled down big bucks as a banker, so I wasn't surprised she could afford this luxury. No telling how Brian had finagled the money out of Eldon, but there it stood, a testament to Roxy's acquisition skills. Houses, husbands, ranches—was there no end to her talents?

Headlights shone behind us and Roxy jogged up the walk to the porch. "You greet him. I've got to pee."

Sure. I'll be the downstairs help—take his coat, offer him sherry, and tell him the mistress will be down soon.

I followed Roxy up the stairs and across the porch. The porch light flashed on, as did small yard lights along the front walk. The windows glowed bright, one by one, presumably as Roxy ran through on her way to the bathroom. Though I'd seen this house plenty of times when I brought Carly out here or picked her up, I'd never been inside.

Peering through the cut glass window, I pushed open the red

door and stepped into a wide entryway. The polished wood floor—maybe cherry or rose or whatever kind of wood—glowed with a coppery tone in the soft light cast by a massive Tiffany chandelier. I assumed it wasn't a real Tiffany lamp, but what do I know about decorating? From the entryway, the room opened into a wide expanse, with the focus drawn to a river stone fireplace and bank of windows. I suppose it looked over a hay meadow, but the night hid the view. The kitchen, which could have held my whole house, was separated from the living area by a wide island. The stainless steel appliances, with, God help me, a dishwasher and a refrigerator the size of Gibraltar, sparkled amid all the granite. Thick Navajo rugs were spread across the hardwood. The *Bonanza*-style ranch furniture went well with the beams that ran along the extra-tall ceilings. A set of stairs led from the right side of the living room. I assumed these would take you to opulent bedrooms.

I wasn't the least bit jealous of all this luxury. I couldn't picture myself living like this. Didn't want to try; not at all. Not one bit. My eyes rested on the refrigerator. But I could see where Ted might enjoy it.

The doorbell rang. Doorbell? I couldn't remember one home in the Sandhills that had a doorbell. I reached to open the door and noticed this had a lock, as well. Definitely not your typical Sandhills house.

I opened the door. "Come in."

Baxter breezed in, gray as a cloud of toxic smoke, wearing his new jeans and boots. A leather vest and Western bolo tie completed his outfit. Money can't make you look good if you're a dorky cowboy dude.

He showed only slight surprise at me being there, gave a noncommittal nod, and walked past me into the living room. Without hiding it, he studied the house. In a scratchy voice he said, "Nice place."

My nose twitched at the overpowering smell of rose potpourri. But not like real roses in a sun-drenched garden; more like the fake rose scent from those little pocket flower dolls Louise liked to buy for her daughters. I folded my arms and watched Baxter. Dad would jump all over me for not offering him coffee and setting out a plate of cookies.

He didn't seem inclined to be sociable, and I felt particularly owly so we stood in awkward silence.

Roxy swept down the stairs and into the room. "Mr. Baxter! Glenn. Can I call you that? We're informal here in the country."

Jesus.

She'd changed from her jeans and cleavage-baring sweater to a knee-length denim skirt, cowboy boots with complicated tooling and red and turquoise leather, and, of course, a plunging shirt covered with a beaded Indian vest. It didn't take great investigative skills to notice fresh lipstick and maybe a spruced-up curl or two in her big hair.

Baxter's slick smile screamed arrogance. "Only if I may call you Roxy. This is a lovely home."

She basked in the praise. "I'm sure you're used to much bigger and better than this."

He surveyed the room with pleasure. "Bigger maybe; not better. You have excellent taste." He sat on the leather couch she indicated. "But it might be wasted, hidden up here in the middle of nowhere."

Here we go.

She preened like the prettiest chicken in the henhouse. "I don't get many visitors, that's true."

He leaned forward slightly, a technique my psych text said showed sincerity. "I don't mean to take up too much of your time, so I'll get to the reason for my visit."

Roxy adopted her serious face. "Please. We don't need to beat around the bush."

He gazed deeply into her eyes. “My deepest sympathies on the death of your father-in-law.” Saccharin dripped from his voice.

Roxy drew her chin down. “Eldon’s passing has created a problem for you, hasn’t it, Glenn?”

He sighed. “You’ve got me there. I’ve been working pretty hard to put this deal together. It all hinges on the Bar J and the agreement I had with Eldon.”

Roxy tilted her head. “I must admit, that surprises me. Eldon loved this ranch.”

Baxter nodded. “True. But he confessed to me that he didn’t think it’d be an appropriate life for his granddaughter. He wanted her to have money, to make sure she’d always be taken care of.”

Now that was the biggest load of wet horse apples I’d ever heard. If Roxy bought that, I’d be first in line to sell her a beach cabana in Fargo.

Silence dropped heavily.

After a moment, Baxter took up the slack. “I understand you are executor of the estate until your stepdaughter comes of age.”

If Carly were here, she’d rip his throat out for calling her Roxy’s stepdaughter.

Roxy looked up at Baxter in a coquettish manner. “You must have some pull. I haven’t seen Eldon’s will. How do you know this?”

Baxter puffed up at her gushing. “I have my ways.”

All of them underhanded and slimy.

Baxter produced a sad smile. “You’re a young, beautiful woman. Surely you don’t plan on staying here, your taste and talents going into a home no one sees.”

She studied her hands. “I have my stepdaughter’s best interests to think about. I can’t make a decision without her approval.”

I wanted to puke.

He leaned forward farther. “You’re a shrewd negotiator. I would be willing to increase the offer if we can make a quick agreement.”

Roxy glanced at me with discomfort. "Carly is taking some time to herself, to mourn Eldon, and I can't reach her for a few days."

Baxter's cool rasp chilled me. "What are your thoughts on selling?"

Roxy's eyes again bounced to me and then back to Baxter. Her smile showed strain. "I wouldn't mind leaving the Bar J. It's riddled with memories of my late husband, and they break my heart."

"You're in charge, are you not? We can sign the contract tonight and you can be on your way to a whole new life."

I stood by the kitchen island, forcing myself not to throw something heavy at Roxy's head.

She must have felt the violent waves flowing from me, because she held her ground. "I really need to wait for Carly's approval."

Baxter drew in a long, wheezing breath. "What if Carly were no longer in the picture? Say she stays away for good?"

A mantel clock chimed eight o'clock.

I came around the island, advancing on Baxter. "You'd better stay away from Carly."

Baxter's pale face turned from mine in dismissal. "You'll excuse us. Roxy and I have some business. It's later in Chicago, and I typically turn in early." He seemed to remember something, and addressed Roxy. "You wouldn't happen to have a spare coffeemaker and some coffee, would you? I've been missing my morning fix."

Oh no. She did not. I hadn't wondered how Baxter had arrived at the Bar J so quickly after calling Roxy. Or where he was hiding out from the news crew. Outraged, I blurted out before thinking, "Where are you staying?"

He didn't even grace me with a look. "Roxy graciously allowed me to stay at the cabin."

"Glenda's house?" The words struggled from my mouth.

Roxy slapped her thighs. "It's better this way. Even if rooms were available at the Long Branch, you know how awful they are. So noisy, and they smell like grease. I don't think they even clean them."

Since I'd worked for Aunt Twyla and Uncle Bud in high school, I knew the measure of unpleasantness in the rooms above the bar and grill. I'd swear to their cleanliness, though. If it mattered. The important thing was that Roxy was extending hospitality to the enemy and she hadn't even told me.

All the talk of keeping the ranch for Carly—the bargain that I help find Eldon's murderer, the displays of friendship—were all a put-on.

Baxter grimaced at me. "If you see your niece, give her my regards."

The milk of human kindness didn't flow in Baxter's veins. Missing teen—who cares? Colleague murdered—move on to the next deal. Perhaps he could afford to be nonchalant because he'd already solved the first of his problems. I didn't doubt that Baxter was capable of eliminating Eldon if he stood the way of his plan.

Now Roxy had the power to grant his wish or to thwart him. At least he didn't need Carly anymore.

If Roxy wouldn't sell to Baxter, he might kill her. If she did, I'd do the honors.

"You two kids, have fun, and don't stay out too late," I said.

22

My boots clunked on the polished wood floor as I let myself out. A brush of footsteps sounded on the brown grass of the yard, below the wide porch. I jumped to the stairs to get a better view.

A figure hurried away from the house. "Rope?"

He stopped, and hesitated a moment before turning to me. "Evening, Kate."

I studied him and looked back at house. Windows ran along either side of the front door, and an expansive picture window opened in front. From the porch, a person could see everything going on inside.

I made my way down the stairs to Rope. "Were you spying?"

He focused through the windows, like a hawk eyeing a field mouse. "I saw Baxter driving up and thought I ought to make sure everything was okay."

Rope had been on the Bar J since he was a teen. He had brought his bride here, raised his son on the prairies and pastures here, and now was providing Danny with the same stability. He must feel like Roxy held the end of the rug and was about to pull.

Believing that still waters run deep—and maybe mean—I'd feel better if I wasn't alone with Rope. But I plunged ahead. "What did you think Baxter might do?"

He kept his eyes trained on the conference inside the house. "S'pose she's making a deal with him now." He clucked his tongue in resignation. "What a waste."

"What do you mean?"

He frowned. "Eldon worked hard every day of his life. He could of sold out long time ago, but he held on for Carly."

"I figured Eldon loved the ranch and didn't want to leave."

Rope cringed like he was sucking a lemon. "Naw. Eldon had his eye on a slip of land and a cabin up in South Dakota, on Lake Oahe. He let on that he thought Carly might be better off with the money instead of the hard work. He was leanin' pretty hard toward selling."

I didn't hide my surprise. That was almost word for word what Baxter had said. "Really?"

Rope still kept watch on Roxy and Baxter. "I was hoping to talk to Carly and let her know I'm here to help her. Probably selfish, but me and Nat, this is our home. Guess it don't matter. Either Carly will sell or Roxy will."

"Why do you think Carly wants to sell?"

He looked at me like I'd grown Dumbo ears. "Baxter will offer so much money she'd be a fool not to."

I'd be devastated to leave Frog Creek. But at least I had a college degree and was young enough to start over. I wouldn't starve or need to stand on a busy intersection with a sad story crayoned onto cardboard. Rope and Nat didn't have anything to fall back on.

"What about the hay meadow Eldon gave to Danny? Couldn't you put a house there and raise organic chickens or bucket calves or something?"

Animosity gleamed from Rope's eyes. "I wish to hell I'd never laid eyes on that land. It's been nothing but trouble."

I glanced through the windows. Baxter might be a murderer, but right now he and Roxy provided a small sense of safety from the pent-up rage roiling off of Rope. Probably a bad idea to take off down a trail that upset him, but any detail might lead to finding the murderer. "I'd think, after all this time, you'd be glad to have your own land."

He sounded as if slivers of glass sliced his tongue. "It ain't mine. It's Danny's."

I poked at the wound, trying to get him to tell me something useful. "You think Eldon should have given it to you?"

His mouth stayed clamped for a long while. "It's been a good life out here, workin' with Eldon. I didn't need nothin' more."

"What about Danny? Don't you want him to own something?"

Even though his voice never rose, it felt like he thundered. "A body's got to earn it."

I'd have preferred to back away, slip into the pickup, and lock the doors. "You don't think Danny and Carly have worked hard enough to inherit land?"

A dark cloud passed over his face. "Kids now days are given so much in life that they never learn to work hard. Expectin' the world to be perfect."

I knew that wasn't the case with Carly. "Danny isn't happy about the land Eldon left him?"

"Them damned kids are never grateful. I ought to have knocked sense into them when they was young."

His fists clenched at his sides, and I tried to block the image of them shooting toward my face, connecting with delicate bones, bursting through my skin.

His focus settled on Roxy's window. "Did you see Baxter the day Eldon died?"

Rope's lip curled. "You been talking to Nat."

We stood silent for a moment, then I said, "You lied when you said you didn't see anyone here that day."

Rope didn't move for a while. "Baxter's been out here before that," he finally said.

His statement seemed deliberate. "When?"

"A few times in the past few months. The first time I seen him here, he come up to the house when Eldon and me was figuring out what hay equipment needed repairs."

"Did you hear what he and Eldon talked about?"

Rope shook his head. "That was before Baxter made all the offers, and I thought he was an insurance guy or cattle buyer. It wasn't until the meeting at the schoolhouse that I knew who he was."

"Did you ever hear Eldon and Baxter talk?"

"Nope."

We both watched Roxy and Baxter. She rose abruptly and walked away from the living room, toward the kitchen, out of our sight. Baxter jumped up and stalked her. Maybe it was my imagination, but it appeared that he wore a grim expression on his pale face.

A breeze ruffled a few stray curls to tickle my cheek, and the manure-and-birth smell blew from the calving lot behind Eldon's house. Rope's rough voice accented a mother cow's moo. "They weren't friends, though."

"How do you know?"

"The day Eldon was shot, I was comin' out of the barn. I hadn't heard Baxter drive in. But there was his car in front of Eldon's house. It was one of them electric things that don't make no noise."

What fortune that tight-lipped Rope Hayward felt like talking.

"Baxter was banging on the door. Eldon charged out like he was on a boar hunt. He had his rifle in his hand. I couldn't hear what they said, but they weren't friendly. Eldon pulled up the gun and Baxter hightailed it."

Glenda had told me about Eldon's temper. They'd gone head-to-head on more than one occasion. She wasn't one to back down, either.

"You said Eldon was going to sell. Why would he pull a gun on Baxter?"

Rope let out a slow breath, like air escaping from a tire. "Maybe I was wrong about that. Or maybe Baxter didn't offer enough money."

"You need to tell me what you know. Milo is going to charge Ted with Eldon's murder."

Rope reacted like I'd laid a whip to his withers. "They think Ted shot Eldon?"

"He didn't. But I'm going to find out who did."

He pulled his head back into his neck. "And you're helping Ted?" His eyes shifted to the house, then back to me.

"Yeah." Wouldn't it be great to let Ted's confession stand?

Rope lowered his voice as if someone might overhear. "If Ted didn't do it, who do you think killed Eldon?"

"I'm narrowing it down."

The porch door opened and Baxter stepped out. He turned around to Roxy, who leaned on the doorjamb. He said something and she laughed.

Nice, Roxy. Despite declaring my husband the love of her life, she openly flirted with another man. A weaselly, wan, wimpy type. An obscenely wealthy one.

Baxter lingered another few seconds and then meandered across the porch and down the stairs. For all appearances, he was a man enchanted.

Barf.

He made it to the end of Roxy's yard and then spotted us. A scowl flashed across his smooth features. "I thought you left."

I straightened my shoulders. "Just talking to Rope about a visit you made out here a few days ago."

Baxter's mouth turned into a sneer. "Is that right?"

"I heard Eldon ran you off with his gun."

Baxter laughed. "Is that from the moccasin telegraph? Or I guess it'd be the cowboy boot one."

"Eyewitness," I said, with as much venom as I could.

Baxter walked to his electric car and opened the door. "He was a confused old man. I'm not surprised he got himself shot. If you ask me, the way he behaved, it was only a matter of time." He lowered himself behind the wheel.

Rope took a few paces out of the circle of light thrown from Baxter's open door.

I grabbed onto the door before he closed it. "Did you kill Eldon because he wouldn't sell the Bar J?"

Baxter threw his head back and guffawed. "Nice try." He pointed at me. "Didn't your husband confess to the shooting?"

His laughter took me to the level I'd reached right before smashing my fist into Diane's braces. "He didn't do it."

Baxter grew serious. "That could be. But he was there and might know something he's smart enough to keep to himself."

His sinister rasp chilled me. "What would that be?"

He shrugged and looked out the windshield into the darkness. "Information you'd be advised to leave alone. Didn't you have a car accident recently?"

I glanced up to make sure Rope was still around. "How do you know about that?"

His smile looked more like he was passing gas than like a real expression. "I know a lot of things. Haven't you figured that out?"

The metal of the car door froze my hand. "But you don't know where Carly is."

"Yet." He jerked the door from my hand.

23

Just before midnight I rolled the pickup to a stop behind my house. Several times that day I'd wanted to call Ted. How was he doing? Had he gained any feeling in his legs? What did Doc Kennedy have to add? But I didn't want Ted to know I cared. More than that, I didn't want to care.

Weariness pushed at the corners of my brain, but my thoughts kept cranking. I had two strong suspects for Eldon's murder. It all depended on whether Eldon intended to sell the ranch or not.

If Eldon had balked at the sale, Glenn Baxter was the culprit. He wouldn't cotton to someone standing in the way of his legacy. His general suaveness made him my first choice. He was too darned assured and determined.

Rope, with all that submerged rage, ranked a close second. Maybe he'd worked so hard to make me think Baxter killed Eldon to throw me off his own scent. If he thought Eldon was ready to pull the figurative trigger on the sale to Baxter, would he pull the real one on Eldon? Maybe it wasn't about the buffalo common at all, but about Eldon bypassing Rope and giving land to Danny.

Jeremy's pickup wasn't in sight, so I braced myself for evening chores. After taking care of the cows and horses, I trudged up to the back porch, shed my boots and coat, and padded into the kitchen. I snapped on the light and searched for a note from Jeremy. Good boy. He'd left it tacked to the refrigerator, under a picture-frame magnet holding my favorite shot of Carly: her second-grade school photo, with no front teeth.

I pulled the note off and propped myself against the kitchen counter, just inside the living room. My gaze stopped on the Sharpie marks showing Carly's height, with a date written beside them. A blank spot showed between age twelve and age sixteen.

That was the rough time, starting after Glenda died. I'd quit asking Carly to do anything but the necessary things. We struggled along with the hope that Carly would stop fighting happiness and let life be good again. Over time, the clouds started to lift. Then, on the night Carly moved in with us, a year ago, she had handed me the Sharpie and backed up to the wall. Her old light shone in her crystal eyes, a look so much like Glenda's it stole my breath. She had said, "It's about time we get back to living like normal people, don't you think?"

Now, emotion bubbled up and tears blurred my vision. I blinked and studied Jeremy's nearly illegible handwriting. Failing at a third of the words, I pieced together that he'd pulled one calf and had four more with no issues; had fed, kicked out the pairs, and washed the sheets; and that he was sorry he had to leave.

I cooked two eggs and a slice of toast. I played roles of both mother and child as I told myself I couldn't leave the table until I'd eaten it all.

I showered and got ready for bed, but my thoughts stampeded

from Ted to Carly to speculation about a baby and back again, never staying in one pasture long enough to make a plan.

I dragged myself to the bedroom, where the sheets were indeed clean. Unfortunately, they were a tangled heap on the middle of the mattress. I dug a pillow from the pile, wrapped myself in the comforter, and curled up on the bed.

I jerked awake. It wasn't the slow surfacing of a normal awakening. Light or noise or something unusual had jolted me from sleep, and my heart galloped with the unknown. I sat up and held my breath, staring out the window. Usually, no one but deer and buffalo roam outside our windows, and the buffalo not so much, so we don't have curtains. The moon wasn't a big help in illuminating the hay meadow in front of the house. I didn't see anything moving in the darkness, and no headlights or flashlights.

I'd been asleep—more like dead—for three hours. I unwrapped the comforter and pushed myself to the floor. My jeans lay in a wad. I grabbed them, found a hoodie on a hook behind the bedroom door, and wandered to the back porch in bare feet. I might as well check the cows, since I was up. If I didn't, I'd lie in bed and worry about them and wouldn't sleep anyway.

My boots were cold, the leather hard on my bare feet, but I'd make a pass through the lot and I'd be back in bed in ten minutes. I was out the door and past the pickup before my body heat warmed the inside of my barn coat. I pulled leather gloves from the pockets, shoved my hands inside them, and slipped through the gate, into the calving lot.

Frost rimed the damp sand, and lumps of manure caught the scant moonlight. Fresh hills of hay were scattered around the lot, evidence of Jeremy's good care. The cows would munch the hay, and their leftovers would spread out, providing bedding. I made my circuit through the untroubled herd, gratified that their numbers had decreased and we'd be through this busy season in short order. In the far northwest corner I spotted a black figure. I shined the light on one of my best mothers. She swung her head slowly toward me, her eyes glowing red in the beam. I moved the light lower.A dark lump lay under her, curled into the hay. I waited a moment, detected small movement, decided all was well, and turned the flashlight to show my way toward the barn.

Only one cow occupied the whole half of the lot between me and the barn. Something sparked in the back of my brain. I whipped around and shined the light, retracing my path. I moved it over the lumps, those standing and those lying down, and counted. With each beat, my concern grew.

Eleven? Sure, some had calved in the last few days and Jeremy had turned them out, but that should leave more like thirty head. I spun around and studied the cow by the barn. She was not in a calm, motherly mood. Her ears perked forward and her tail whipped back and forth. She trotted up the side of the barn to the corner of the lot, turned, and ran back along the same track. I checked her back end when she changed direction. Afterbirth trailed from her. She'd had her calf recently. I waved the light over the ground, searching for the calf in the lumps in the frozen sand.

What the hell was going on? One calf missing and half a lot full of heavies vanished. I dug my toes into the sand, ran up the hill to the west fence line, and cantered along it. There.

My light had been trained on the three-wire fence, but the wires disappeared at a fence post. I bent over and examined it with my leather-clad fingers.

Cut. Someone had snipped through the fence, letting the heavies out to the larger pasture. A few escaped cows didn't mean a catastrophe, because I could round them up without much bother. But having someone on my ranch, tampering with my herd, creating mischief while I slept, felt like cold fingers squeezing my lungs.

I needed a dog out here. Boomer would never have let a stranger onto the place.

I whirled around and shined my light up the hill. A few cows milled around, undisturbed by my screeching nerves. I held my breath. Did I hear something? I strained to discern anything beyond the cows' heavy breathing. My fingers clenched inside the cold gloves. An engine. I was sure I heard the muffled roar of a vehicle struggling over the hills. But in the still air, I often heard the distant BNSF train whistles twelve miles away.

I trained my light beyond the fence, focusing on the ground. With careful steps I moved through the opening, studying the sand before I placed my feet. A few steps away I saw what I'd been looking for: hoofprints. Not hoofprints that most folks would recognize as a horse, and nothing I could use to prove someone had been here. But they were deeper and wider than a cow's.

My theory—and I thought it held water—was that someone had driven a trailer behind the hill, unloaded a horse, ridden over here, cut the fence, and slipped inside. Why? To rustle my cows?

That would be stupid. There were plenty of cow/calf pairs in the south pasture, easy pickin's for anyone wanting to steal.

The tie rod. Someone sneaking up to the ranch. These had to be connected. Someone was targeting me. Trying to hurt me. The only possible reason was because I was messing in their business. Investigating Eldon's murder.

Sweat slicked my face, even though my ears tingled with cold. My nerves stretched so tight they vibrated. I surveyed the house and the yard. No movement. I let my gaze travel to the dirt and gravel in front of the barn and equipment shed. All seemed as peaceful as it would at dawn.

Rooted to the sand, I tried to figure out my next move. Too early to go to the hospital to talk to Ted. Somehow I had to get him to unconfess and then we'd unravel this mystery as we had the cattle rustling case two years ago.

For now, I needed to repair the fence so at least the rest of the cows would stay put. I normally enjoyed the hours sliding from midnight to dawn. Generally, the peace soothed me. But tonight urgency throbbed too hard. I followed the flashlight beam toward the barn.

The agitated cow still traveled up and down the outside of the barn wall. It's possible she'd wandered out into the pasture when the fence was cut, had her calf out there, wandered back, and forgotten where she'd left it. Or maybe the calf had followed another cow out of the lot. Neither scenario was likely. I nudged the hay mounds close to the barn to see if maybe it had snuggled under the hay. No calf.

Coyotes sometimes attacked newborns. But that's one reason I kept the heavies locked in the lot. The predators rarely risked getting this close to the house, and even if one had, the herd would put up a ruckus of mooing and bawling.

I couldn't work out what had happened to her calf, but I was more worried about Carly, about Ted, and, well, about me—and about who wanted to hurt any or all of us. The same someone who had killed Eldon, no doubt.

I popped through the steel gate at the edge of the lot and into the corral that led to the barn. The old wooden barn door squealed on its hinges. The welcoming smell I'd expected didn't hit me. I know most people wouldn't consider dried sweat on horse blankets, manure, old saddle leather, and musty hay a good smell, but for me it was home and tradition and a life of satisfying work.

As much as I appreciated Jeremy's excellent care of the herd, I couldn't give him points for keeping the barn clean. It smelled foul. The sour whiff of blood and wet hay mingled with the sickly sweet odor of death. It curdled my stomach, and I hated that I wouldn't be able to clean it today.

I didn't want to be an investigator. I wanted to stay here on my ranch, tend my cows, clean my barn, plan my branding.

I pulled off a glove and reached to flip the switch that would brighten the series of bulbs dangling from the center lane. Four stalls were lined up on either side, all empty now, but ready in case of a blizzard or bad weather, when I'd bring in the baby calves.

I turned from the light, already starting down the lane, heading for the wire stretchers I needed to repair the fence. My next step didn't hit the ground in front of me; I pulled it back at the same time that I gasped. My foot landed behind me and I fell backward against the barn door. It wasn't latched, and when it swung outward, I slammed onto my tailbone. The cry I let out wasn't due to pain.

I sat with my legs in front of me, my gloved hand over my mouth, the bare hand planted on the frozen ground, propping me up. I couldn't close my eyes, couldn't look away. A whimper lifted from my lips and my stomach clenched.

My natural inclination would be to stay that way forever. But I forced my knees to bend, my arms to thrust me forward. I couldn't quite make it to my feet, but I crawled until I could register what my eyes had seen.

The missing calf wasn't a mystery anymore.

It was sprawled across the lane. Glassy eyes stared at nothing, the black tongue clamped between white teeth, under lips drawn back in a grimace. Blood had seeped into the trampled hay from the gaping slit across the calf's throat.

My knees trembled as I pushed myself to stand. My innards swirled like a washing machine filled with vinegar.

There was no doubt.

I was getting closer to finding the real killer.

24

Not much stirred in the hospital this late—or was it early? The hall lights blazed, but most rooms I passed clung to a sort of fake twilight. The floor nurse watched my approach. I sounded like a parade marching down the empty hospital corridor. When I got closer, I recognized her as Beth Salzberg, a girl from Danbury I'd played basketball against in high school.

She met me with a bucktoothed smile, much too perky for someone who'd pulled the night shift. "He's having a good night," she said, even though I hadn't asked.

Normal Sandhills manners dictated that I ask after her kids or parents, but I didn't stop. Rolling into Ted's room like a tank on attack, I said, "Wake up. It's time for you to stop this game."

"Kate!" He'd been sitting up in bed. "You're here!"

I might have been surprised to see him reading a book, something I'd only witnessed a couple of times in our marriage, but I didn't care. "What the hell is going on?"

Dahlia wouldn't be in until official visiting hours, so Ted's dark whiskers shadowed his face. He raised his hands in surrender mode. It seemed to me he moved quicker than yesterday. "Roxy's not going to sell to Baxter. She'll talk to Carly first."

Darkness blanked the scene from the window, throwing my stormy reflection back to me. I gripped the rail on his bed. "Tell me why you confessed."

His jaw worked. "Let it go. I can plead self-defense and might not spend any time in jail."

"Maybe yesterday I might have gone for that. But someone made this personal, and I'm not going to let that stand."

Beth Salzberg walked in, chirping like a sparrow. "I need to take your vitals."

Ted and I both turned to her and, in a synchronization seldom displayed in our marriage, said together, "Not now."

Her mouth dropped open, but she backed out of the room, stammering, "I'll c-come back later."

Ted put his hand next to mine on the rail. "What do you mean, personal?"

"In the last two days I've nearly been killed because someone tampered with Elvis, and someone sent a pretty clear message, via a dead calf, that they don't want me looking into Eldon's murder."

"What are you talking about?"

I explained about Elvis and the calf. I told him my theories about Rope and Baxter.

When I finished, he said, "That doesn't make any sense."

I banged the rail and he jumped. "Why? What are you not telling me?"

He scowled. "Nothing. I killed Eldon, so no one should be trying to scare you."

I leaned my hands on the bed and shoved my face close to his. He smelled like Ted, and my thoughts froze. The slight musk, spicy skin—that unique personal Ted smell. So familiar I never thought about it. The smell I might lose forever.

I pulled back. "If you won't tell me, I'm going to have to keep digging and someone might kill me."

His alarm popped like hot grease. "Stop it, Kate."

"Who?"

"Let it go."

"Tell me."

His chest rose and fell, and I realized mine did, too. Like two bulls in a standoff.

I whirled around to leave.

"Stop."

I didn't.

Defeat withered his voice. "Okay. I'll tell you."

He spared one look out the window, where there was still no sign of daybreak. "I can't remember every detail, but some of it's coming back. I told you I'd left Roxy's and heard yelling on Eldon's porch."

I stepped toward the bed.

"When I got closer, I saw Eldon wasn't alone."

"Baxter?"

He paused. "No. Carly. The wind picked up, so I couldn't hear what they were saying, but I think they were arguing."

"Why do you think that?"

"Because they were yelling."

"But the wind was blowing hard, right?"

He squinted as if seeing the night again. "Yeah. Real hard. It blew my hat off and I had to chase it down."

"Then what happened?"

"I got my hat, and by then they'd left the porch. A light went on upstairs, in Eldon's office. I thought I should let them work it out, but it was Carly, and sometimes when she flies off the handle, she'll listen to me when she won't pay attention to anyone else."

True enough. He'd acted as peacekeeper between Louise and Carly a time or two.

"I went up to the house. I knocked, but no one answered, so I went inside."

A thought occurred to me. "You didn't think Carly and Eldon would wonder why you were at the Bar J?"

He stared at his feet. "I thought I'd tell them I was investigating missing cattle in the area."

Yeah, Ted would have a ready excuse.

"I heard Eldon's voice upstairs. He was kind of bellowing, because he couldn't hear and wouldn't wear his hearing aids."

Obviously Roxy kept him informed about Eldon's annoying habits, such as not wearing his hearing aids.

"I thought about leaving again, but Eldon sounded really mad. So I started up the stairs. The closer I got, the better I understood him, and that's when I started to run toward the office."

Hot pins pricked my skin. "What did you hear?"

He swallowed. "Eldon said, 'This is my land and I'll do what I damned well please. When you get your inheritance, you can decide for yourself.'" Ted closed his eyes. "But what he said next is what scared me. 'Quit waving that gun around like some damned outlaw. You know you're not going to use it.'"

I tried to picture Carly threatening Eldon with a gun.

"I forgot all my training, because I wanted to keep Carly from doing something stupid."

"You burst in?"

He nodded. "Everything happened all at the same time. I threw myself at the door, got a quick glimpse of Eldon sitting at his desk, then fire burned through me. I remember the roar of the gun, but that's it."

He stopped talking, but his chest heaved like he'd run a mile.

I played out his story twice, seeing everything, from Ted

walking to his cruiser and changing his path, through to him being shot.

The door to his room opened and we both shouted, "Go away."

I couldn't believe what I had heard. "You confessed because you think Carly did it?"

"I can claim self-defense."

This was why I loved Ted. Just when you thought he was the biggest shit in the world, he did something noble. Stupid and misguided, but noble.

I glared at him. "Carly didn't do it."

Uncharacteristic gentleness touched his voice. "I know you don't want to believe she could kill someone. Neither do I. But the evidence is there, babe."

I growled. "Don't call me 'babe.'" He knew I hated pet names. I'll bet Roxy loved them. "How could you even suspect her?"

"She was there."

"On the porch. You didn't see her in the house." I tapped the rail with the underside of my wedding band, as if the ticking noise could make my brain work better.

He whispered, "She shot Eldon."

No. "She worshipped him."

He met my stare. "Think about it. She's got all that fire and temper. Passion, you'd call it. She flies off the handle. She doesn't always make the best decisions. You know as well as I do how upset she was at Eldon for even considering selling the ranch. Is it so hard to believe she lost her temper?"

My conviction was set in my tone. "She didn't shoot Eldon."

His voice cracked. "I know how much you love her. I love her, too. So drop this investigation. Let Milo charge me."

I didn't wait for more conversation. I don't remember opening the door and running out, though I have a vague recollection of Beth Salzberg chasing me.

25

Taking only enough time to fill the gas tank, I was on the road before three a.m. Allowing for the time change from western Nebraska's Mountain zone to Lincoln's Central, I ought to reach Susan's before anyone roused out of bed.

I had to see Carly. Hug her. Talk to her. She'd been to the Bar J moments before Eldon was shot. She must know something.

The three-hour drive was torture, with my thoughts stampeding from Carly to the possibility of a baby. I tried to quiet myself with deep breathing. If I'd been in Elvis, I'd have my blues CDs. Ted only played country music. I'd rather listen to the rattle in my own head than suffer the twang. When I succeeded in switching gears from Eldon's murder, my brain kept coughing up aha moments that swirled my empty gut into a sulfuric sludge. There was the time Ted's phone rang while he'd gone to the barn to find pliers. I'd answered the local number, but the caller hung up. When I punched to reconnect, I got generic voice mail.

Then there was the night I'd gone to bed at eight o'clock and had fallen into an exhausted sleep. I woke an hour later to use the bathroom. Ted wasn't in the house, but I spotted him in the equipment shed. The light shined from the open door and Ted paced back and forth, talking on the phone. Every now and then he threw his head back and laughed.

Now, I rubbed the moisture from my eyes and focused on the dawn breaking over the eastern hills. Cattle moved around in the pastures, waiting for someone to bring them feed. Calves cavorted in the weak sunshine. I didn't feel their joy as the pickup labored up one hill and coasted down the next.

Damn me. I'd even checked his phone the next morning to see who he'd called. It was an unknown number and he'd talked for over an hour. Did I ask him about it? No. It was probably one of his college friends and he'd gone to the barn so he wouldn't wake me. Asking him about it would make me a suspicious wife. I either trusted him and or I didn't.

The truth was, I didn't. But I hadn't admitted it. Now I was every bit as mad at me as I was at him.

I circled back to Carly. During my teens, my refuge from the war zone of the Fox house was the Bar J. For the cost of gas for the twenty-mile trip, I could find peace and someone to listen to me. Glenda and Brian's few cramped rooms with a wood-burning stove were always clean and smelled of something wonderful baking. Glenda welcomed me like she was a mother cat and I was a lost kitten.

When Carly was born, I feared I'd lose my welcome. But Glenda still kept the lumpy couch for my bed. I went from honorary ward to integral cog in the family. Always a fussy baby, Carly accepted me as a surrogate mother. Glenda delighted in the bond between her daughter and me.

Glenda always acted happy to see me driving Elvis down her dusty road. It meant that I'd stay with Carly and Glenda would have hours of freedom to ride her horse or help with cattle work, knowing her baby was in good hands.

I pulled into Lincoln in the middle of morning rush hour. Traffic slowed to the speed of a sloth on Xanax as I hit three thousand stoplights between the thriving downtown businesses and the state capitol building. Sharp-suited men and women bunched at crossings on their way to the banks and law offices along the shaded streets. I maneuvered to the dowdy southern downtown neighborhood where Susan and her roommate lived, in an old brick house that had been divided into four apartment units.

Spring hit Lincoln a few weeks earlier than it hit Grand County. Here, the lilacs had already gone from masses of purple and white to lush green bushes. Peonies popped in wild profusion in almost every yard, sprinkling their pink and white petals on thick green lawns. The trees boasted full leaves and the flowering crab apple trees were nearly spent. The whole neighborhood throbbed with spring's vitality and cheer. It bounced against me as if I wore a cone of doom.

I found street parking two blocks away and felt lucky. I'd lived not far from here over ten years ago, when I'd been an undergrad. I'd always liked Lincoln. If I left Ted, maybe I'd move back here. And do what? With my psych degree, no practical experience, and no PhD, I wasn't qualified to do anything more than answer phones or sell clothes. And with my fashion savvy, those clothes would be at the Orscheln Farm and Home.

I didn't bother locking Ted's pickup, and I lumbered up from the drive while walking to Susan's building and up the stairs to the second floor. Even this early, music thrumped from more than one unit, tunes boxing with one another in the dark, rundown hallway. A lingering odor of mildew, from the century the house had stood in Lincoln's humidity, mingled with stale beer, a faint tinge of pot, and old garbage. The wood stairs and walls bore chips and holes, scuffs and dirt from countless semesters of young renters on their own for the first time.

I needed to pull Carly to me and assure her that everything would be all right. As if I could guarantee anything but my love for her.

I pounded on Susan's door, hoping Carly could hear me above the wailing alternative rock music slithering under the frame. Footsteps that sounded like a kangaroo approached, and the door was flung open with such force that I felt sucked inside. Saskatchewan loomed in front of me, all six-foot-five-inches of hair, including a dark beard that ran halfway down his chest.

"Hi, Sask." I stepped inside.

"Hey." He was unruffled to find his roommate's sister at his door before eight o'clock. "Didn't know you were in our fair city." Sask's mother had named him Rodney. His family ranched in Choker County and Susan had met him at a track meet their junior year of high school. They were best friends, each other's backup dates for proms, and now roommates.

He lumbered to his phone, tapped a few times, and the music slunk to a less ear-damaging decibel. I eased into the cramped living room strewn with piles of coats, clothes, books, dirty dishes, blankets, fast-food containers, and things better left unidentified.

"Susan's not up yet." He glanced at his phone. "She doesn't have class on Wednesdays until noon."

I kept my arms to my side, afraid to touch anything for fear of disease. "That's okay. I'm really here to get Carly."

He looked confused. "Carly Edwards?"

The bedroom door swung open and Susan stumbled out, rubbing sleep from her eyes. She wore plaid pajama pants and a red wife-beater. A younger version of me, her wild hair tumbled around her head and shoulders. Her sleepy eyes flew open to match her O of a mouth when she saw me. The door gaped open, and she looked like Lot's wife after she'd caught her last glimpse of Sodom.

Sask's music drifted to the ceiling.

The first flash of fear flicked in my belly. "Where is she?"

My voice released Susan and she shoved a pile of clothes on the floor with her bare foot. "I can explain."

A hard edge colored my words. "Explain what?"

She passed a glance to Sask. "She was really upset. She needed some time, so she asked me to stall for her."

Blood pushed into my brain faster than it could drain. "When did she leave? Where did she go?"

Susan swayed from foot to foot, like she used to do when she was three and got caught playing with Diane's makeup. "Well. I talked to her, like, really late Monday night."

Dread clenched my stomach. "What about Tuesday? Was she even here at all?"

The rocking stopped and she bit her lip. "No."

I pushed my hand through my hair, maybe trying to get my brain to settle down and think. "She called you? She didn't have her phone."

"I didn't recognize the number, and I almost didn't answer. But it was a western Nebraska area code, so I did. She sounded really upset."

"Of course she's upset."

"She said her granddad had died and she couldn't deal with the funeral and all the family. She said Roxy was making her nuts."

All that was true enough. "Did she say where she was or where she was going?"

Susan shrugged. "You know Carly. She has these meltdowns, but she always comes around. I tried to get her to book it here. Told her she could crash on the couch."

We both glanced at the couch, which was covered with so much debris the brown fabric hardly showed.

"When did you see her last?" Susan asked.

"Monday morning, the day after Eldon was shot." I leaned on the door.

Sask tapped the music off.

Susan hadn't moved. "She sounded freaked out. I didn't want to lie to you but, you know, I wanted to help her out. She had to deal with Glenda and then her dad. I didn't think she'd go, like, AWOL or anything."

"Maybe she's hanging out with a friend or something." But why would she call Susan to stall? Why not just tell me she needed space?

"God, Kate. I'm so sorry."

"She didn't give you any clue where she was?"

Susan shook her head. "I think you know her the best of all of us. I mean, she told me how much she liked living with you and Ted."

I shoved a pile of junk aside and plopped onto the couch. I rose and pulled a thick geography textbook from under me, then sat back. "Where would she go?"

"Don't worry. She's strong." Susan swept a jumble of debris to the floor and crouched on the arm of the couch, slipping her feet under my thigh. "Remember the night Glenda died?"

I wished I could forget it. "Bad night." I'd left Glenda's crowded room. Drowning in grief, I'd needed to be alone.

Susan's voice got that ragged edge. "When Doc Kennedy told us Glenda wouldn't last through the night, I didn't know what to do, so I went to the chapel with the rest of the sibs, but you weren't there."

It all came back. The faded Southwest-print couch and garish blue carpet of the hospital lounge. The smell of artificial air, perfumed with cleaning supplies, the faint soggy vegetable smell from the cafeteria, and fear. I had traced the zigzag of the couch pattern, fighting a rage so basic it seemed ingrained in my blood.

"When the nurse came to tell us it was all over, we couldn't find Carly." Susan paused. "That was the first time we all went looking for her."

The shadows bathed the waiting room off the main lobby. Silence muffled the chilly space, because the receptionists, accountants, and visitors had vanished hours ago.

Without any sound to alert me, I had turned my head, knowing what I'd see. Carly stood at the edge of the carpet, a ghost of sorrow. No tears dribbled from her eyes, which seemed like puddles of pain. Even in the dimness of the security lights, she appeared bloodless, as if I could see through her.

I had held my arms up and she drifted into them. Twelve years old, and now without a mother.

Susan leaned into me. "We found you on that couch in the lobby. You were a crying mess. But Carly, man, that kid was like iron. She didn't shed a tear."

Carly had trembled in my arms. Still smelling like a kid: sweat and clean at the same time.

Susan hadn't learned to distrust happiness as I had. "She's going to be fine, and she'll find you when she needs you, like she always has."

This was Susan's version of Dad's motto: If it's not okay, it's not the end. Did they forget that things don't always turn out for the best?

Instead of yelling at Susan for being so foolish, or throttling her as I itched to do, I pushed myself from the couch.

Susan jumped up and met me at the door. "I'm really sorry. I thought I was doing the right thing."

I hugged her because she needed forgiveness—and I needed to forgive her—and patted her cheek because I knew she hated it. "I love you, Suzy-Q. Call Mom. She finished up a piece and is back in the real world. Let me know if you hear from Carly."

26

When you live in the Nebraska Sandhills, you spend a lot of time behind the wheel. The region covers a quarter of the state, and the scenery doesn't vary a whole lot—just mile after mile of rolling, grass-covered sand dunes. Every ten or twenty miles, you might meet another vehicle. You only know it's settled country because of the endless barbed wire fences strung to the horizon. That was fine with me. I'm not always a big fan of people.

I bought a sleeve of crackers and some string cheese when I fueled up, and washed it down with a slug of apple juice. I set the cruise control and barely moved the steering wheel over the miles of straight road.

Carly could flake out, that was true. But disappearing for days, with her granddad's funeral coming up, didn't seem like something she'd do. Ted couldn't be right; Carly didn't kill Eldon. But she was in some trouble. As the miles ran under the wheels of the pickup, my anxiety climbed. I reached for my phone and scrolled until I found the number.

Mary Ellen Butterbaugh answered on the first ring and, after I identified myself, said, "Carly's teachers brought her homework to the office. You can pick it up whenever you're in."

I couldn't care less about homework. "Could you call Danny Hayward out of class, please?"

"Oh dear." She must have jumped to the conclusion that Danny and Carly were together. When I'd seen him in town yesterday, I thought Carly was at Susan's. He'd said Carly wanted him to meet her. Was there any truth in that? "He hasn't been back to school since Eldon's death."

"Okay, thanks." I exited at North Platte and gunned the pickup through the green-tinged hills. With one eye on the road and other on my phone, I searched for Rope and Nat's phone number. Maybe Danny was at home.

Bright sunshine made reading the display difficult. April was giving us big doses of precipitation and sun, perfect to grow grass to feed the pregnant cows all summer. I ought to be pleased with that but I couldn't generate enthusiasm.

I lost the signal, gained a few bars at the top of the hill, and tried again. Frustration mounted as I got voice mail giving me a cell number to try. I sailed down another valley and I had to wait. The pickup struggled to the top of the hill and I dialed.

Nat answered on the first ring. She sounded alarmed to hear from me. "Is something wrong?"

The speedometer quivered just under ninety. "I need to talk to Danny. Is he at the ranch?"

She spoke so quietly I could barely make out her words. "No. No one is home. We're away. Broken Butte. Not home. So sorry." She clicked off before I could ask more.

Still driving way too fast, and thrumming with fear for what might be a baby I was putting at risk with my reckless driving, I wrangled my phone again and punched Dial.

Milo answered. "Howdy, Kate. I hear you been traipsing all over with Roxy, trying to clear Ted's name."

I don't know why it surprised me that he knew about that. "You can't really believe Ted killed Eldon."

He sucked on his teeth. "I haven't charged him as yet."

I felt like a traitor, but I felt desperate. "Carly is missing." The words stuck in my throat. "Can you help me find her?"

Milo hesitated. "Why do you suppose she's gone?"

I wish I knew. "Overload of grief?" I should sound more sure.

A shriek of a spring rang out, indicating that Milo had leaned back in a desk chair. "This don't look particularly good for someone who was recently suspected of murder."

"I can't tell you who killed Eldon, but I can tell you it wasn't Ted or Carly."

He wheezed into the phone. "Maybe. But Ted confessed and Carly is missing."

A jab to his belly with my spurs would feel good. "Can you file a missing persons report or issue an APB or a BOLO or something?"

He hesitated. "I can do that. I wouldn't mind finding that girl, myself."

I still hadn't come up with a plan, twenty minutes later, when I forced myself to slow down through Hodgekiss. I was probably heading back to Broken Butte to talk to Ted, because I didn't know what else to do. Carly was gone. Someone was trying to stop me from finding the real killer. The clues had to be in Ted's head, and I wasn't above knocking them out, if that's what it took.

I swung my gaze up Main Street as I buzzed by on the highway, then slammed on the brakes. Good thing it was Hodgekiss and not Lincoln, because there wasn't any traffic behind me to smash into my tailgate.

I squealed tires as I pulled a left and gunned the pickup into a parking place. I'd seen Nat's thinning brown-gray waves entering

Dutch's Grocery. She wasn't in Broken Butte. She was right here. And she'd lied to me.

I flew from the pickup and yanked open the glass door, searching the first aisle. Aileen Carson was at the checkout, visiting with the checker. She greeted me as I rushed past. Since there were only five aisles, I had no trouble spotting Nat at the end of the last one, studying Dutch's meat case.

"Nat," I hollered, while I rushed toward her.

She swung her head around and started to run away.

I lunged toward her and grabbed her arm. "Why did you lie to me?"

"I . . ." She faltered, and her face turned the color of a ripe tomato. "It's. I." She finally stopped.

"Where's Danny?"

She didn't look at me, and her voice shook. "He's got such a soft spot for Carly. There's nothing he wouldn't do for her."

This wasn't what I wanted to hear. "They're together?"

She slid her focus to the meat in the counter, the canned green beans on the shelf behind me, the display of bread on my right. "I understand how it is when your kids get into trouble. It's like my Mick. He was a good boy. He didn't mean to hurt anybody."

He might not have meant to, but he'd shot a convenience store clerk in Omaha for meth money.

Her voice was a whiny buzz. "Carly's like that, too. She loves that ol' ranch so much. Might have made her do bad things."

"Nat." Rope's voice sounded like a slap. His boots crashed like thunder as he strode toward us.

She lowered her hands and they started to pull and rub against each other. She whimpered and shrank into herself.

The fury of a spring blizzard was nothing compared to Rope's face. He closed a rough hand on my upper arm and jerked me down the aisle. “What are you doing to her? You leave her alone. Do you hear me?”

Aileen and the clerk gaped at us, but they didn’t protest Rope dragging me past them. He shoved the door open, the bell struggling to stay attached. He didn’t stop until he had me in the alley next to Dutch’s and had bounced me against the side of the building. He stood in front of me, huffing like a freight engine.

Snow was trying to accumulate on the sidewalk, but the temperatures hovered too high.

He put a finger in my face and spoke with a voice as full of threat as it was quiet. “Natty gets upset easy. You got any questions about Danny or Eldon or any other fool thing, you talk to me. Leave her alone.”

I’m not about to say he didn’t scare the bejesus out of me. But this was about Carly. I gave him my meanest glare. “I want to know where Danny and Carly are.”

Fat snowflakes landed on his hair and melted immediately. He stepped back and exhaled in frustration. “How would I know? Gone. Just gone.”

“Why? Where? You must know something.”

His lips curled back like a dog’s right before it bites. “What I know is what Baxter told you last night. That he’d find Carly.”

It felt like a slap across my cheek. Baxter. Roxy had told him she couldn’t make a decision without Carly’s opinion. Baxter wanted the Bar J as soon as possible. He had the resources of private investigators and maybe even a custom police force. He’d find Carly.

And when he did, he’d try to convince her to sell the Bar J.

Carly was all that stood between Glenn Baxter and the buffalo common.

I barreled past Rope on my way to the pickup.

27

The road stretched black against the gray clouds pressing in on all sides. Heavy, expectant air smothered the pastures on either side of the highway. The speedometer on the pickup only dipped below ninety when I navigated the tightest corners, and still I felt like a sailboat stuck with no wind.

I sped past the Bar J turnoff, three miles north to a rutted, two-track trail road. Fresh tire tracks marked one side of the road. Baxter's electric car with its itty-bitty wheelbase would need to ride one side in the road, the other side on the grassy rise separating the tracks.

I raced down the road and around the first bend. Damn it. I slammed on the brakes. This seldom-used pasture didn't warrant an expensive AutoGate. A three-wire fence stretched across the road, and there was no Roxy to open it.

I ran to the wire gate and pulled the metal lever to unhook it. The steel froze my palm. He may drive a toy car and be a city slicker, but Baxter knew to keep the gates closed at least. I didn't take the time to relatch it behind me. This might be the first time I had ever left a gate open. Some things are more important than keeping cattle in the right pastures.

With every ounce of willpower, I prayed Baxter wasn't the monster I feared he could be. Carly was smart. Maybe survival instincts would lead her to appease Baxter. Maybe she'd figured out a way to stay alive.

The pickup ate up the rough road better than Elvis ever would, but the only time anyone used this route was to check windmills during the summer months. I couldn't believe Baxter had managed to drive his golf cart of a rental car out here, and at every turn I expected to come across it buried in sand.

I hadn't thought I'd ever see Glenda's house again. But I kept the gas pedal down, gripped the wheel, and bounced down the rough road, barely keeping in the tracks. I climbed the last hill and then descended into a narrow gully and around a tight curve. The cabin crouched in a sliver between two hills, hidden until the last few yards.

I roared around the curve, my back wheels sliding out. Too fast. The road in front of me had washed out. A four-foot gash interrupted the two tracks, the sand borne away by a summer flash flood. I slammed on the brakes. The world slowed so that I had time to anticipate the crash, my head driving through the windshield, and my skull shattering. Or the steering wheel impaling me and perhaps the new life I carried. I couldn't save Carly. Ted would spend his life in jail. All because a sudden summer storm had ripped the road apart. I clenched my teeth, my hands, my whole body, waiting for the impact to batter and kill me.

The front tires fell over the edge. Airborne for maybe two seconds, but feeling like a slow motion eternity, the pickup flew into the ditch and the grill banged into the other bank.

Warm liquid ran from my nose and I reached up to the sudden

stinging. My hand came away covered in blood. I'd bashed my face into the steering wheel in the crash. But that was the extent of the damage.

Water filled my eyes and I blinked away tears with the pain. I placed my palm against my belly. "If we make out of this in one piece, I promise you, I won't drive over twenty-five miles an hour until you're born." I waited a second. "If you're in there, I mean."

I grabbed a leather glove from the console—the only thing handy—and wiped at my bloody nose. With most of the goo smeared away, I pinched my nose closed, shut the engine off, and jumped from the pickup.

The pickup was good and stuck. I might be able to rock it into the washout and drive down the sandy gully until I found a way out. But it would take time.

Still pinching my aching nose, I shambled up the side of the wash and down the road. My ears and fingers tingled in the frosty air. The cabin was only fifty yards away, but it remained hidden around one final turn.

Five years of neglect hadn't helped the old house. Glenda and I had dug flower beds around the wood-sided cabin. Dead brown weeds drooped where happy snapdragons and cornflowers used to bob in the breeze. Large chips and gashes marred the sunny yellow paint I'd helped Glenda slap on the house, which was now faded to the color of a smoker's teeth. The seven-foot roof that covered the front steps was missing a support and hung at a crazy angle, clinging to the house and relying on one narrow pillar to stay upright. Sand and mud covered the concrete steps, nearly burying the bottom one.

Baxter's car was nowhere in sight. I hurdled the steps and exploded into the house. "Carly!"

I don't know what I expected. She wasn't chained to the plaid couch. The old rocker was empty. The bathroom door stood open, revealing nothing but the stained pedestal sink and stool. From where I stood, in the middle of the front room, I could see into the kitchen and out the window above the sink. A coffee cup and a mess of papers spread across the spindly kitchen table. "Carly!" I shouted, even though I knew no one was there to answer.

I banged my shin on the pressed-wood coffee table, on my short trip to the bedroom, the only other room in the house. The sage-green chenille bedspread covered no body shape. The mirror above the chipped dresser showed only my wild curls and blood-smeared face. My eyes swept across the room, which was barely big enough for the double bed, dull light from the overcast sky creating gloom.

"Carly!" I screamed, whirling around, not knowing where to go. *Where are you?*

The dark figure in the bedroom doorway froze the blood in my veins.

Baxter raised a pistol and trained it on my chest. He kept that characteristic smooth expression and wore his stupid Hopalong Cassidy getup. "What are you doing here?"

I wanted to fly at him. "Where is she?"

Baxter grimaced at my face. "What happened to you?"

I gritted my teeth to keep from attacking him. "Where is Carly?"

Baxter's hand wavered slightly, as if the gun were too heavy. "You tell me."

Baxter was taller, but I wagered that, since he sat behind a desk all day and I worked a ranch, I was tougher and stronger. If I hit him before he shot me, I could wrestle him to the ground and grab the gun. But it would take less time for him to twitch his finger on the trigger than it would for me to lunge across the room. "What did you do with her?"

He strained to hold the gun on me. It wasn't like the pistol I owned to ward off weasels in the henhouse; this puppy was more like something the Lone Ranger would carry. I guess if you're rich, you can afford authentic Colt revolvers, probably owned by General Custer. "Leave Carly alone," he said.

I clenched my hands, frustrated that they weren't around his throat. "If you've hurt her, I'll kill you."

He drew his head back, still looking over my battered face. "I didn't hurt her."

"Just tell me where she is."

I stayed standing, wondering what kind of game he was playing. Would he pull the trigger if I moved? I took a chance and lunged for him.

He pulled the gun up, steady enough to put a hole in me at this range. Ridiculous Saturday morning cartoon outfit, oversized showpiece of a gun, but deadly intent.

I held my palms open in a stopping motion. He scowled and swung the gun back and forth, motioning me to the kitchen. He kept the pistol trained on me while I took slow steps to the table and lowered myself into a chair.

He propped himself against the counter, keeping the gun on me. He looked even grayer than he had before. We stared at each other for several seconds, and then he shook his head and asked in a quiet voice, "Why did you do it?"

I started to rise and he thrust the gun toward me. I sank down again and tried to figure out his question. Why did I come after Carly? "Because she's my niece. She's family. Do you even know what that means?"

He seemed taken aback by my vehemence. "Of course I know about family. That's why I'm here. I've known Brian since we were fourteen, at Kilner. We were brothers in every sense of the word, except blood. Brian loved Carly. He was her family."

If Brian was so much like family, why would Baxter threaten Carly? "Yes. He was."

Baxter's face hardened. "Then why did you kill him?"

I dropped my jaw. "What?"

He wagged the gun. "Was it the money? Where did it come from?"

I studied him. He didn't look crazy. Angry, yes. Dangerous, certainly. "You're going to have to back up and tell me what you're talking about. But first I need to know, is Carly is safe?"

The gun wobbled. He was too frail for a cannon that size. "You tell me."

My nose throbbed and I was sure blood still oozed. I swiped my sleeve along my upper lip, no doubt smearing a grisly mess across my cheek. "She'll sell you the ranch. Hell, she'll give it to you. Just don't hurt her."

Sweat beaded under his nose and ran from his temples. "I don't want the ranch."

"Then let her go."

He raised his voice for the first time. "I don't have her!"

His shout echoed, and snow started falling beyond the kitchen window. He didn't have Carly. Where was she? "What's going on?"

He panted with effort, and sweat dribbled down the side of his face. "I'm trying to find Carly. I'm afraid she's in trouble."

A cold wave of fear crashed over me. "You thought I would hurt her?"

He assessed me for a moment longer, then lowered the gun and placed it on the counter. "Yes. Or no. I don't know."

He looked ready to pass out, but his eyes burned into me. "I'm a good judge of character. You don't get to this level of success unless you can read people."

He didn't wield the gun, appeared to have very little physical strength, and yet he seemed controlled and capable.

"And what does Carnac the Magnificent have to say about me?" I asked.

"I trust you." He said it with finality.

"You don't make mistakes?"

He shook his head. "Rarely."

Well, happy day. "So I don't seem like a psychopath who would hurt someone I love?"

He almost smiled. "I don't think you'd hurt Carly. I'm not sure about the psycho part."

"Now that that's settled, why don't you fill me in on why you're here."

Baxter closed his eyes, as if drawing on strength reserves. "All I know is that Eldon feared for her."

"Eldon? What?" This guy talked in riddles.

He rubbed his hands on his thighs. "Here's what I know. And it's not much. Eldon called me a few months ago. He asked me to come out here and try to buy up land. He wanted me to make a big show, hold meetings, be visible."

"Why would he do that?"

Baxter shuffled toward me and eased himself into the other spindly chair. "Eldon knew me from Kilner, when Brian and I were close. He called me up out of the blue. He had this idea that Brian had gotten involved with some bad people and that maybe his death hadn't been an accident."

I could only stare at him in shock and wipe at the dribble of something warm from my nose.

Baxter inhaled with effort. "I know Brian and Eldon had an uneasy relationship. It was Eldon's belief that giving children land or money would make them lazy and spoiled. He wanted Brian to learn to work for what he had. Brian always felt slighted."

Glenda had never let on that Brian wasn't happy with Eldon, though Roxy had a few things to say about it. "What's this got to do with Carly?"

Baxter frowned. "Something changed with the death of your sister. Maybe she had a settling influence on Brian, or maybe he decided life was short and he wanted to enjoy it more. He married Roxy and immediately started spending big money. They built an extravagant house, invested in high-dollar cutting horses, began construction on a state-of-the-art indoor arena and barn."

"How did Brian get Eldon to agree to that?"

Baxter pursed thin lips. "That's just it. Brian never asked Eldon. The money didn't come from the Bar J."

"Where did Brian get it?"

Baxter shook his head. "Eldon didn't know. Brian wouldn't tell him. I tried to get it out of Roxy, but she apparently doesn't know. Then Brian crashed his plane into a hill two years ago."

"How did that change anything?"

"It didn't, for some time. Until Eldon discovered an account, set up under the Bar J and housed in Grand Cayman, that he knew nothing about."

"He just found out? How?"

Baxter shrugged. "Something about an account number Eldon found written on an old invoice for a maintenance issue at Roxy's house. It had been a copy of an old contract, to show the terms, and Eldon recognized Brian's writing. I don't know exactly how he tracked down the account. It doesn't matter."

I tamped down my curiosity for the details and waved him on.

"When he investigated, he found that Brian had opened the account. He wasn't able to provide passwords and get past security firewalls, but he had at least one bank statement that showed an enormous balance."

"Brian was hiding money from Eldon? Why?"

Baxter wheezed. "The important thing is that, a couple of weeks ago, Carly came across some of Brian's papers. There was a bank statement and I don't know what else. She brought it to Eldon and he tried to dismiss it. But Carly wouldn't be put off and Eldon was afraid for her. If someone had killed Brian, they'd kill Carly if she began investigating."

That's why Carly had seemed so distracted. "Did Eldon have any idea who it might be?"

Baxter didn't look good. "If he did, he didn't tell me. Except he felt sure that one or more of the people involved were Carly's relatives."

I sat back. "That's crazy."

Baxter folded his arms across his chest. "Is it? You're related to half of Nebraska, and there are probably a few cousins, aunts, or uncles who've ventured into the world at large."

"Why did Eldon think Foxes have something to do with it?"

Baxter shrugged. "My guess is that something in the papers Carly discovered held a clue."

Why hadn't I looked at that blue folder? "How are you involved?"

"When he first called me, he wanted to find out where Brian got the money, and if someone had killed him to get it back. I urged him to wait until I . . ." For the first time, Baxter lost a bit of his overpowering confidence. "Until I felt better and could put more effort into helping. But he wouldn't be put off."

More of Eldon's stubbornness. "So what were you supposed to do?"

"I thought Eldon was delusional. Brian knew a lot of men from Kilner. Many are successful. He probably could have attained a loan from any one of them."

"You don't think so now?"

"Of course I think so. But Brian was my brother. I felt duty-bound to humor his father. Eldon's plan was to make people think he was selling the Bar J. He assumed that whoever wanted the money Brian stashed wouldn't want Eldon to sell, because then he'd lose all chance of recovering the cash."

I must have had a disbelieving expression.

Baxter nodded and drew a labored breath. "I know. It made no sense. Eldon was an old man and, dare I say, paranoid and reactive. I'm certain he was in the early stages of dementia."

I was ready to cross Baxter off the suspect list, but I had another question. "What did you and Eldon fight about at the Bar J, the day of the shooting?"

He leaned his head on his hand for a moment. "I need to return to Chicago for medical treatment. He wanted me to stay on."

"Rope said Eldon threatened you with a gun."

Baxter brushed that off. "Small towns and their rumors. I went to see Eldon that day and caught him as he stormed out of the house with that rifle."

"What was he doing with the gun?"

Baxter shrugged. "He seemed extremely upset, scared even. He talked about protecting Carly. He said he was giving Carly a stack of cash and sending her away from the Bar J for her own good. He asked me to keep an eye on her."

That night Ted had seen her on the porch, she'd been arguing with Eldon. He wanted to send her away, and she'd fight against that.

Baxter drew in a wheezing breath. "Of course I'd do whatever I had to do to help Carly. She's Brian's daughter."

My mind whirled with questions. "Then who killed Eldon, and why is Carly gone?"

"This harebrained scheme of Eldon's got him killed. Someone actually believed he'd sell the Bar J. It's got to be someone local. Who has the most at stake?"

It took less than a second to come up with the answer. "Rope Hayward."

I hesitated. "If Rope killed Eldon because he thought Eldon was going to sell the ranch, then he assumed Carly would inherit it and wouldn't sell."

Baxter sat up straighter. "What if Carly figured out that Rope was Eldon's murderer? Would she go to the police?" Even Baxter knew the answer to that.

"She'd try to avenge her grandfather."

My mind raced. Why had Danny wanted Carly with him right after the shooting? Why had he talked about protecting her?

Because he knew his grandfather was the murderer.

Now Danny was missing. But maybe he hadn't gone far. I remembered Nat's near-panic when I asked about Danny. Her abject fear when Rope appeared.

The fresh tracks leading from Eldon's house to the calving lot. Only Danny would drive through there. "Carly and Danny are at the Bar J."

Baxter shook his head. "Rope wouldn't allow that."

"Rope doesn't know."

28

The cabin closed in around me and I sucked in air, trying to settle my brain. I don't know how I got from the kitchen to the front door, but Baxter's words grounded me.

"Where are you going?"

I flung the front door open to a blast of swirling snow. "The Bar J headquarters. Danny has Carly and Nat knows."

He struggled to his feet, clearly at the end of his energy. "I don't understand."

To clarify it for myself, I took the time to tell him. "If you didn't kill Eldon, then Rope did. Carly found out. She went to the Bar J to confront him. But Danny stopped her. He told me he'd always protect her. Nat said she'd always protect Danny. They're keeping her hidden so she won't turn Rope in but he won't find her."

"I'll go with you." He took a wavering step.

I took a gander at his pasty face and trembling legs. "You're in no shape."

He might be a frail desk jockey, but he radiated frustration at not being able to help me. "There's no signal here, so I can't even call anyone for backup."

I'd already opened the door, well on my way to ignoring him.

"Take my car. It's on the other side of the washout. Your pickup looks buried." That would leave this sick man stranded at the isolated shack. He reacted to my hesitation. "I'll be fine. Go. Hurry."

I dashed into the growing storm, moving slower than my brain. Rope. The man who went out of his way to point the finger at Baxter.

He'd been at the debate when I announced I'd find the killer. The next day, my tie rod was broken. Plenty of people had heard me say that, and anyone could have tampered with Elvis while he was parked in Hodgekiss that night. But only Rope had been standing with me outside of Roxy's when I repeated the vow, just hours before someone killed the calf.

Carly spent a lot of time at the Bar J. She and Eldon were close. He wouldn't tell her his suspicions about Rope, but she'd probably figure it out. I jumped into the tin can and looked for the key. When I couldn't find that, I cast about for the pull cord. I finally located the push button and the engine cranked up with a sorry little whine.

I cleared a skiff of snow from the windshield of Baxter's putt-putt car, with one swish of the wipers. I'd be lucky to get back to the pavement without high-centering on the ridge between wheel ruts. Running would be faster, except once I hit the pavement I could get up some momentum.

Damn it! Baxter had closed the gate again. I let out a string of cursing as I flew from the car and unhitched the wire. After an eternity, I finally turned onto the pavement. I raced down the highway, heading for the Bar J.

I found my phone in my shirt pocket and sailed all over the empty road while searching for Milo's number. After finagling a phone call out of the spotty reception from widely separated cell towers, and shouting over the rattling dishes in the café where Milo was drinking coffee, I eventually convinced him to meet me at the Bar J. He sounded reluctant but agreed to at least make the drive out. I only hoped he'd take me seriously and cut short his coffee klatch.

A band of steely dark clouds hovered along the western horizon. The last April storm, which would swoop in to murder baby calves minutes after they hit the ground.

I jerked Baxter's car off the highway and onto the Bar J road, a move that seemed sure to loosen some molars. Sweat dampened my flannel shirt. Despite the golf cart bottoming out on bumps and sliding on the narrow tires, I was able to think about what had happened that night.

It must have enraged Rope that Eldon skipped him and gave Danny land instead. He tipped over the sanity rim when Eldon planned to sell the Bar J and take away even Danny's promised share. Rope had hidden in Eldon's office and shot him. When Ted burst in, Rope had shot him, too.

If Rope killed Eldon and shot Ted, he might not hesitate to kill Carly. But Danny loved Carly and Nat loved Danny. I prayed that Danny and Nat had hidden Carly successfully. I gripped the steering wheel harder.

I bypassed the driveway leading to Eldon's and Roxy's houses and slipped behind the barn to the muddy and rutted cookhouse drive. I bounced through a puddle, the mud thudding on the underside of Baxter's car. I pulled up at the back of the barn and slammed on the brakes, sliding like a runner into first base.

The wind smacked me when I launched from the car. I glanced at the barn, wondering if Carly was hidden inside. I fought the biting wind to reach the cookhouse's rickety front porch.

Nat flew from the house and her flowered apron smock flapped in the wind. "What is it? What do you want?"

I pushed past her. "Where is she?" I hit the front door. "Carly! Carly!"

Nat ran after me, pulling on my shirt. "She's not here. What's wrong?"

I grabbed Nat by her shoulders, so much like chicken wings in my hands. "Nat, listen to me. Rope killed Eldon. We've got to grab the kids and get out of here."

Her eyes were glistening saucers of disbelief. "No. That's not true."

"Danny's here, isn't he?"

She made mewling noises.

"Rope doesn't know, does he?"

She still didn't answer me.

"Where is Danny? You have to tell me before Rope comes home. We have to get away from here."

Nat's eyes twitched and scanned the room, but she didn't focus on anything.

I pushed past Nat and tracked straight through the front room, heading for the kitchen.

She scurried after me. "He's not here. Danny's not . . ." She sounded more out of breath than the short trip warranted.

I stopped in the middle of the kitchen. A monster of a gas stove took up the majority of the far wall. The sink and fridge settled between counters that ran along two walls. I scanned the room, desperate to find any clue to Carly's whereabouts.

A spacious center island provided a breakfast bar, with three stools shoved under the lip of the counter. A cramped space beyond the bar made scant room for a listing La-Z-Boy, an afghan-covered couch, a boxy television, and a few trays that acted as side tables.

"Rope will be home soon. You shouldn't be here." Anxiety tinted each word.

I pushed past the breakfast bar to the couch and leaned over, my hand closing around an Xbox control. It felt warm against my palm. I held it up. "You aren't a gamer."

She paled.

I advanced on her. "Where is he?"

She backed against the fridge. "You should go."

I took a few more steps. "Please Nat, tell me."

A floorboard squeaked in the front room. Nat's eyes widened in alarm. I whipped my head around and leaped toward the doorway. Nat reached out, and her clawlike hand closed around my arm and clutched at my sleeve.

I jerked loose and thrust myself forward, in time to see the front door creak on its hinges as if someone had slipped out and hadn't closed it tight.

I ran across the room, knocking a chair with my hip.

"Stop!" Nat called behind me.

Through the door's window I saw jean-clad legs racing toward the barn.

I flung the door open, dashed across the porch, and jumped down the steps, eyes trained on the closing barn door. Snow fell in fat plops, splashing on the dirt. One landed wetly in my eye and I blinked. The slick soles of my cowboy boots slipped and I fell to one knee. I pushed myself up and kept running.

In seconds I hit the barn door and slammed the latch open. I rushed inside the dark alley and stopped, my ragged breathing blending with the huff of cows moving behind a few of the stall gates.

"Danny?" I called, trying not to sound threatening.

A cow let out a low moo, probably talking to her newborn. Something rustled in hay.

“Come on out.” Where was Rope? Not in the house. I prayed he wasn’t lurking in the barn. He could be anywhere, from five miles away checking windmills to just outside in the calving lot.

Still nothing but the soft sounds that could be cattle or a teenage boy.

Every nerve stretched tight. My ears and eyes strained. “I only want to ask you some questions.”

The barn door banged open and Nat’s silhouette was outlined in the swirling snow. She sounded out of breath. “Please leave us be.”

I turned away from her and faced the cavernous barn, which was dark and damp. My brain screamed at me to hurry, before Rope discovered us. “I promise to keep you safe. He won’t hurt you again.” How would I make good on that promise if Rope crashed in on us now? I had no gun, no weapon of any kind. I prayed Milo was on his way.

The only light streamed from the white sky behind Nat. My eyes adjusted to the dim barn. Where was Danny? A ladder was propped to the haymow above us. I tried to keep the desperation out of my voice. “You aren’t responsible for what your granddad did. But you need to help me. You need to help Carly.”

A soft footstep in hay and a creaking in a barn stall brought my attention to my left. I started for the sound, sure it was Danny.

The scarecrow figure of Rope stepped from the stall.

My heart jumped to my throat.

“Danny.” Rope’s voice whipped around the still barn. “Come here.”

After a moment, a shadow disengaged from a stack of feed sacks in the dark corner. Danny crawled out and unfolded himself. His voice caught. “I’m sorry, Granddad.” His blond hair looked as if he hadn’t washed it since Christmas. Red spots blotched his face, and dark circles puffed under his eyes.

Nat stood in the open door, behind me. With Rope and Danny

in front of me, deep in the shadows, I stood between Nat and her baby. If she were a big boss cow, I would be worried.

With silent grace, Rope walked to Danny and put an arm around him. Danny sobbed into Rope's shirt. "I'm so sorry." Even severely abused children cling to their known parent. Danny wouldn't think of Rope as a murderer.

Facing a killer with no gun of my own, I had to stall until Milo arrived. Inside, I felt like a rushing, spring-swollen river of icy rapids. Outside, I needed to be calm as a goldfish pond. "It's okay, Rope." Somehow I kept the quavering out of my voice. "Danny hasn't told me anything."

Rope held on to Danny, keeping him close, like a hostage. His voice accused me from the shadows. "You should have stayed out of this." He bent his head to Danny. "And you—you're in some trouble, son."

Nat let out a sob. "Danny didn't do anything wrong. It was Carly. She's the one."

If Nat blamed Carly, that must mean she was alive. I was like a bird dog, pointing toward Rope but wanting to break and run after Nat. "Where's Carly?"

Rope hesitated. Maybe he was waiting to see where Danny's loyalties lay.

Nat squawked behind me. "She's gone, and good riddance. She killed her own grandfather. She's an evil witch."

Danny shook his head, looking miserable. "Don't, Nana."

Rope sounded like the voice of God. "You both quiet down."

Danny shrank against Rope.

Without looking at me, Rope said, "It ain't my job to look after your kids. I got mine here. You go on."

Fighting to ignore the heat and ice clashing inside me, I said, "I'm not leaving without her."

Nat's high-pitched screech came from behind me. "Don't let her go. Do something."

Rope raised his head and gave her a stern frown.

I'd never heard Nat use a voice that was so loud or harsh. "But you won't, will you? You'll leave it to me."

Danny pulled away from Rope. "Nana, stop."

I kept my eyes on Rope, afraid that if I didn't he'd draw a gun and I wouldn't be able to dodge. But Nat's rant sent a chill across my scalp.

"Tell her," she said. "Tell her how Carly did it. Tell her how Ted shot Eldon. They did it. Danny is innocent. He's not in trouble. He's not." She sobbed.

Rope seemed to break apart. His arm fell from Danny. His voice was like crushed stone. "What did you do?"

If possible, Danny paled even more. "I didn't mean to."

"Danny," Rope commanded.

Danny rubbed a hand over his red-rimmed eyes. "Carly and I were going to be together. We always used to talk about when we were married and running the Bar J. But then she started to act like she thought she was better than me. She cheated on me with Ford Butcher, you know, from Lakeview."

Nat interrupted him; tears made her voice rough. "Don't, Danny."

"But then she called me that day when she had a fight with her aunt, and we went to Denver. I knew that she'd always need me. She was as upset about Eldon selling out to Baxter as I was. So when I saw her go over to Eldon's that night, I had this idea that if I saved the Bar J for her she'd understand how we're meant to be together."

Nat moved behind me, but I stayed still, not wanting to rattle Danny.

"So I took the gun . . ."

"The one you stole from Roxy's pickup?" I asked. It was starting to make sense.

He shook his head and swallowed threatening tears. "No, I took the gun from Eldon's desk, where he always keeps it. Carly was on the front porch, and I snuck in the back door and waited in Eldon's office. I wasn't going to shoot him. I only wanted to scare him."

Rope's arms dangled at his sides.

"But . . . ?" I prompted Danny.

He rubbed his eyes again. "I tried to get him to promise not to sell the ranch. But then Ted flew through the door. I don't know what happened next. I really don't remember. But I was holding the gun and felt the heat and heard the shot." He broke down and buried his face in his hands, sobs wrenched from his gut. "I shot Ted."

If he had Eldon's gun and shot Ted, then who shot Eldon? We stood in silence for several beats.

Rope jerked as if poked with a Hot-Shot. "No. Oh, God, no."

The clack of a rifle engaging exploded in the barn. Nat's voice slapped the back of my head, all sign of weakness gone. "Don't move."

My breath caught. How could I have discounted the mama cow? The one who would face a pack of wolves to save her calf, smash the rancher into the fence rails if he didn't pay attention. The protector, who would put a bullet through me to save her grandson.

Danny moaned. "Nana, no."

I slowly dropped my hands to my sides and turned. She didn't need any more incentive to shred my flesh with a bullet.

I focused on the unlikely sight of Nat, in her smock apron with spring flowers, her arms upraised, with a rifle pointing straight at my heart. Her cold eyes told me she had every intention of using it. "It's Carly that shot Eldon. Why else would she run?"

Good question, but not my top priority now.

"It wasn't her, Nat." Rope's speech was softer than I'd ever heard him. "I understand, hon. You were only protecting Danny."

Nat's tone hardened. "I let the law take my son. Mick was a good boy. He made a mistake and got into some trouble, but it wasn't his fault. I didn't do nothing about it when they took him off. He come out of jail and couldn't get right. I won't let you do that to Danny."

Rope soothed her but couldn't hide the desperation painting his voice. "You've always taken care of our boys."

She jerked her gun. "Danny is a good boy. But that girl of yours, she made him crazy, teasing him along."

There was no ambiguity in her eyes. Only stark determination. My arms wanted to hug around my belly, but that wouldn't stop the bullets. *Come on, Kate. Do something before she pulls the trigger.*

"What he done, he done for love, and what I done was for the same. I won't let anyone take another boy of mine to jail."

Rope made a tentative step toward us. I prayed that wouldn't set her off. He spoke quietly, with more courage than I could. "I understand why you did it. Just tell me what happened."

Her eyes flitted from me to Rope, as if considering whether to shoot first and talk later. She braced the butt of the rifle against her shoulder and adjusted her aim.

I couldn't throw myself at her; the bullet would hit me before my feet left the ground. I closed my eyes but opened them quickly. It was worse waiting for death blind than to see it coming. And if I didn't do something, it would be here soon.

"Did . . ." Rope stopped, then started again. "Did you shoot Eldon?" he asked.

Nat narrowed her eyes and sighted down the barrel. My teeth clenched and I hunched over to protect my belly. *Do something. Do something.*

"Please, Nana," Danny sobbed. He yanked on Rope's arm. "Nana must have been down in the kitchen, bringing his supper. She came in and saw Ted on the floor and Eldon yelling about calling the cops. She had this gun and she made Eldon sit down at the desk and I thought she did it to calm him down so we could call the ambulance. But then she pointed it at him and shot him."

Nat's attention shifted momentarily to Danny, but it was the break I needed. I launched myself at her, knocking her backward with an *oof* that came either from her lungs or from mine. Maybe both. We landed in not-so-soft hay and her head snapped on her neck. Since she was a sprite of an old woman, I figured that was all it'd take.

But she wriggled back and grabbed the rifle from where it had been thrown. I didn't expect any help from Rope. He wasn't the murderer I thought, but he might be willing to let me disappear if it would save his family.

I scrambled in the hay and pushed myself to my feet, ready to spring on Nat. She'd done some maneuvering of her own and now faced me. I tried to back up, but she stayed with me, the barrel jabbing me in the belly.

Danny screamed for her to stop.

Her eyes reminded me of the rabid coyote I'd shot in the chicken house a few summers back. There'd be no reasoning.

I squeezed my eyes closed. The shell would explode in me, burning and shredding my flesh, mangling my intestines, forcing my blood to splatter on the barn door. I slammed my hands across my belly as if that could protect the baby that might be growing there.

Danny sobbed; a cow mooed. Nat panted, and the barrel pressed into me. Life ticked away, my last seconds.

"Nat, honey." Soft words floated from behind her head.

A footfall brushed hay and I opened my eyes. Rope landed a hand on Nat's shoulder.

Tears sprang from Nat's eyes, but she held her gun up, total focus on me. "This is the only way."

"It won't solve anything," he said, in the gentle way you'd talk to a spooked horse.

She started to shake. "They always win. You know Eldon deserved what he got. He treated you like a slave all these years, didn't pay you a living wage. And then he was going to sell out and leave us with nothing, after all these years."

Rope leaned over her. "Ah, honey, you know he was gonna take care of us."

Tiny earthquakes shook her as she held her sobs in. "We gotta protect Danny. They can't take him."

Rope reached out and put a hand on the barrel of the gun, lowering it to point at the ground. "It's gonna be all right, Natty."

She dropped the gun and it crashed against a stall door. I jumped, afraid it would discharge. Thank goodness it didn't, because it might have hit Danny, who sobbed on his knees in the straw.

Rope grabbed Nat and pulled her into his embrace. She dissolved in wails of despair.

29

All four of Hodgekiss's streetlamps burned, highlighting fat snowflakes dancing under the beams. The putt-putt car made a suspicious whine and an occasional grinding noise when the wheel cranked a hard right. The unnaturally narrow tires left baby tracks down the empty street. Maybe Elvis wasn't preferred ranch transportation, but I'd vouch that Baxter's electric car should be banned from Nebraska.

I directed him to my parents' house and Baxter pulled up, shutting off the engine. A Sandhiller would keep it running, but an environmentally conscious person such as Baxter would naturally do the right thing.

"You're sure you don't want me to call Triple-A to tow your truck?" Baxter asked.

My hand still shook as I reached for the door latch. "Thanks. But my brother Michael has a boom to pull it out."

Baxter rested a hand on my arm. "I have an investigator on staff. We'll find Carly."

It was a big world, and Carly had a bunch of cash. Whether she was running toward trouble or away from it, she had the smarts to stay hidden. I should have known, when I noticed Birdy Bird gone, that Carly had taken off for good. "The first place to start is that bank account Eldon found."

Baxter's eyebrows shot up. "You're a natural investigator. My guy checked it today. The account vanished."

"Someone closed it?"

He shook his head. "No. It's as if it never existed."

"That's not right. Banking is too regulated for something like that to happen."

"You'd think so. But offshore accounts are different."

I thought of the overturned houseplant, the chaos in my office the night Eldon died. The missing blue file. Had Carly ransacked the house? What if someone else had come looking for that file? How much danger hunted Carly?

I climbed from Baxter's car and let the snow dampen my curls as he drove away. He'd never make it to Broken Butte in that Coke can. His pilot and plane waited there to whisk him back to civilization, where I hoped he'd be able to repair whatever plagued his lungs. But he had resources, and I was plumb out of worry space.

The wind had followed the sun beyond the horizon and the night felt warm, despite the snow. Not a killer, this storm would bring nice moisture to grow grass. I followed recent footsteps up the walk to the kitchen door and let myself in.

Mom stood in the middle of the red, retro kitchen, drips from her hair adding to the puddle of water beneath her feet. She was completely naked, all of her gray hair kinked with damp.

"Snow angels?" I asked.

She laughed. "It's too wet, really, but I thought it might be my last chance for the season."

"With any luck." I reached for a thick robe draped over the back of a chair and handed it to her. It's a modern miracle she'd never been caught on her nocturnal nude snow angel ventures. Or if she had, no one had turned her in.

For the first time since I'd walked in the door, she looked directly at me. "Oh my. What happened to your face?"

I gingerly probed my swollen and aching nose. Bless Milo that he'd scurried right out to the Bar J and had arrived in time to make all the arrests and take care of the official business. It had taken the balance of the day to give my account and to help Milo out with the Haywards. I'd had the chance to wash my face before I drove back to the cabin for Baxter.

The door exploded inward and three imps rushed in. "You've got cooties!" "No, you've got cooties!" "Aah!" "Get 'em off!"

The cootie war ended with "Dibs on the remote!" "No fair!" With hellos and a hug or two thrown indiscriminately to me and Mom, they vanished into the living room before Louise crossed the threshold. Louise didn't allow television in her home, so a visit to Grandma's was cause for excitement.

Mom pulled her robe close and sat at the table. She crossed her legs, and her face glowed with contentment. When she wasn't working, she loved a houseful.

Louise placed a foil-covered plate on the counter. "Something for Dad when he gets in." She kissed Mom on the cheek. One look at me seemed to confirm something for her, and she planted her hands on her hips. "It's true, then. I dropped Ruth and David at open gym and I find out that Nat and Danny Hayward were arrested for Eldon's murder and Ted's shooting? And you were there?"

Mom turned to me with interest.

I shrugged.

Louise lowered her voice and glanced at the doorway to the living room. "They said Nat tried to kill you."

"I'm not sure she really meant it."

Louise's mouth opened in outrage. "But she messed with your car and did something disgusting at Frog Creek."

I needed to talk to Milo about the leak in his office. Except he was probably the perp. "I'm sure she was only trying to scare me."

Louise peeled the foil back and picked a brownie off a big pile. She settled at the table. "What I want to know is if Carly had anything to do with it."

"She didn't," Mom said.

Louise bit into her brownie and talked around it. "Well, she and Danny were tight, and I know she was upset with the land sale."

"She didn't," I repeated, and plopped onto the bench opposite her.

She held up her hand in surrender. "Okay, okay."

"Have you heard from her?" Mom asked.

I shook my head. Louise leaned forward, then rocked back, her mouth tight. I imagine she wanted Mom to ask more questions, to show angst, to tear her hair or rend her clothes.

A forceful knock on the kitchen door made us all jump. It creaked open and Dahlia swept in, outfitted in a long leather duster. I glanced at the kitchen floor, muddy from everyone tromping through the snow. But Dahlia didn't appear the tiniest bit damp. Were flakes afraid to fall on her?

With her curled hair, flawless makeup, and lipstick smile, Dahlia raised her eyebrows at Mom. "Ready for bed already, Marge? I suppose it feels cozy on a snowy night."

I jumped to my feet. There wasn't a nice way to put it, so I tried to sound pleasant. "What are you doing here?"

She beamed at me. "I was in Hodgekiss for dinner with Violet and Rose when Roxy called me. She told me about what happened at the Bar J and how Ted is cleared. I'm so happy, I had to stop by and give you a hug."

She grabbed me before I could step back. I didn't wipe her cooties from me, even though I felt the urge. "How did you know I was here?"

"Roxy told me."

I'd called Ted on my way to town and filled him in. Obviously he'd talked to Roxy, or she wouldn't have the information to pass on to Dahlia.

Dahlia clapped her hands together. "All this nasty business is finished."

As far as she was concerned.

She tilted her head to the side. "How about if you get those posters out tomorrow? We want everyone to know Ted is their choice for sheriff."

Whatever I mumbled worked to propel her out the door.

Mom's foot bounced. She locked eyes with me. "'As far as possible without surrender be on good terms with all persons.'"

Maybe I imagined it, but I thought she emphasized the "as far as possible" part.

Louise brightened. "So, putting out posters for Ted. Getting hugs from Dahlia. You must have decided to work things out."

I hesitated. Mom said to figure out what I wanted most. I'd spent the last few days shoving the question of my future far from my mind, but somewhere in the middle of the danger and angst, probably during those endless hours on the road, my subconscious had been busy.

"Yeah," I said slowly. "I think we're going to work it out."

30

The ground kept its snowy blanket, the white reflecting so brightly I almost wished for Roxy's blinged-out shades. Instead, I squinted down the flat road at Broken Butte's water tower growing in my windshield and adjusted the visor in Mom's '83 Vanagon. Since Elvis was out of commission and the pickup rested in the washout at the Bar J, my choices for a ride were slim. I felt unstable, perched on the towering driver's seat, strapped in so I wouldn't tumble off.

I'd woken before dawn with a dull ache in my lower back and the unmistakable warmth on my thighs. Disappointment and relief seesawed inside me. There was no denying that a baby would complicate my life and my relationship with Ted. But I wanted to be a mother. Someday.

Only one campaign sign rattled on the floor behind me. After putting off distributing them for so long, it felt good to have at least that chore behind me. It had taken the better part of the morning, because I had to repeat the story about Danny and Nat at every stop. People didn't seem surprised that Rope hadn't known Danny was hiding out at the ranch.

"I've known Rope all my life," Dad's cousin Marlene told me. She owned the bakery in Danbury, the next town along the highway east of Hodgekiss. "If it didn't have to do with the Bar J, he didn't pay any attention. That's what went wrong with Mick, and probably Danny, too. I'm not surprised it sent Nat over the edge. He should have stayed a bachelor."

Marlene hadn't heard the gentle way Rope talked to Nat. I'd lay chips that Rope knew Nat was one crack away from shattering.

I turned up Main Street, sorry to see that, with the heavy snow, the daffodils were done for. They never last long anyway. Sort of like happiness.

But the flowers would bloom again. If not next year, then the year after. It was bound to come around.

I made one stop on my way to the hospital. I wanted to give Ted a little surprise, something special to mark the beginning of our new life. I'd had to make an appointment first thing that morning, and I did some fast talking to get exactly what I wanted. But I dealt with Annette Stromsberg, another of Dad's cousins, so she promised to drop what she was doing to help me out.

I parked Mom's van in the hospital lot and grabbed the last campaign poster, along with Ted's surprise. Because today was the first day of the rest of my life—or anyway, it wasn't the end—I put a little spring in my step across the wet parking lot.

Before I reached for the handle to the glass entry doors, the text alert beeped on my phone. Balancing the campaign sign, I reached into my jacket pocket and pulled out my phone. I didn't recognize the number. Area code 201. Someplace on the East Coast? I opened the message and blood rushed into my head, roaring in my ears. I squinted at the tiny emoticon image of the colorful toucan.

With shaking fingers, I pushed buttons. I held my breath while it took twenty years for the circuits or cybers or magic to finally connect and start ringing. A woman answered.

"Carly?" I nearly screamed it, even though this clearly wasn't Carly.

"Excuse me?" The voice sounded firm.

I tried to lasso my raging emotions. "I got a text from this number. Did you send it? Did someone else?"

"I didn't send any texts lately. My daughter's been playing with my phone, though. Maybe she accidently hit something."

The message was no accident. "Where are you? Could someone else have used your phone?"

The woman let out an irritated huff. "We're at O'Hare and our plane's delayed, so I gave my daughter my phone to keep her occupied. A nice young girl started playing one of those silly games with her. I suppose she might have sent a text."

My words tumbled over themselves. "Is she still there?"

"I . . . Let me look." I waited a half a second. Her voice came from a little distance. "Honey? Where did that girl go?"

A child's voice said something and the woman came back on. "I don't see her."

It felt like I had dropped into a pool of tepid water, disappointment closing over me. "What did she look like?"

The woman sounded concerned. "She was blonde, probably about twenty. She seemed so nice."

O'Hare. Carly could be boarding a plane now. Or she could have just landed. She might be in a taxi or sitting in a restaurant. Where was she going? Was someone chasing her, or was she doing the pursuing? The answers drifted far from my grasp, and there was no way to pull them back to me. I took the woman's information for Baxter's investigator.

Carly had sent me a message to let me know she was okay. A coded message no one else would understand. I focused on what

I knew: she must look good and healthy and relatively happy or no mother would allow her near her child. For now, that would have to do.

I stared up at the endless blue of the Nebraska sky and sent a prayer for Carly. She might be young, but she was strong and smart. I channeled Mom and decided to trust Carly. Plus, I had the added insurance of Baxter's finest on her trail.

I pocketed the phone, patted Ted's surprise, and pulled open the hospital doors. Aunt Tutti scurried across the lobby in her purple scrubs. She changed directions and charged up to me, grabbing my chin and inspecting my face. "Nice shiners."

"I won't need eyeliner for quite a while," I said.

She chuckled. "It's going to be purty when they turn green and yellow."

"Guess I'll forego the eye shadow, too."

I tucked the sign under my arm, the two stakes pointing down, and hurried to Ted's room.

No whiskers hid the healthy color in his cheeks. His eyes sparkled, and all that charm that held me—and Roxy—in such thrall oozed from him. My heart stuttered a bit at his good looks.

He beamed when I walked in the door. "I've got a surprise for you!"

I would let him go first.

He whistled when he got a good look at my raccoon eyes. "Wow. Did Rope punch you, or Nat?"

"The steering wheel."

"Wait until you see this." He sat up tall and whisked the blanket from his legs. His forehead crinkled in concentration and his jaw clenched.

I watched with fascination, focusing on the big toe's yellowed nail. Did Roxy get grossed out like I did when Ted didn't trim his toenails?

Slowly, the toe bent down and labored back up. Ted let out a whoosh of air and grinned. "How about that?"

"Congratulations!" Not that I believe in signs from the universe, as Mom tends to, or believe that God has my back, as Louise claims, but it did seem to confirm that I had made the right decision. It would make life easier for both of us if Ted could walk again.

I pulled my surprise from the back pocket of my jeans and laid it carefully on his bedside table.

The smile slipped from his face as his eyes rested on the stack of folded papers encased in a light-blue page. "What is this?" He didn't touch the bundle.

I'd expected a thudding heart, tears tugging at my eyes, shaking hands. Instead, I felt perfectly calm. "I'm not asking for anything more than my fair share."

"You can't." He stared at the papers as if they'd bite him. "I don't own the ranch."

"You can buy out my share and make it easier for everyone."

"Dahlia said you'd stay until the election. She made you a deal. You can't renege."

"I can't vouch for what Dahlia thought, but I never made a deal with her."

"But the ranch is all you know. You can't make a living if you want to stay in Hodgekiss. You'd hate living anywhere else."

I nodded in agreement. "It tears me up to leave Frog Creek." But I needed to find my own place. Frog Creek was never really mine.

"What about all our years together? You can't leave me now."

"You'll be fine. You just hate the idea that I made the choice instead of you. You'll get used to it."

He sounded desperate. "How can you leave me when I'm laid out like this?"

I pointed at his yucky feet. "You're on the road to recovery. No doubt Roxy will be glad to nurse you."

"Give me a little more time," he pleaded.

I tipped my head toward the papers. "Have your lawyer look it over and he can call Annette Stromsberg."

Now that the pleas didn't work, he folded his arms in a commanding way. "I'll give you a few days to think about it. If you leave Frog Creek, the only thing for you is to work for Bud and Twyla at the Long Branch."

"We'll see." I stepped back and propped the campaign sign on the chair below the TV. I had an overpowering craving for a greasy cheeseburger and giant basket of onion rings, and I planned on rushing to Ben's Burger Barn.

Ted couldn't read the sign until I moved toward the door. I was already two strides down the hall when I heard his bellow of outrage.

Ted didn't seem to appreciate my recycling skills. With a few strokes of a paintbrush, I'd cleverly repurposed all of Dahlia's signs. I kind of liked the new look.

VOTE FOR KATE FOX

GRAND COUNTY SHERIFF

TRUSTED AND EXPERIENCED